The path curled around an outcropping of shale and then skirted a bramble patch before opening up into a shallow clearing inside a stand of oaks that had to be forty years old. I had the shortcut and if I hustled I'd be in the timber before they came out of the overhanging pines.

Last year's acorns crunched beneath my feet and my breath caught in my throat, but I'd been quick enough. They were still twenty yards away and I got my back up against the biggest oak I could find and tried to breathe real shallow. The gun in my hand felt like a bar of iron. I took the time and made sure the safety was off. Then I heard the owl in the timber hoot again and they stepped out into the clearing. I made myself wait until they were ten yards past.

"That'll be far enough, Menifee. I've got a gun and it's loaded. Just turn around real slow and keep your hands out where I can see them."

Yard Man

Chris Helvey

A Wings ePress, Inc.
Mainstream Novel

Wings ePress, Inc.

Edited by: Jeanne Smith
Copy Edited by: Christie Kraemer
Executive Editor: Jeanne Smith
Cover Artist: Trisha FitzGerald-Jung
Credits: ID 117049564 © Vitaliy Nazarenko
Dreamstime.com Clouds, plane

Wings ePress Books
www.wingsepress.com

Copyright © 2019 by: Chris Helvey
ISBN 978-1-61309-599-7

Published In the United States of America

Wings ePress Inc.
3000 N. Rock Road
Newton, KS 67114

Dedication

To Mike Embry, Mark Kinnaird, and Keith Hellard—fellow writers, friends, and lovers of the written word.

One

It had to be the hottest day of the year. Maybe the decade. Naturally, it was the very day I'd run flat out of coffee and flour and light bread. I'd been out of eggs for a week, but catfish had kept me going. But even they had given up biting in such heat.

My aim had been to wake up before daylight and get moving early, before the worst of the heat. But it had been so hot during the night that it must have been three o'clock before I dozed and when I woke the sun was bright in my eyes. Now it was dead on noon and I was headed home from A.C. Dupree's Grocery and Meat Market. Sweat covered my face till I looked like the Methodist had baptized me three times, and my shirt was stuck to my back. Sweat was even trickling down the crack of my ass, which my Granddaddy Cain, back in Martin County, Kentucky, always said meant a man could quit hoeing and go to the shade for a spell.

Only thing was, there wasn't any shade on Evangeline Street and my sack full of groceries felt heavier by the minute. I was glad for my old straw hat, even if it was shot full of holes with the brim plumb broke down. Otherwise I might have died of heat stroke. Reminded me of forced marches I'd done in the army, and why I'd not bothered to reenlist.

At first, I thought I was hearing voices, on account of the heat, but when they kept up I got to looking around and saw the woman. She was standing on the side porch of a house on the far side of the

1

street. Usually, I don't come home this way—only did this time cause it was so hot and cutting down Evangeline saved me about a quarter mile—and I didn't know her.

I didn't know her and she looked like trouble to me, so I ducked my head and kept walking. Then she started hollering again and when I looked, she was waving a handkerchief and making motions like airmen do when they're guiding a plane in.

"You there with the grocery bag, come here for a minute."

I pointed at myself like I wasn't sure she meant me, even though they wasn't any other fool out walking up and down the road under such a broiling sun. No dogs, even. Hell, I might as well have gone and joined up with the French Foreign Legion they're always making movies about. Least then I'd have gotten paid for marching in the midday sun.

Thinking about the midday sun made me think of a poem I'd heard years ago. Something about mad dogs and Englishmen strolling about in the noonday sun. I wasn't up on Englishmen, but I had seen a mad dog once and they plain didn't know what they were doing.

Anyway, the woman nodded and hollered for me to come over, and after a few seconds I thought why not. At least I could stand in the shade for a few minutes and maybe she'd let me get a good drink out of her garden hose. So I strolled across the street and up her drive.

It was a big old two story brick place with a garage around back and roses growing in the front. The brick was that shade of yellow that wasn't quite mustard and was real popular down on the Gulf a few years ago in places like Biloxi and Mobile. There was a carport on one end of that house and a covered porch on the other where the woman was standing. At the end of the drive I stepped off and started walking across the grass in front of the house.

Up until last week we'd had plenty of summer rain and the grass was tall and fallen over in spots. Right off I could see the roses needed a good pruning and there was a forsythia bush that had grown up until it was a small jungle. A big limb had fallen off a black oak that grew in front of the bay window and as I stepped over it I wondered if the woman was a widow.

She was standing at the rail, shading her eyes so I couldn't get a good look at her, but I was sure I didn't know the woman. Just guessing, but I'd say she was in her forties, maybe a little over average height for a woman, and starting to put on a few pounds around the middle. She looked down at me over a long nose.

"You one of the Rayburn boys?" she asked. She had a nice voice. Pleasant, with a nice deep throaty sound to it. Sounded like a Mississippi woman to me and that got me to thinking about Annie Curry, which wasn't good for my disposition.

"No, ma'am. I'm no Rayburn."

"Well you look like one. At least you did when you were on the other side of the street. Are you a Dinkins, then?"

"No, ma'am. I know a Eudell Dinkins, but we're no kin I ever heard tell of."

"Oh my," she said, and I could tell she was all exasperated. She went to fanning herself with a fold of newspaper and I could see a line of sweat above her upper lip.

"Guess you've heard about Henry Lucas?"

"Never heard of him."

"Well, see here now, he was my yard man for better than ten years and then last week he went and had a stroke. In church they tell me. Right while they were singing, 'Leaning On The Everlasting Arms'."

"That's one of my favorite hymns," I said and went to singing the chorus, "Leaning, leaning, leaning on the everlasting arms, Leaning..."

"Hush up there, you. Hush up right this minute. I didn't call you over to hear you sing. Besides you sure don't have much of a voice."

3

"Reckon I can sing all right, ma'am. It's more carrying the tune along that I never was real good at."

"Oh, for pity's sake, hush."

I shut my mouth then and shifted my groceries to the other arm and looked up into the woman's nostrils. She had a good enough nose, nice and straight, only bigger than most women's. Not that such a thing bothered me at all. Not with mine having been broke three times. No, I'm sure not a pretty sight. Oh, I'm not some monster. But, on the other hand, Hollywood studios aren't beating a path to my shack with contracts in their hands. Anyway, I didn't say anything more right then. Learned a long time ago not to aggravate a woman with money, and if she lived on this street she had money. Or her husband did.

"What I'm trying to find out is whether you know a man who can cut our grass." She nibbled on her lower lip, looking something like a giant rabbit, and said, "And it needs to be cut today. Tomorrow, as you surely know, is the Fourth of July and my husband and I are having a party. And as you can see, what with Henry dying and all, it was really a most inconvenient time for him to pass, the yard looks awful and some of the women are coming from my Sunday school class. We're Methodists, you know. And I will just curl up and die if they see the place looking like this." She gave me a pleading look and then sighed deeply.

Now I hadn't even realized it was coming up on Independence Day—a man living by himself doesn't pay much heed to holidays, one day being so much like another—and I sure didn't give a diddly about a bunch of Methodist women, but for some reason I did feel sorta sorry for that woman. Maybe it was cause her nose was a little big, or maybe it was because she looked soft around the middle, like her body and her life were both getting away from her. Or maybe it was because she had this look on her face like she'd lost her way and didn't have the first idea about how to get back on the path.

Anyway, I could see that it was going to be a long afternoon, but I was durned if I was going to up and be a Good Samaritan, even if that person was about my favorite person in the whole Bible. Old and New Testaments, saving Jesus, of course, who really wasn't actually a person. Not really. What he actually was, when you got down to the truth, was God, which merely thinking about always gave me a headache. God and Jesus were both beyond my powers of understanding. However, I did have a feeling for the old Holy Ghost. Maybe cause I was sort of like a ghost myself, slipping in and then out of people's lives. People are all right, but for me they were sorta like castor oil. Meaning, naturally, that I could only take them in small doses.

Sweat felt heavy on my forehead and I tugged out my sweat rag and swiped it across my face. "Guess I could mow it for you," I said and gave her a look out of the corners of my eyes. "That is, if the pay is right."

"Oh," she said, "oh. My husband always paid Henry and I'm not sure what he paid him." She dabbed at her checks with a lace hanky. "Would a dollar be enough?"

"Well," I said, drawing the word out and letting it hang out there in the air like a punted football.

"Two?" She sounded half cross and half desperate.

"I generally get three dollars when I mow a big yard like this." Now that wasn't a lie. One time I'd mowed around the graves for the Baptists and they'd given me three dollars. Course, they probably figured it was missionary money, but it spent just the same.

"Can you start now, Mr. ...er, I'm afraid I don't know your name." She sighed again and seemed to sag in on herself. Her prominent bosom positively drooped, putting me in mind of a big sunflower starting to wilt.

"It's powerful hot, but seeing as how you're in a bind, I'll get started. You can call me Judas. My full name is Judas Cain."

"Oh my," she said. "What an unusual name. I'm Mrs. Arthur Ayers." She swallowed and smiled. It was a phony smile, but then she wasn't having a particularly good day.

"The lawn mower is in the shed out back. You should be able to find it easily. The shed's unlocked, Mr. Cain. You can leave your groceries in there while you mow."

Suddenly, she clapped her hands and her eyes got big like a bee had gone up her dress. "Oh, I must go now. My husband will be home any minute and he'll want his lunch. I must go. You can handle things from here?"

"Can I have a drink of water before I start? I'm powerful thirsty."

She gave me a hard look and I could tell she was anxious for me to get mowing. Still, I was thirsty and the air was oven hot.

"Surely you wouldn't want another yard man to have a stroke." I grinned real big like we were old fishing buddies. "Neighbors might start to talk, you know."

She looked like she was about ready to have a stroke herself, or maybe simply melt into a pool of butter like those lions or tigers or whatever wild beast was in the Little Black Sambo books. Her throat worked some like she was trying to swallow a big lump. Finally she got it down.

"There's a garden hose right over there. Help yourself."

I nodded real polite like and kept on grinning. Thought about aggravating her a little more, but I needed the work, so all I did was give her a smile and nod. Then she fluttered off toward the back door and I headed for the hose. My throat was as dry as the Oklahoma panhandle dust I'd seen back in thirty-four.

Two

I was making laps down in the bottom when the Pontiac roared around the curve and started up the hill. The man driving was wearing a straw hat and he gave me a hard stare as he rolled by. Figured right off he was the man of the house. His fat face went with the neighborhood. A few seconds later he wheeled the Pontiac into the driveway and screeched to a stop under the carport. He hopped out of the car and hustled around to the porch, moving like a man intent on his lunch.

I kept mowing, taking it slow in the heat, pausing in the shade of the trees that formed what looked like the property line and figuring how I was going to spend that three dollars. It was a big yard and, desperate as she acted, I probably could have charged the woman more. But I'd made my deal and Judas Cain was a man of his word. Always. Maybe not a whole lot besides, but most definitely a man of his word.

Way I saw it, not everybody got blessed with brains or looks or money, but each person could live up to their promises. A rain crow started cawing down by the old cotton gin and I kept on making laps, pretending I was a prisoner of war, or maybe a soldier in that French Foreign Legion. Like Gary Cooper, only not hardly so handsome.

~ * ~

I was resting in the shade of a persimmon tree when I heard him coming down the slope, grunting like a bear searching for berries. Sweat was dripping off me like I'd got caught out in a summer rain and I leaned against the tree and waited.

Once he got down the slope he moved better, but he wasn't any great white hunter for sure. By the time he made the shade he was breathing heavy and his forehead was streaked with sweat. He had brown eyes that looked like polished stones and a gut that belonged on an older man. The gut made him a banker or a merchant, or a used car salesman. The light gray suit he was wearing made him a banker. He was too young to have a gut like that. I'm no doctor, but a fool could see it wasn't healthy packing weight like that.

He came to a stop about ten feet away and looked me over like he aimed to be able to pick me out of a police lineup. He rubbed his hand across his mouth and I noticed the big onyx ring on his right hand. It was a beauty. He cleared his throat. I looked down at a swarm of black ants crawling around in loose dirt.

"My wife tells me you're the new yard man."

"Well, I agreed to mow your yard all right, Captain."

"She says you charged her three dollars."

"That's right."

"Don't you think that's too much money for mowing a yard?"

I gave him an up from under look. His face looked mighty red. He was too much a fat man to be out tromping around in such heat and getting all worked up. "You got a mighty big yard, mister. Not to mention it's hotter than the back end of hell today. Plus, your wife seemed mighty anxious to have your yard mowed. Said something about a party."

"That doesn't give you the right to hold her up. Three dollars is too high a price. The last yard man never charged such."

I swiped at some more sweat and looked off over his shoulder. Maybe thirty yards off there was a line of trees. Under them the shade looked blue and cool. "Meaning no disrespect, boss, but that man is dead."

Mr. Ayers swole up then. His face got bigger and fatter and redder. His body shook and I thought for a minute he was either going to pick up a stick and hit me a good one or simply explode.

After a minute, though, he let a long whoosh of air slide between his lips and then looked at his watch. "I've got to get back to work. See that you do a damn good job mowing this yard. For three dollars you ought to cut it by hand with a pair of pinking shears."

"Yes, sir," I said real polite like. Didn't need to be Einstein to see that Mr. Ayers was a man that liked his respect. You do work like cutting grass or hauling groceries you learn to read people.

He nodded and acted like he had something more to say. But if he did he never spit it out. Instead, he turned on his heel and trudged back up the hill. His slacks were too tight across his ass and he slipped a couple of times on account of the leather loafers he was wearing, but he caught himself before he fell and kept on trudging. I watched him all the way to his automobile. Then I went back to mowing. Sooner I finished, sooner I could get on home.

Three

It was deep in the afternoon when I finished up and pushed the mower back into the shed. Granted, if I hadn't stopped a few times to rest in the shade or get a drink of water from the hose I'd have been through a good hour before. But that heat was purely too much for any man I knew to stand up under for long.

As I picked up my sack of groceries, I figured the woman would be watching me. She had been most of the afternoon. Every time I eased off on the mowing and walked back to the house to hit the hose, I'd caught her sneaking a peek out a window. Most of the time I only caught a flash of movement, but a couple of times I saw her face. Once we made eye contact, but she turned away real quick.

Her keeping an eye out didn't bother me. Fact is, I understood it. Lately, crime had been on the rise and in a neighborhood like this one, folks generally did have something worth stealing. By mid-afternoon she'd probably begun to regret hiring me to mow the yard. Every time I made that march to the water hose, why she'd have been worried I was going to steal her blind, or maybe even try to rape her. Lots of women felt that way. For a Kentucky Hill Jack I was plenty dark, especially in the dead of summer.

Now, don't get me wrong, I'm no African nigger the color of a ripe eggplant. But my mother had turned the color of café au lait

10

under every summer sun, her mother being a Creole lady of sorts from Louisiana. Her daddy had been white, though. A professor from Tulane down in New Orleans. I'd seen his picture one time when I was going through boxes.

My own daddy had been more of a bronze color, which was probably because his daddy had been considerable Seminole. Least he claimed that, and the very few times I saw him he sure enough looked like an Indian, or one of those Melungeons people back home spoke of. Far as I knew, I didn't have a drop of colored blood in me, but that didn't matter, especially to white folks. I looked sorta colored, and that was enough.

So Mrs. Ayers' nerves were probably singing all afternoon and now as I walked toward the back door she'd be gathering up her money and steeling her resolve. In spite of how hot and tired I was, I had to grin at that. Tell the truth, I was about as dangerous as one of those moths that fly around lights at night.

Never even made it to the back door before she stepped out. Expect she counted on me stopping where I was, but I took three more steps and then I was under the roof of the carport. It was hot enough there and the air was still and close, but at least I had my head out of the sunlight.

She had changed clothes. Her new dress was speckled with little yellow flowers. She wore an apron over it, like she was fixing to cook supper. "Yard mowed?"

"Yes, ma'am."

"Now you did a good job, didn't you? I mean my husband won't have any cause to complain, will he? He always inspects the yard after it's mowed. A nice looking yard means a lot to both of us."

"Oh, it's mowed real good, Mizz Ayers. And I picked up all the sticks and tossed them over the bank." I surely wasn't scared of the woman and I didn't care much if I ever did any more work for the family. She was cold and unfriendly and he was a chubby blowtop.

"You all got a couple of rotten trees down there, beyond the flat. Might want to hire them cut afore they fall on some kid. And that old fence is leaning something fierce."

"I see." Her face went all hard under the softness and the line of her jaw jabbed out.

"Just saying."

"I heard you. Here's your pay."

She held out three dollar bills. I took them, being extra careful not to let my fingertips brush against hers. She wiped her hands on her apron anyway.

"You may recall I'm giving a party tomorrow."

I nodded.

"And I'll need someone to set up the folding chairs out on the lawn. It will have to be done in the morning before any of the guests arrive. I think having servants work like that when guests are present smacks of putting on airs."

I didn't say anything. What was there to say? I rubbed my fingers ever so easy over those fine bills.

"Do you think you could do that for me, Judas? It is Judas, isn't it? Such a strange name."

"Reckon I could set out a few chairs in the morning. Don't think I've got anything on my calendar."

She gave me a dirty look, which I expected. We both knew my social calendar never was very full. Way I saw it was that just cause I had to suck up considerable, I didn't have to be meek and mild about it. Sure, according to Jesus, the meek were to inherit the earth, but I couldn't see where too much of it was worth having.

"I'll pay you, of course."

"That would be nice. How much you figuring on paying me, Mizz Ayers?

"A dollar should be plenty."

"It's a right smart walk for me to get here and I need my rest, just like the next man. You want me to get up real early, the way I understand it."

"Yes, that's important. Do you have an alarm clock, Judas? I can let you have an old one."

"That's all right, Mizz Ayers. I can get up on my own. Sorta set a clock in my mind afore I go to sleep, see?"

"Yes, yes, all right. But will you come? Can I count on you?"

I shrugged and looked down and drug my feet back and forth across the concrete. "Think you could see your way clear to making that two dollars, Mizz Ayers? Like I said, I'll have a long walk."

Her eyebrows went straight up then and she jutted her jaw out till I thought she was going to throw it out of joint. I never said a word. Only shifted my grocery sack to the other arm and scratched behind one ear."

"All right, all right, two dollars," she said. "I swear you're trying to send me to the poor house, Judas. If I didn't know better I'd think you were part Jewish."

"Jesus was a Jew, Mizz Ayers."

"What?" Her voice was harsher than those rain crows I'd heard earlier in the afternoon. Made goose bumps pop up on the back of my neck.

"I only said Jesus Christ was a Jew. Cause they couldn't have been no Christians before him. Don't you agree?"

"I mostly certainly do not. Our Lord and Savior, Jesus Christ was a pureblooded Christian, just like I am. Why, he was baptized."

"That's right," I said, "by John the Baptist. That's where the Baptists got their name. Lots of Baptist churches in this town. Freewill and First and Old Regular and..." I stopped naming then and looked directly into her eyes. She had eyes that all the time looked ready to cry, whether she was about to or not. They were a deep blue, almost a violet you might say, a real pretty color, but sad looking, in a way that struck me as lonely.

"Now, didn't you say you a Baptist, ma'am?" I knew she wasn't a Baptist. Only said that to aggravate her. She had a way of rubbing my nerves kinda raw.

"Most certainly not. I am a Methodist, as I believe I told you and right now I have to go get the roast in the oven. Standing here talking to you has already made me late and my husband is a man who likes his supper on the table when he comes home." She glanced off down toward the road as though she expected to see that Pontiac crest the rise.

"I declare, Judas, if I don't wonder if you aren't more trouble than you're worth."

"You're not the first to wonder that," I said.

"What?" she said, and looked at me funny. But before I could reply she started shooing me out of her yard like I was a neighbor child, or maybe a stray tomcat. "Run along now, Judas. I've got to start supper. Now you be here early in the morning, you hear?"

"Yes 'um, I'll be here good and early," I said and grinned at her real good. Then I turned and started walking toward the road. She called after me, but I didn't pay her no mind.

Four

By the time I made Conklin Road, the air had gone the color of musty grapes. My legs felt like stone and the bottoms of my feet were sore. If I hadn't been so close to home by then I might have eased down under one of the big gum trees that grew along the road and taken a nap. But I wasn't any more than half a mile from home, so I kept on putting one foot in front of the other. Ever so often I rubbed the tips of my fingers across that money.

With sunset, a light breeze had come up and I could hear it ruffling the leaves and murmuring among the pines. The dirt road ran between columns of trees on both sides. Beyond the trees to the south was the river and to the north the railroad tracks. Even though it hadn't rained in several days, the murmur of the river was still clear and comforting.

Always liked living close by a river. A river is forever moving and I done a lot of that myself over the years. Lately, I'd felt the itch. I began to figure how much I could save up doing yardwork for the Ayers and how much money it would take to travel on. Traveling was part of me, in my blood and bone, and it seemed like there was nothing in this world that could tie me down for long. It wasn't a lack of cash money for sure.

That was because I knew from personal experience that a man could travel for free if he was willing to hop freights and snatch pies off window sills and pilfer a henhouse once in a while. Or he could bum around the country for months, years even, doing odd jobs and sleeping out under the stars, in haystacks, barns, or abandoned houses. Lots of those all over the South and Midwest, even the West. I'd traveled a lot back when I'd walked in a younger man's shoes.

I came to the fork in the road. Go right and you walked through a break in the willows and sycamores down a cutbank and then you were on a sandbar. I went left.

A few houses, all of them built years before and most nothing more than shacks to begin with, huddled in the trees. At one time somebody surely lived in each of them. There were probably twelve or fourteen; I'd never counted. Now, only three of us were living along the spur. Old Tom Delong lived in a cabin off in a clutch of cedars. He'd been there for years. Old Tom couldn't rightly say how long, but he claimed Warren G. Harding had been president when he moved there after he got too up in years to work anymore for the Georgia Southern.

Across the road, on a little knoll, was a house painted white where a man and his wife and three kids lived. All I knew was they'd moved in back in April, coming in after dark one evening after I'd gone to sleep. One night that white house was empty; the next morning a family lived there. I'd never been to their house and none of them had come to mine. I'd met the man a couple of times walking. Tall and rawboned, his sandy hair was going thin in the front. Said his name was Timmons and he worked at the sawmill when somebody showed up with timber, and on cars at Green's filling station when they didn't. He wasn't a man to shake hands. He was a nodder.

A hundred yards after it split, the road petered out, going to sand and shell and dirt the color of aged copper, ending abruptly in a grove of hickory and black oak. Dead in the center of the grove stood what I'd been told had once been a slave cabin. Then again, I'd heard other stories, that it had belonged to an evangelist, or a soldier from the Spanish American War, or a famous writer who had a drinking problem and came there once a year to dry out.

If any of those tales was truth, I couldn't swear it. When I'd moved in summer before last it had been empty, except for a nest of finches under the eaves, a one-eyed tomcat who came and went according to whim, and a passel of mice. Took me until way up in the fall to get shed of the mice. The old cat wasn't much help. I left the birds alone. Liked to hear them chirping to one another in the mornings.

It was black dark under the trees when I slogged down the path. A breeze ruffled my hair and it was cool and refreshed me some. I pushed the door open and crossed the floor on memory and fumbled around until I'd found the coal oil lamp and the box of matches and got a light going.

By then I was almost too tired to eat, but my stomach was grumbling so I rummaged through my sack of groceries and found a can of Vienna sausages and opened it and ate them along with a hunk of cornbread left from the day before. I wanted a good strong cup of coffee, but was simply too bushed to make it. So I drank water and listened to the dark falling outside.

A night is full of sounds if a man will simply sit still and listen. Frogs were croaking and the finches were still twittering in the wake of my passing. On the far side of the railroad tracks a man named Benton ran about a hundred head of cattle and now and then one of them would make a low mooing sound. A dog barked off from down to the Timmons place and I figured it was their sad-eyed hound they kept chained to the clothesline. An owl started off down in the timber and from on down the road a whippoorwill began its song. Small animals rustled in the weeds outside and the tin roof popped as it cooled.

I finished all the Viennas and ate another piece of cornbread and the last piece of a dried apple pie I'd got a few days ago for working on a fence for a widow. Didn't have much washing up to do, so I strolled over to the window and looked out across the patch of yard I'd wrestled from the brush.

The moon was up good now and moonlight fell like spilled paint through the hickories and oaks and striped the ground. Honeysuckle was blooming sweet and I could smell it strong and it reminded me of a time I'd walked all night along the tracks down in Texas with a girl I'd met. The honeysuckle had been in bloom then, too. Ever since I'd been fond of honeysuckle.

Right then I surely wished for a smoke, but I was flat out, so I leaned my head out the window and tried to think about other things. That was what a man had to do when an urge came on him. Whether it be a longing for a cigarette or a beef steak or a woman, or even an itch to move on down the line, if circumstances didn't permit, a man had to shift his mind. Now while that was pure truth, it was also easier said than done. Still, it had to be done. So I tried to think about the money I'd made today and the money I'd make tomorrow and then what I would do with it.

Figured I'd better lay some of it back for the hard times that always came, just like the rain. But I surely could use some new underwear and socks. Might stock up on canned goods, too. The Bible speaks of laying back for the fallow years, and I'd had my share of those. Wouldn't mind a shot of good whiskey while I was wishing, and it would be mighty nice to take a fine looking woman to a picture show.

After a while the moan of a train whistle cut through the night and I felt the old urge to hop a freight and roll on to land I hadn't seen. But I was way too tired to run after any freight train tonight, so I turned from the window, crossed the floor and sat down on the bed and took off my shoes and socks and pants and shirt. Then I reached down and picked up my Bible and let it fall open according to God's will, for that was the way this preacher I met down in Florida had told me was according to the Lord's plan.

And the Good Book fell open to the tenth chapter of Luke, the fourth verse, so I read "Carry neither purse, nor scrip, nor shoes, and salute no man by the way. And into whatsoever house ye enter, first say, Peace be to this house. And if the son of peace be there, your peace shall rest upon it: if not, it shall turn to you again. And in the same house remain, eating and drinking such things as they give: for the laborer is worthy of his hire."

Those words sure seemed to fit me, I thought as I closed the Bible and sat it on my chair. Then I raised up and blew out the lamp. I eased back down and thought about Mr. and Mrs. Ayers and whether my work for them had been prophesized. The whippoorwill was singing sweet in the holy night while the smell of honeysuckle was a lovely perfume.

Five

In the sweet blue birthing of morning I came wide awake. I rolled out and stumbled to the window and peered out, wondering if I was already late. It was a good two mile walk to the Ayers place and the woman had been real anxious that I get there early.

One glance told me I was all right. Daylight was nothing more than a promise in the tops of the hickories and oaks. The air was summer soft, like invisible velvet shot through with the scent of honeysuckle. I closed my eyes and said a short prayer. Learned years back that it never hurt a man to express gratitude.

The wrens began twittering sleepily and I opened my eyes and got cracking. I stepped outside and took care of business, then washed my face and hands good with water I'd hauled out of the river the day before. Then I built a quick small fire in the cookstove and started a pot of coffee. Nothing any better first thing in the morning than a good strong cup of coffee.

The clothes I'd worn yesterday were nasty and I rummaged around until I found a cleaner shirt and trousers. Didn't take all that long; I don't have many clothes. I wet my hair and ran a comb through it, not worrying all that much. By the time I hoofed it clear to the Ayreses' place I'd be sweating anyway. By then the coffee was done, so I drank a cup and ate a piece of cornbread standing at the window, watching the day get light.

I drank a second cup while I put on my shoes and socks and said a couple of Bible verses I remembered. Daylight was coming on strong now and I figured I'd better be getting a move on. Mornings were the best and prettiest time of day to be out anyway.

A light dew had fallen during the night and the grass glittered in the sunlight like shards of green glass. Birds fluttered about and I could hear Benton's cattle off to the north. Smoke was coming from the Timmons place and Delong was already standing in front of his cabin smoking a cigarette when I passed. The smell of that burning tobacco made me want a cigarette myself, but time was passing, so I simply lifted a hand and Delong waved back.

Since I hadn't been working regular, my legs and back were sore from the yard work the day before and it felt good to step out and work the kinks out of my joints. Morning air was still cool enough to be pleasant and off to the south the river was a soothing sound.

By the time I hit the main road the sun was above the tree canopy and I started stepping quicker. Now and then a car passed me and once a wagon full of melons and tomatoes pulled by a pretty team of red mules, their coats shining in the sunlight.

A little old man drove them. Actually, the person was so wizened I couldn't tell to swear if it was a man or a woman. Whoever it was had on a wide brim straw hat and their skin was the color of old leather, which might have been due to sun or blood.

By the time I could see the Ayers house, people were moving around outside. As I got closer I could see they were women in maid outfits. Tents were set up and a delivery truck from Apex Catering was pulled up in the drive. I cut across the bottom and climbed the slope and worked my way around to the back door. Some of the maids gave me the evil eye, but I never paid them any mind, only kept moving. As I was coming up on the back porch, Mr. Ayers stepped out the back door carrying a cup of coffee. I stopped walking and watched the steam rising from his cup.

"About time you got here. Mrs. Ayers has been looking for you for twenty minutes."

"It's still mighty early. I told her I'd be here early and I am. Why the heat ain't even started to build yet."

"Oh, yes it has," he said. "Mrs. Ayers is hotter than a frisky fox in a forest fire. To her this is the biggest day of the year. Beats Christmas, Thanksgiving, and New Year's all hollow. Now you'd better get to moving double time before she catches you. Unless you want a real chewing out, that is."

I shook my head. "Nope, but I could use a cup of that coffee. Had to start out mighty early, Captain."

"All right, I'll send one of the help out with a cup for you in a bit. First though, I'm gonna smoke me a cigar and you better be getting to setting up the folding chairs and the tables. Get one of the catering staff to help you with the tables."

"Where you want it all set up?"

He looked off over my shoulder, "Down in the bottom, I suppose. Didn't she tell you yesterday?"

"No sir. Just said to get here early. Which I am."

"Sounds just like Marilee. I'll check with her, but some of them will have to go down there anyway. Rest of the yard won't hold all of them, at least not on level ground. Must have ordered eighteen or twenty." He blew on his coffee and then he took a sip. "You'd best get going. Judas, isn't it?"

"Yes, sir, Judas Cain."

"That's what I thought she said. Why did your folks ever give you such a name as that?"

"My mother give it to me. Reckon she was a Bible reader."

"But Judas betrayed Christ. Why would a mother name her son Judas?"

I looked him hard in the eye. "Spect my father did a bit of betraying himself."

His face twisted into interesting shapes while he studied on what I'd said. Then he drank more coffee. Finally, he said, "Okay, I get you. Now, Judas, you get going on those tables and chairs."

I looked around, but didn't see any tables or chairs. "Where they at, boss?"

He jerked his head. "In that truck yonder."

"Right," I said. "I'm on it, but don't forget my coffee, Captain."

He nodded and slugged more coffee.

~ * ~

Setting up didn't take all that long. The caterer had three or four helpers, and one of them was a long-headed Negro who wasn't quite right. I knew him from seeing him fishing down to the river. Folks called him Mudcat, or Mud for short, cause he liked to catch mudcats, which were a type of catfish, better than any other kind of fish that swam in the Watchahaini.

I got Mudcat to help me and we arranged the tables and the chairs down in the bottom long before the Hope Circle of the First Methodist Church and their husbands arrived. Mr. Ayers remembered my coffee, and after Mudcat and I got the chairs and tables set out, I slipped around back of the catering truck and drank it and ate three or four of the little finger sandwiches Mizz Ayers had ordered. The egg salad was right tasty. I also ate two egg kisses plus a macaroon. It was right pleasant sitting under the shade of a red oak on the far side of the shed, nibbling on sandwiches, drinking coffee, and watching the hired help serve the honored guests. Two or three of the waitresses were right cute, especially in their little black and white uniforms. Where women concerned, it had been a long dry spell and seeing those waitresses sashay around was extra fine.

I'd sorta figured on getting Mizz Ayers off to the side and collecting my pay and then heading on out before the sun really hotted up. But she was busier than a one-legged man in an ass kicking contest, fluttering from one table to another, as well as any woman her size could flutter that is, gabbing first with this horse-faced woman and then with that dog-faced one. The sun kept on climbing and getting hotter and I could see that I needed to run down Mr. Ayers to try and collect from him. He was probably paying anyway.

Should have asked him when I first saw him, but I wasn't thinking straight then and after that he was inside the house or sitting around shooting the breeze with a bunch of the other husbands and I sure couldn't interrupt such as that. Not if I wanted to work more for them down the road and at the moment that seemed like a fine idea. For sure, it was the easiest money I'd made in quite a spell.

There wasn't a cloud in the sky that day and by the time the sun got directly overhead the air felt like it had just escaped from a baking oven. That heat was pure brutal, so bad a number of the Methodist ladies started to melt and come apart at the seams. Right after the egg kisses were served they began drifting away.

By then it was so hot I didn't fancy a stroll myself, so I lounged in the shade. Gradually, the heat began to make me sleepy and I unbuttoned my shirt halfway and closed my eyes.

I wasn't what you'd rightly call asleep, but I wasn't fully alert either. For some time I could hear the women talking. As they were mostly off down in the swale, the sound of their voices was like the hum of a hive of bees. Then all the voices started to run together and I could feel the surface of my mind smoothing out, the way the surface of a pond smooths out after a kid skips a flat rock across it. Now, I don't think I went hard asleep, but mayhaps I did doze. Never dreamed, though. Fact is, I seldom dream. When I was younger I used to wonder if such a lack of dreams signified something.

~ * ~

Something hard jabbed me in the ribs and I blinked and came back clear-headed into the boiling afternoon.

A shadow had fallen across me and I looked up in the face of Mizz Ayers. Actually, I was staring into the dark twin tunnels of her nostrils and I quick moved my head. She was staring me down with those purply-blue eyes. They sure were a nice color.

"And what do you think you're doing?" she asked in a smarty-pants way. When she used that voice it naturally grated on my nerves.

"Waiting on my pay," I said. My voice was thick with remembered sleep.

"Ha. You're simply lazing around eating my food and ogling the waitresses. Now don't deny it, mister. I saw you eating egg salad and staring at the skinny blonde earlier."

I shrugged and sat up. My face was glistening with sweat and I wished I hadn't unbuttoned so many shirt buttons. Being that way around a class lady like Mizz Ayers made me feel embarrassed. I cleared the phlegm out of my throat and spat off to the side. "If you'll give me my money, I'll get out of the way."

"Not yet, mister. You need to help load up the tables and chairs before you go," she said.

I stood and brushed off the backside of my trousers. "Loading will be extra, a dollar, say."

"What?" Her voice was pitched high and shrill and the sound of it hurt my head.

Out of the corners or my eyes I could see her husband ambling over. If she wouldn't pay me, he would. To get me off his property, if for no other reason.

"You hired me to set up," I said.

"Well, I never."

Mr. Ayers laughed. "The man's right, Marilee. You hired him to set up, not to take down."

"But it's all part of the same job."

I shook my head. "Not to argue, ma'am, but those are two different jobs."

"Oh, pay the man a dollar extra and let's get this mess off the lawn before it kills the grass." Mr. Ayers had a glass in his hand and it looked like bourbon was in that glass. I surely was thirsty.

His wife glared at me. Her face was pinched and her body all puffed up. "Of all the unmitigated gall," she said. Seeing her like that put me in mind of an old swole-up she-coon.

I didn't say that, of course. Only grinned at her and wiped sweat off my face with a rag I carried around in my back pocket for that very purpose.

Sweat stood out on her upper lip like liquid jewels. Sweat stains ran along the sides of her dress, too. I looked off over her shoulder. All of the ladies were gone and the caterer was putting bowls and tablecloths in the back of his truck. Bees hummed over the honeysuckle and a car horn blew way down the driveway. Her hair was going limp, the curls falling out like scared soldier boys.

She took a deep breath and held it for a second while she looked at me. Then she glanced at her husband and let the air whoosh out between her lips. She looked like a punctured balloon.

"All right, but you're the next thing to a thief."

"So was Jesus," I said.

She stared at me so hard her eyes almost crossed. "What in the world do you mean by that?"

"On the cross," I said, "When he was hanging on the cross Jesus was right next to a thief. Says so in the Bible."

"Oh, but you are the most aggravating thing. I must have been suffering from the heat when I hired you. "She dabbed at her brow with a hanky. It was snow white, with blue trim. "Well, all right, I said I would pay you another dollar, so get going and load those tables and chairs before Apex charges me extra."

Standing behind her, her husband was grinning. He took a puff off his cigar and blew smoke out of his mouth.

"Okay," I said as I started moseying down the hill.

"Hey," she hollered after me.

I stopped and turned around.

"You know anything about roses?"

"Considerable, I reckon."

"Well, can you come in the morning? Mine need trimming in the worst way."

"Sounds like you looking for a regular yard man, Mizz Ayers."

She rolled those violet eyes like she was trying to see God Himself. "I suppose so. Are you interested?"

"What's the pay?"

She told me and I stood there and scratched my chin like I was figuring. But that was only for show. Jobs weren't growing on trees that year and I needed the pay, whatever it was. Her husband shook his head, turned, and started for the house. A streak of sweat ran up the back of his shirt like it had been painted there. After a few seconds I nodded and allowed that would work. I thought she looked like she had something more on her mind, but she closed her mouth up tight and whirled around and walked off after her husband. Her back was so stiff and straight it looked like she'd stuck a broom handle up under her dress. I hollered for old Mudcat and then mopped sweat till he ambled over from the truck.

Six

Smoke hung in the corners and drifted along the walls like the last signs of a dying campfire. I sat on the last stool and stared at my reflection in the smeary mirror behind the bar. The face staring back at me looked a little ornery and a whole lot ordinary. No movie star, for sure, but then it didn't belong in a carnival freak show either.

Maybe it looked slightly older than I remembered, and maybe it looked a little drunk. When a man hasn't had any liquor for months, a couple of good shots will hit him hard. Way this Friday night was going I figured on a hangover in the morning. But that was all right, because the Ayers were out of town for some wedding all weekend and in my pocket I had my first real payday in so long I couldn't exactly remember the last one. Now, I surely didn't aim to blow it all in this concrete block, tin-roofed juke joint, but I did intend to ease the majority of my aches and pains.

While I was still staring at the man in the mirror, a tall, slim, thin faced woman high-heeled it to the bar. For a slim woman she sported a real nice chest. Not to mention she had a pair of mighty fine looking legs. I caught her eye in the mirror and she grinned at me. She sure had a sweet smile. I grinned back and inclined my head. Then I looked back down at my glass. It was nearly empty. No need to look like I was extra eager. No need to be dog drunk, either. After a moment, a sweeter scent drifted through the odors of stale smoke and spilled beer and sweat and grease and a sourness I couldn't name.

I looked up and into her face. She had real nice features. There was a smoothness to them, like the way two pieces of wood look real smooth when a skilled carpenter joins them together.

Her hair was dark brown, it shimmered when the light touched it, and there was some curl to it. Her nose was straight and not too broad and her lips looked like they had been sculpted out of pink soapstone.

Her eyes, though, were what got to me. They were big and round and set deep in her face. Years ago, when I was tramping through a woods in Virginia one foggy morning, I'd come up all quiet on a doe. She just stepped out of a thicket and there she was, no more than two feet from me. For a few seconds we were both too surprised to be scared. That deer had eyes just like this woman's. I tried to think of something clever to say, but my mind was as blank as an erased slate. In the end, I simply nodded.

She let me see her fine white teeth and stuck out a small hand. "Hi, I'm Jessie."

I took her hand. Her skin was smooth as velvet. My hide was so rough I was afraid of scratching hers up, so I just squeezed it lightly and let go. "Judas," I said.

She laughed then and the sound was like sleigh bells tinkling. "Is that your name, or some secret password?"

"That's my name."

The stool next to me was empty and as she sat down I got a better whiff of her perfume. She smelled like roses. She stared into my face. Her eyebrows went up and down.

I swallowed the lump in my throat. "Buy you a drink?"

"That would sure be nice." She winked at me. "I've been thirsty all day."

I waved at the bartender. "What's your poison?'

She looked at my glass. There was a quarter-inch of amber liquid there. "What are you drinking, Judas?"

"Whiskey."

"Then I'll have the same."

The bartender leaned his elbows on the bar and I pointed at my glass and held up two fingers. He nodded and I drained my glass.

In a minute the bartender brought us our drinks and I paid up. We clicked glasses.

"Cheers," I said.

"Down the hatch," she said and took a drink. It was a long drink and she closed her eyes when she drank.

She opened them and leaned closer. One of her breasts pressed against my shoulder. "You new in town?"

"Been here little over a year."

"Don't remember seeing you in here before."

"That'd be because this is the first time I've ever been in here."

"Oh," she said and laughed and brushed a curl out of her face. "And where do you usually do your drinking, Judas?"

"At home," I said, "not that I do much." I made the money sign with my fingers.

She took another drink, another long one. She hadn't been lying; she was a thirsty girl.

"But you're drinking in here tonight."

"Finally got a payday," I said.

"Oh, where you working? Out to the lumber yard? No, wait, you look like a factory man to me. Bet you're working at that place over toward Eden that makes parts for guns, you know, rifles and such."

I took another slug myself. I was starting to feel dangerously good. "You'd lose your money, Jessie," I said. "I'm the new yard man over to the Ayers place on Nineveh Street."

"Oh," she said, "well, I bet that's a good job, too."

"Any job that pays is a good one."

We both took a drink and when we came up for air our glasses were empty. I got the bartender back over and ordered us another round. While he was pouring, she hummed a tune I didn't know and I tried to figure out how much money I had left.

He brought our drinks and I paid up. Sure was a wonder how fast a man could spend his money, especially when you considered how hard he had to work to earn it.

We both took a sip and then for some reason we laughed. Somebody dropped a coin in the jukebox and an old slow song started playing. It had been a hit a few years before, but I hadn't heard it in a long time. The first few notes called out memories I didn't know I still had.

"My, that's a pretty song," she said. She ran two fingers down my left forearm. "Sure is a nice song to dance to. You wanna dance with me, Judas?"

Now, I'm no dancer. Two left feet. But right then there was nothing more in this whole wide world I wanted to do. I could already feel that woman in my arms. So I nodded and mumbled something and we got up and walked toward the dance floor. Before we got there she slipped one of her hands into one of mine and between one step and the next I felt my heart flutter.

We danced that one, then another. She was a good dancer and she felt so good in my arms I was ready to join whatever church she worshipped at. During the second song, I felt her body relax and she laid her head against my shoulder and her hair brushed against my face while her body pressed against mine. I pulled her tighter, wishing the song would go on and on and on.

But it stopped of course, and we walked back to the bar holding hands and finished our drinks. Then I bought us one more, wishing I was a rich man, knowing I had to stop. Already, I was into my grocery money.

While we were waiting on the third drink I leaned over and kissed her real soft on the cheek and the next thing I knew our lips were pressed together and that made an awful lot of hours in the sun seem worthwhile.

I nursed that next drink real slow, squeezing her hand then kissing her one more time. She sucked her drink down quicker than I was counting on and I went against my better judgment and bought her another, figuring it wouldn't hurt me to miss a meal or two. I'd done that before. And all the time she was telling me this story about this great big fat woman she knew who had a little bitty dog who went everywhere with the woman. To the grocery. To the bank. The dog even slept with the fat woman. Jessie giggled a lot over the story and I smiled and forced a laugh once, even though I didn't really think it was all that funny. But then, women see things different than a man.

The fourth drink hit her pretty hard and she leaned over and kissed me and this time the tip of her little pink tongue made laps around my lips. My head was starting to spin and I pushed my drink back.

Another good slow song came on then and we got up and started dancing. Only we started dancing before we ever got to the dance floor. I was feeling real good by then, and I didn't figure she was feeling much pain. We waltzed around the floor a couple of turns before I leaned closer and brushed my lips across the side of her neck.

"Gettin' hot in here. Want to get some air?"

"Sure," she murmured in my ear.

We slid apart and worked our way through the dancers. Outside the air was still warm, but it was moving some and there wasn't any smoke drifting through it. It was pleasant to smell honeysuckle instead of burning cigarettes.

Part of an old wall still stood at the edge of the gravel parking lot and I nodded at it. "Wanna sit down?"

"You got a car? A car would be nice."

"No," I said, "no car."

"All right then," she said and we started drifting over to the wall. As we walked, I wondered what she was thinking. Not that I came up with any answers, but then women confuse me.

We sat on the top of what remained of the wall. At one time it had been the side of a building. I wondered what it had been. Somebody's dream, I reckoned. A business some poor fool had thought would make him rich. And now all that was left was a section of crumbling wall. But then all dreams die. Some just die harder than others.

Music drifted out into the parking lot and mingled with the sounds of tree frogs and cars passing on the highway. I slid one arm around her shoulders. She put a hand on my thigh. No woman had touched me there in a long time. I brushed back her hair and kissed her on the ear. She squeezed my thigh.

Something sweet and light with a long piano roll was playing inside. One of those songs that made a man feel like falling in love. I ran the palm of my hand up and down her bare arm and she turned her face to me. I kissed her right on the mouth. She tasted of whiskey and chewing gum. I wanted her bad.

Our mouths came apart and I heard footsteps on the gravel. A tall man walked very slowly across the parking lot. In the poor light, his face looked serene. At a newish Ford, he paused. The man had on a nice shirt and I thought he was going to get behind the wheel. But he only peered in through the open window. After a moment he pulled his head back out, turned, and walked sedately to the end of the parking lot where he paused. He looked both ways, then turned left and walked off toward the lights of town.

I looked up into a blacking sky polka-dotted with stars. The wind shifted and carried the scent of mimosas in bloom, which was about my favorite scent in the world.

"Like I said, Jessie, I don't have a car. But I do have a house not far from here. Only about a ten minute stroll. Could fix us some coffee."

She bent her head and her hair fell across her face like a shower of dark water. Then she flipped her hair back, tilted her head and smiled up at me.

"Three dollars."

I didn't understand what she meant. But then I did.

"Three dollars?"

"Yas," she said, still smiling. Her teeth were very white in the night. "A girl's gotta make a living, you know."

"But I thought..." I let that sentence die. I wasn't sure what I'd been thinking. Maybe the whiskey had been doing my thinking for me.

"Three dollars," she said, standing up and letting all those stars light up her profile, No denying it was a sweet one. "Just three dollars. You'll never forget this night."

No, I thought, I won't. Only I didn't need to spend three dollars merely to remember. Anyway, I guess my feelings were hurt. I'm no prude, but I'd thought she'd liked me. Guess it was like Arizona Charlie had always said when we rode the rails together, just cause a man wishes something don't make it so. And that's all I'd been doing. Wishing, and hoping.

"What about it, mister? You ready for the night of your life?"

There was lots I wanted to say, but I couldn't make my throat work. Not then. Not for her. So I shook my head and looked down at the gravel. Finally, I choked out, "Reckon I'll pass."

"You sure? You'll be sorry later."

"Probably so," I said, "but no thanks."

I could sense her standing there. A car rolled down the highway, its headlights cutting up the night. When it had passed, she ran one finger down the side of my face.

"Maybe I'll see you around," she said.

"Maybe," I said. Seconds later I heard gravel crunching. Then the music got louder and I pushed up and walked out to the road.

Coated with starlight and moonlight, it looked alive. I felt about two feet tall. My head was high and hollowed out from the whiskey and my legs seemed far away. Down in the timber an owl hooted and as if in response the long low moan of a train whistle floated out of the dark. Right then I surely wished I was on that train, wherever it was headed.

Seven

I woke with sunlight in my eyes and a nasty taste in my mouth. A strange quiet seemed to envelop the world and I lay very still, trying to understand why. Time passed. I knew that because I could hear it ticking inside my head like one of those metronomes piano teachers use. After what seemed like a long time, the answer came to me—the birds weren't singing.

I opened one eye, slowly. The light was blinding. Felt like someone was jabbing an ice pick right behind my eyes. I closed the open eye. It was morning, but not early. The heat of the day was already building.

I rolled over and felt my stomach lurch. It felt like I was on a small boat in a heavy sea. If I moved again I was sure I would vomit. I swore I would never move again. A strange little man had crawled inside my skull and was pounding away with a sledge hammer. I pretended I was a corpse. Slowly, my stomach began to settle down. The little man's swings slowed. Sweat eased down my face. I could smell stale cigarette smoke on my clothes and stale whiskey on my breath.

I tried to think of something cool and smooth and still. Ice would work, or polished glass. My brain wouldn't cooperate. It kept going back to Jessie. I squinched my eyes shut so tight I could see little black specks.

When I opened them again the light had changed. The morning had grown up and wandered off. The air was hot and stale. Time had the feeling of noon. Moving like an old man in a rest home, I sat up. The room swayed and I focused my eyes on the photograph beside the door. It was a picture of a family in a kitchen. The woman was just turning from the stove. She wore an apron and held a large ladle in one hand. A little girl clung to the hem of the woman's dress. A little boy sat at the kitchen table. His hair needed combing and he looked hungry. The only life in his face came from his eyes. They were open very wide. A man sat at the table, too. He was half turned in his seat as though he had heard a noise and was looking to see what had made it. He looked angry and, at the same time, lost.

I had no idea who the people were in the picture. It had been hanging on the wall when I moved in. Sometimes at night when I couldn't sleep I made up stories about the family. Must have studied that picture five hundred times without ever figuring out what made those people so interesting to me.

When the room grew still, I stood and walked cautiously across the floor. There were a couple of dippersful of water in the pail and I scooped one out and drank it slowly. The water tasted of the bucket, but it washed some of the nasty out of my mouth. I laid the dipper on the counter. Then I picked up the bucket and walked outside. I sat the bucket down and took off my shirt. Then I picked the bucket up again and dumped the remaining water over my head.

I came up spluttering. I wiped the water out of my eyes and rubbed my arms and chest. It wasn't a bath, but I was cooler now, and more alert. I put my shirt back on and picked the bucket up and started for the river. Before I got out of sight of the shack I thought of something and turned around. When I started out again the bucket dangled from my left hand and my cane pole from the right.

Dust puffed up with each step and mosquitoes whined. Blue jaws flew between the trees. Cornflowers bloomed along the side of the road and Queen Anne's lace grew tall in the ditchline. Butterflies, blue and orange and white, fluttered among the weeds. In a few minutes I could hear the river as it ran over the rocks in the shallows and then there was a path leading off to the moving water, running between willows and sycamores. I turned and went down it.

The soil was sandy now, loose under my feet. Tree roots were exposed and crawdad holes dotted the soft earth. At the end of the path there was a deep pool of water and I filled the bucket and set it in a depression time and water had carved.

The earth was soft here, covered in places with dead leaves and fallen trees and I pushed some of the leaves out of the way and started digging with a stick. In five minutes I had a tobacco tin full of worms.

Then I worked my way on down the bank, stepping over roots and around rocks. In a couple of minutes, I came through a little thicket of young willows and onto a sandbar. I walked out to the edge of the sandbar and sat down on a piece of driftwood. Then I threaded a worm on my hook and flipped it out into a likely looking pool.

Along the water a breeze had sprung up and where the willows and sycamores grew shade dappled the surface. Across the river somebody was running a tractor and the smell of fresh cut hay drifted on the breeze. Between the sunlight and the breeze and the murmur of the water, the pounding inside my head had almost disappeared. My stomach rumbled and I wished I'd brought something to eat.

Even in the middle of summer, bluegill and sunfish will bite, and at night you can catch catfish. I was fishing the backwaters here and the current didn't amount to much. My bobber floated slowly downstream. Occasionally I'd see it wobble and then it would duck under as a little fish tried to grab the worm. Then it dunked under good and I jerked and swung a nice bluegill onto the bank.

I unhooked him and strung him up and cast again. In less than an hour I had four nice ones and was planning on catching one or two more and heading home. I was baiting my hook when I heard a twig snap. Trying to look casual, I turned around.

An elderly Negro stepped out of the willows. He was tall, but bent some, as though the years were weighing heavily on his shoulders. His hair was gray and wooly and cropped close. His shirt was blue and red plaid and the tail flapped out behind him. His trousers were wrinkled and greasy looking. Raggedy looking boots encased his feet. A cane pole dangled from one hand, a minnow bucket from the other.

When he saw me he took a step sideways. Then, as though he had had gotten a better look at me and seen that I was no threat, he grinned and walked on across the bar. He walked younger than the gray in his hair, but he was missing about every other tooth.

He stepped up alongside of me and his shadow fell dark across my legs. I was downwind and he smelled of smoke and sweat and threading through those an even more basic odor, perhaps the earth itself.

"Are they bitin', brother?"

"Some," I said. "Mostly bluegill."

"Well," he said, "them's mighty fine eatin'." He pointed at large flat rock maybe ten feet away. "Care if I join you? This looks like a likely place."

"Help yourself. Don't reckon this here river belongs to me."

I turned my head and looked out across the river. The water was a dozen different colors, the surface glittering silver in the sunlight, white in the shallows where it ran over the rocks, deep green in the pools, almost black against the far bank where shadows already lay thick, and more shades of blue than I'd ever dreamed.

I heard his minnow bucket clank against the rocks. As he sat down, he grunted. His shadow fell across my feet and for some crazy reason it felt heavy. Maybe I was still a little drunk.

He baited his hook and flipped a minnow a few feet out from the bank. I heard him jamming his pole down between the rocks, whistling softly between his teeth. The tune was a new one to me. Then the whistling stopped and I heard him clear his throat.

"Not from around here, are you?"

"Wasn't born here, that's right. But I've been here a spell."

"Thought I'd seen you around, but knew I didn't know you. And I know near about every man, woman, and child in this town, leastways those who's been here all their life, or close to it."

Something splashed out in the middle of the river and I waited to see if whatever it was had another jump in them. But the water smoothed out until there was nothing but sunlight shimmering on the surface.

"You from here?" I asked.

"Bred and born," he said. "Eighty some years ago. Ain't rightly sure how old I am. See, I was borned at home, with only an old conjure woman to help Momma, and don't guess anybody ever got around to reporting me, at least official like. Far as I know, there's no birth certificate for me. Course maybe there's one down to the courthouse, but if there is I've never seen it."

"Didn't you ever ask your folks when you were born?"

"Sure I did. Only by the time I thought of asking, Momma's mind had started to wander. She could remember some days real good, mostly when she was a little girl, back on the Sullivan plantation. Other days, not so good."

"What about your daddy?"

"He got killed in a logging accident a week afore I was hatched."

He stretched his long legs out and sent a shower of gravel into the water. "Knows I was borned on November nineteen. Leastways, that's when Momma would bake me a birthday cake. When she had flour, that is."

The fish had quit biting and I turned my head enough to see his face. It was a long one, putting me in mind of a horse, and here and there furry patches of gray grew along his jaw. He scratched at one of them.

"Judge Pemberton told me one time, back when I was doin' his yard work, that Mr. Lincoln give his Gettysburg Address on that day, way many years ago. Guess you've heard tell o' that?"

"Heard of it." I'd read that speech too, once. Back when I was in school. But I couldn't see the good in telling that. Might shame the old man in some way.

"The old judge is dead now, and so is Momma. Death, well he gets us all. But, back to the judge telling me that, why I think it surely do fit, cause see my momma she was one of the slaves Mr. Lincoln freed. Said she was a big enough girl to be a helpin' in the kitchen all during the war. Heard her tell a hundred times about Yankee soldiers a comin' up the old Bartlettsville Pike, and how the sunlight reflectin' off the barrels of their guns was pert near blinding, and how blue their uniforms was." He shook his head. "Always wished I'd a been there to see such a sight." He turned and stared at me. "Course I wouldn't have a wanted to live as no slave. No sir, I sure don't hold with sech."

A couple of rain crows commenced to cawing at one another and we sat there and listened till one of them got mad and flapped off. Crows are birds I've never rightly been fond of and I was glad when they quit cawing.

"You work long for that judge?" I asked, trying to keep the conversation flowing. Last couple of years my life had been more silent than not.

"I'll say, more than thirty years."

"What happened then?"

He looked down at the gravel, then out across the river, then somewhere far off, beyond the river, beyond the tress, beyond anything I could see. I watched his eyes go glassy and out of focus and I wondered if he was looking back across time, which was something I'd done myself. He came back into the afternoon slowly, as though he was reluctant to leave where he had been.

He blinked, shook his head, then turned and smiled. It was a tired looking smile. "Then I got old, the judge died, and the kids didn't want me hanging around no more. Always thought that I must have reminded them of the judge. He was a hard man, you see. And when a man's hard, he's hard to like. Respect? Sure, those kids all had respect for their daddy, but love? Course I got no way a knowin' what was in their hearts, but judgin' by what they did and the way they talked, before and after, no, they didn't love him."

He sighed and rubbed the palm of one hand across the back of his neck. "Now, I know you would never believe it if you'd heard the way the old judge yelled at me and cursed me like a mangy dog, but, to the tell the truth, I reckon, in a way, I did love the old varmint."

The old man paused and cocked his head to one side so that he looked like a large, dark bird. "See, he gave me a job when nobody else in this town would and he kept me on all those years. Now, the man never told me that he liked me, or even that I did a good job, but in the last couple of years afore he died, he was trusting me to make all his deposits down to the bank. Said he couldn't trust his children. Claimed they were robbing him blind. And they probably was doing just that. See, he kept them on such a short leash for so long that when he started going down and they got loose, why they took every advantage they could. And, even though his old body was going, the judge had his right mind till the day he died. And he knowed he could trust me. Sure as Sunday morning he did. Cause I'd been as honest as the day is long all those years. Plus, you know I never once took a single dime off of him, though I sure 'nuff could have. Why, sometimes he'd give me two or three hundred dollars to take to the bank for him and every time I'd go straight there and straight back, not stoppin' even once to chit-chat with nobody, not even with Reverend Leroy if I was to see him."

The old man grinned then and rubbed his hands together as though he could still feel the judge's money. "And when he died, why the judge he left me a hundred dollars cash money and a little old three room house out in the county. And what with him being a judge and all, he wrote that will so tight that even his own stingy childrens couldn't take that money or that house away from me. Live in that place to this day."

"Guess that made you feel good, him leaving you the money and that house," I said, wondering how it would feel to receive something like that.

The old man nodded. "Yas, it sure did. Made me feel proud, tell you that."

He nodded again and looked right solemn, the way I figured a judge would look sitting up on the bench. Or rather the way I'd seen them look the times I'd been in court standing before them, waiting to be judged.

"Yas, sir, real proud that a fine, learned white man like the judge would be that generous to me, the son of a slave. Yes, my mother was a sure 'nuff slave, borned afore the War Between the States up on the Crawley plantation in the bend of the south fork of the Green."

Sunlight was coming in at a slant now, striking me in the eyes, and I wished I had a cap. I shaded my eyes with one hand and curled my neck and looked at the old fellow. His skin shone like it had been polished. He pulled a plug of tobacco out of a pocket and gnawed off a hunk. Then he offered it to me.

I reached out and took the plug and worked me off a chew, then handed the plug back. "She talk much about those days?" I crammed the tobacco into my mouth. It was cheap leaf, but I was out of smokes. Besides, chewing tobacco had a way of easing a man's mind.

The old boy nodded and chewed and spat. "Took it by spells. Wouldn't say a word about it for weeks, months, not even when you asked. Then out of the blue, say at supper or on the way to church a Sunday mornin', why she start telling the life like it happened yesterday."

I worked the chew around to the side of my mouth. I could feel it pushing against the side of my face. Dragonflies skimmed across the water and a blue heron I hadn't noticed before rose silently from the shadows along the far bank and flapped noiselessly skyward. I watched him until he was nothing more than a dark speck in the sky.

"Did she have it rough?"

The old man closed his eyes and leaned back against the trunk of a long dead sycamore. "Rougher than some, I reckon, but not so rough as others. Course I was borned into slavery, too, only I was mostly too young to 'members much about it."

"Damn," I said, "you're not kidding me, are you?"

"No, sir, I was sure 'nuff borned a slave. My master was named Leland Jurand. He owned better than six hundred acres of the finest bottom land anywheres and over a hundred slaves. Raised cotton and corn and potatoes and beans and enough melons to feed an army. Had cattle, too. 'Member them old long horns. Scared me somethin' awful."

"So, you were a slave?"

"Yeah, but I was just a kid. Didn't have to do no real work. Oh, I might shoo the flies off with a peafowl feather or maybe fetch the white folks some little something, and I real hazy remember feeding some chickens. Helped out some in the kitchen. No, I had it real easy compared to the older ones."

"Like your mother?"

The old man nodded. "Yeah, she sure 'nuff had it rough. Had to do the cooking for the big house and if the food wasn't jest the way the mistress wanted it, why that mean woman would slap my mother and pull her hair something awful. Sometimes she'd even kick her in the shins." He turned his head and spat a stream of brown.

"Once, I recollect mistress busted my momma up the side of the head with a stick of firewood. Took her days to get any sense about her. For a while she couldn't even 'member I was her son."

He shook his head. "Sure enough, them was bad times. Course in some ways they was better. Back then, at least a poor nigger never had to worry about where his next meal was a comin' from or where he was going to lay his head at night. See, the white man valued the blacks then, cause they was worth money to him. 'Cept maybe for the land itself, slaves was the most valuable thing a white man could own. Big buck nigger field hand who could work all day in the heat, or a nigger what could shoe horses or do fancy woodworking, or a colored woman who could produce a passle of slave babies, why they could be sold for hundreds of dollars, maybe more than a thousand, and I mean to tell you that was sure a whole lot of money back then. A dollar was really worth something in those days."

He scratched at his jaw while he studied my face. He gave me a good looking over, like he was memorizing my features. He pursed his lips and spat tobacco juice.

"Hope you don't take no offense," he said, "but your skin looks different when the light strikes it certain ways. Sometimes you look like you got nigger blood and sometimes you got more of a coppery cast to you. Course some niggers does have a red look about 'em." He cocked his head. "Care to tell me about your family?"

"Don't know a lot to tell, and, no, I don't take any offense. I've heard I've got a little Indian blood, but I couldn't swear to that. I tan real good in the summer, just like my mother did, that much I know. Some folks say I'm one of those Melungeons."

"Who are they?"

"Don't rightly know. All I've ever heard was they were from Europe and settled down in the mountains of Kentucky and Virginia and Tennessee."

"You from Virginia?"

"My folks was from Kentucky, Martin County, but I was born in Missouri."

He nodded. "Never heard tell of them Melungeons. I was only wondering. Didn't want to offend you. When I first saw you I thought you was a brother, but after a while I weren't so sure. Guess you've got what folks around here call dirty blood. You ain't purely one thing or the other. Sorta like you don't belong to any peoples or any place." He twisted his face up and grinned. "Ever feel that way?"

"Sure," I said, "lots of times. But don't reckon there's much I can do about it."

"No," he said, "don't reckon there's much a man can do about his blood. What he's born with he's got to live with it all his days."

Grunting a little, he checked his line. Something had got his minnow. He dug down in his bucket and came up with a big shiny one. He jabbed the hook through its head and flipped it back out into the pool. Sunlight glittered on the surface until it looked like fire.

The afternoon was sultry, like the inside of a furnace where a hot fire had been, and I began to grow sleepy. After all, I was still trying to recover from the night before. Fact is, I was half asleep when the old man started talking again.

"Now days we still got slavery, only it's wage slavery. Poor man out there a workin' his fingers right on down to the bone and for what? Pennies, I reckon. Hard to keep body and soul together these days. Course, some folks like my old judge pays better than others, or else they throw in a little food or a shirt or coat that ain't hardly been worn."

He turned his head and spat again and hitched his britches up over his narrow hips. They were tied with a slash of rope. "What about those people you a workin' for? They treat you right?"

"Haven't been working for them long enough to say for certain. Just got my first payday yesterday."

The old man gave me the once over. He grinned like he had good sense. "Looks like you had yourself a hard night, mister. What did you do, spend it all on wine and women?"

I laughed. "Did have me a few drinks. More than I should have. Don't have a good head for whiskey, especially when it's been a while between drinks."

"What about a woman? One slip her hands down inside your pockets?"

I shifted my gaze across the river. Three cows had worked their way down the bank and were standing in the shallows, dipping their heads into the water. A pair of ducks floated on the surface. One was far enough out from the bank to be in the sun. His green head shone like brushed emerald velvet, Out in the middle of the river, a big rock jutted out of the water and a turtle lay on the rock, sunning. The scene looked like a painting I'd seen once in a magazine.

"No," I said, "women are too rich for my blood these days."

"I hear you, brother," the old man said in a way that made me wonder what he'd gone through. He mumbled something else, but by then he'd turned away and was walking up the bank and I couldn't catch his words.

In a minute I heard twigs snap and then I heard him making water. I checked my hook and flipped my line back out again. Off toward town a dog started barking and then I could hear the faint murmur of children's voices. The afternoon grew heavy on my shoulders and my eyes felt full of grit. I closed them and tried to imagine slavery. Then I thought about a couple of women I had known. Then I could feel my brain going all warm and smooth.

By the time I woke up the clouds had gone purple and banked along the western horizon. I came wide awake with my mouth tacky and one of my legs aching where'd I laid on it funny while I slept. I sat up, yawned and stretched. The worst of the heat had gone out of the day. Tiny black flies were swarming in the air. They had a nasty sharp bite. One got me on the forearm and I slapped at him.

~ * ~

"Pure devils, ain't they?" the old man said.

"I despise them."

"They sure sweet on you, though." He laughed at his own joke. I rubbed the back of my neck and tried to ignore him.

"Get your nap out?"

"Reckon so," I said.

"You snore right fierce," he said. "But then I suppose you've been told that before."

"Don't worry much about it," I said, and stood. Limping the kinks out of my legs, I walked down to the water and splashed some on my face. Then I cupped my hands and scooped a little into my mouth. Right then I surely could have used a good shot of whiskey.

Down along the water the flies were worse and there were mosquitoes whining among them. I heard a big fish flop, but I was hungry, so I turned and walked back up the bank. The sun had dropped behind the trees across the river and dusk was falling like a purple rain.

"Reckon I'll take it to the house," I said, staring at the old man. "You catch anything?"

"Not one. Hardly got a nibble."

"Got too hot," I said. "I caught four or five before it got so bad. Bluegill. They're in the water right by the bush on this side of that piece of driftwood looks something like a snake. You want 'em?"

He looked up at me and something in the fading light let me see how old and fragile he really was. "Don't you want 'em? You caught 'em."

"Not really," I said. "Don't feel like cleaning them. They're yours if you want 'em."

"Well, that's right nice of you, mister." He pouched out his lower lip. "Say, I never did ask your name. Mine's Moses Jurand."

He stuck out a hand and I shook it. Moses had big hands, full of bones. "Mine's Judas," I said, "Judas Cain."

"My, my," the old fellow said, shaking his head, "you and me, we sure got Bible names, ain't we?"

"That's true enough," I said as I let go of his hand. "Well. Moses, guess I'd better head for the Promised Land. Going to be dark soon."

"Judas, you right about that. Only I wouldn't worry none. Whatever might grab you in the dark will sure let you go quick come daylight." He slapped his thigh and started laughing, a high-pitched cackle that put me in mind of a pet crow a man named Jules DeLambre had kept in a homemade cage down along the Nacogdoches. Never did like that bird. Had a smart-alecky turn.

I picked up my water bucket, raised a hand and started up the bank. "See you around, old man," I said over my shoulder.

"See you, Judas," he said.

Then I was in the tree line and my passage riled up some birds in a blue ash. Their fluttery wings sounded like an airplane starting up. Under the trees, it was dark and some cooler, then I stepped out onto the road and dusts puffs rose around my feet. Nobody was waiting for me at the cabin, but I stepped along right lively. Moved quick like I had a woman cooking supper and a passel of children playing hide-and-seek out in the yard. Dreaming had never done much for a man, I suppose. But a fellow had to keep his spirits up some way. By the time I reached my turnoff, the sky had gone plum and a crescent of a moon shone through the hickory branches and moonlight whitewashed the ground.

Eight

In the early blue of morning a cardinal streaked across the drive and landed in a crabapple tree. From there, he eyed me like he figured I was a fairly dangerous man. The sun wasn't high and a faint coolness lingered. The paperboy wobbled by on his bicycle and flung the paper. It hit on the driveway, then slid off onto the grass and I walked over, picked it up, then strolled on toward the house. Dew had fallen during the night and it sparkled in the first slanting rays of sunlight.

At first I thought they had the radio on and some show was playing. As I got closer I could tell they were arguing again. For a couple that claimed to be happily married they sure carried on. Most of the time it was her yammering at him about drinking too much, or eating too much, or spending too much time with his friends. Usually he kept calm, but sometimes he flat out lost his temper and went to yelling and cursing. Mr. Ayers sure got red in the face when that happened. Being on the porky side, he didn't look real healthy carrying on like that. Wasn't any of my business, of course, so I tried to stay out of the way.

I headed on around to the back. As I walked by the car, I noticed a few weeds had worked up through some cracks and figured I'd pull them soon as I passed the boss his morning paper. I stepped around the car and up to the back door.

They were in the kitchen and she was dishing up his breakfast. Fried eggs and bacon and biscuits. Just smelling them made my mouth go watery. He was sitting at the table with his back to me, but she was facing me and I could tell from her face that she saw me. Didn't stop her from giving him what for though. She paid me no more mind than if I was a squirrel.

"I swear, Arthur, you sound like you want war."

"Of course I don't, Marilee. But in my mind it's only a question of when it starts. After all, look at what happened in Spain."

"Oh, Arthur, you know the war in Spain doesn't mean anything. That was merely like our war between the states."

"Not really. Not with Germany and Russia both getting involved. Italy stuck her nose in, too. To me, that means those countries are getting ready for war."

I knocked on the screen door. Eavesdropping is only good for a man hearing things that'll get him in trouble for sure somewhere down the road.

"Someone at the door, Marilee."

"It's only Judas with your paper. I'm glad he's here. I've got quite a list for him."

"Such as?"

"Such as I want all that honeysuckle ripped out and burned."

"Ah, not the honeysuckle. It's got a real sweet smell. Always makes me think of summer."

"Hot as it's been, I should think you wouldn't need any reminders."

"Smells better than your French perfume."

"I'll have you know Montparnasse Bleu is among the finest perfumes available on the market today."

"You sound like one of those ads on the radio."

"Don't you want me to smell nice?"

"Of course, I do. Only I like the smell of honeysuckle. Puts me in mind of when I was a boy."

"Well, the bees have been swarming it all week. As you know I'm allergic to bee stings."

Mr. Ayers jammed a biscuit in his mouth and turned. He chewed for a moment before he could swallow. He waved at me. "Come on in, Judas."

I didn't want to, but I figured I'd better do what he said. Stepping into other people's houses always makes me nervous. The door squeaked as I swung it open and I told myself I'd oil the hinges after he headed for the bank. That kitchen sure smelled good. My can of pork and beans didn't compare to fried eggs and bacon. I crossed the floor and handed him his paper. He grunted and flipped it open.

"Look here, damn it, look here." Mr. Ayers jabbed at the paper with a finger. "Look right here, Marilee."

"I wish you wouldn't curse, Arthur."

"Marilee, I swear you get more like your mother every day."

Mrs. Ayers made a sniffing sound like she'd smelled something nasty. "And what's wrong with my mother?"

He fluttered his paper and sighed. "I didn't mean anything. Only saying you remind me more of your mother all the time. Nothing wrong with that, is there?"

She smoothed her apron down. "No, of course not." Then she flicked a quick glance at me, but I'd seen her start to turn her head and by the time she was looking at me I was looking out the kitchen window. From there I could see the yard fall away and the peach trees on the slope and then the bottom where Mr. Ayers raised a few tomatoes. Next to the tomatoes there was a flower bed that needed attention. Lots of things got neglected in the heat.

I figured she was going to tell me to get busy on some job, but he started going on about Hitler over in Germany and then

Mussolini in Italy. Seemed like every news story lately was about one or both of them.

"Says here, Hitler is making noise about wanting to annex Czechoslovakia. The man is never satisfied. If you'll remember, Marilee, I said that the last time they gave in to him on that other land he claimed was really part of Germany."

"Yes, yes, I remember. You made quite a point of it at the reunion. Now hush, Arthur, and eat your breakfast. If you don't get going, you're going to be late."

"There's a whole lot more to worry about than eggs and bacon, Marilee. I tell you the man is dangerous." He turned and winked at me. "And maybe nutso."

"Really, Arthur, a person would think you want war."

He turned back to his paper then. "No, I don't want war. But I've got a bad feeling in my gut that it's coming." He forked eggs between his lips.

"That's probably heartburn," she said and laughed. But that laugh sounded thin to me.

"Joke if you want, but don't say I didn't warn you."

He twisted in his seat and stared at me. "What about you, Judas? You're a right smart fellow. What do you make of this Hitler?"

"Seems like he's a man might turn on you," I said. "Puts me in mind of a mean tempered dog."

"Exactly," Mr. Ayers said. "See, Marilee, just like I told you, this Hitler is not to be trusted."

"Oh, pooh, what does Judas know about world affairs? He's only a yard man. Speaking of which..." she whirled and looked straight at me. "You'd better get to work now, Judas. We're not paying you to stand around in the kitchen killing time by discussingHitler and the European situation all day."

"Don't forget the Japs," Mr. Ayers chimed in. "They've been fighting the Chinese for better than a year now."

"Ugh." Mrs. Ayers shivered. "Orientals. They're even worse than Negroes. At least with the Negroes we've had years of experience dealing with them. We can tell what they're thinking. Lots of times before they get it clear in their minds. But, oh those Orientals. They're so inscrutable."

Mr. Ayers laughed, stuck a piece of biscuit in his mouth and stood. He chewed while he straightened his tie. "Got to go on that one," he mumbled around his biscuit. Still chewing, he walked over and gave his wife a peck on the check. As he walked by me, he punched me on the shoulder. "Good luck, Judas," he mumbled real soft. "Expect you'll need it. She's on the warpath today."

Then he was by and in a second the screen door slammed. Before he could get the Pontiac started, she was giving me the orders for the day.

"Now, cut down all that honeysuckle and weed the flower bed in the bottom."

"Those flowers surely need water. Been no rain for better than a week."

"Well, give them some. And I want all the rest of that old fence pulled up and hauled over to the barrel and burned. It's been falling down for ten years and I simply can't stand to look at it anymore."

"Powerful hot to be burning today," I said.

She lifted her chin then and straightened her back. Her eyes went real wide open. Sunlight poured in through the window behind her and lighted one side of her face. In that silent moment she looked real young and I could see how she'd been before too many years and too many cares and too much cake and mashed potatoes had worked on her.

"Then I expect you'd better get started." A strand of brown hair had fallen across her forehead and she flipped it back and stared hard at me.

Mrs. Ayers looked at me like I was something she'd discovered on the bottom of a shoe. I didn't say anything. Needed the job, after all. Maybe old Moses down at the river had been right about the wage slavery. Even though I didn't have any colored blood in me, she still considered me beneath her. After all, she had the money.

Suppose it was like old Moses had said, my veins were full of dirty blood, and maybe that was close enough. So, I simply nodded and grinned like I had about half-sense. Then I mumbled "Yes 'um," turned and went outside. You can be sure I never let that screen door hit me on the ass on the way out.

~ * ~

By the time I finished with the honeysuckle and the fence posts, both the day and I were worn out. Down in the swale, the air was blue-tinged and lightning bugs flicked on and off like they were sending code, only I couldn't begin to read it.

The worst of the heat had gone out of the day, but heat still radiated from the dying fire. Sweat was running off me like salty rain. In the woods beyond the lawn, birds were settling down for the night. From the other side of the street, a dog barked and kids hollered to each other, playing one of those games kids play before they grow too old and the games suddenly become too real.

As I tossed dirt on the ashes, I thought back to when I'd been a kid playing games. Baseball and throwing rocks at tin cans and seeing who could walk the longest on the steel rails of the L & N. Not many games, though. Most of the time we'd had to work. Growing up, there was always corn to hoe, or wood to cut, or ground that needed plowing.

For a moment I wondered where my cousins were. Had to have been three years since I'd even heard about any of them. Duane had been in Parchman, and Dexter had been down on the docks in New Orleans, and somebody had told me Trey was down to Texas working in the oil fields. Eileen had taken off for California with that sweet-talking Jackie Williams and Lucy was working on her third young'un. None in my family were much inclined to write, and, even if they had been, I wasn't much on staying in one place long enough for the postman to track me down.

Out in the woods, an owl hooted and the tree frogs started up like they had something important to say. Lights were coming on in houses all around. Lamplight always looked pretty to me. Seeing it made me imagine coming home to a wife and kids and a nice hot supper, and then a warm bath and a soft bed. But lamplight of that sort was meant for some other man.

The dog had hushed and the kids must have gone in for the night. Once, a car passed on the street and somewhere west of town a church bell started ringing. Probably a revival meeting, or else the snake-handlers were gathering. Down in the swale all the light had gone, and I unbuttoned and pissed on what was left of the fire. Then I buttoned up, picked up my tools, and headed up the slope. My clothes stank of sweat and smoke and my guts growled. Already, I was wishing I had the walk home behind me.

I could see her standing at the sink, washing dishes. I wondered if she'd look up and see me coming out of the dark with a scythe and an axe and be afraid. I figured he was sitting in the living room reading his paper or one of those detective books he liked, but as I got closer to the back of the house a puff of wind came up from that direction and I could smell one of his cigars. He spoke out of the deep shadows under the sugar maple.

"You working mighty late, Judas."

"Yes sir, your wife had a mighty lot for me to do today."

"Get it all done?"

"Most of it," I said and leaned against one of the clothesline poles. "Leastways I burnt up all the honeysuckle and those old fence posts. Those things sure must have been there a long time. They were most rotted through."

"Been here ever since I bought this place back in the spring of twenty-nine and they weren't in good shape then. Story was Charlie

Hester, who had this place before, used to keep a cow or two down there. For the milk, I reckon."

"Must have been some time back," I allowed. "Don't nobody keep cows or chickens or even horses in this part of town. Now, over to the gulch or down along the tracks you still see some of that."

"That where you live, Judas, along the tracks?"

"My place is between the tracks and the river."

"Then you've got a walk before you."

"For sure."

With that, I pushed off the pole and started for the tool shed, but Mr. Ayers' voice stopped me.

"Hitler made another speech, the paper says."

"What'd he say?" I asked, although I didn't see how one German could affect me much.

"Says if the British and the French don't agree to let him have Czechoslovakia he'll have to go to war."

"Sounds like he's spoiling for a fight," I said.

Mr. Ayers laughed at that and then I could hear him sucking on his cigar. "Based on what I've seen over the years, Judas, a man spoiling for a fight usually finds one."

"Um," I said, "that doesn't sound good."

"It's not. If he keeps pushing we'll have another war just like the Great War. And that was supposed to be the war to end all wars." He laughed again and I stepped into the shed and put the tools up in their place.

Trudging back to the house, I could see him sitting in a lawn chair by the back door. He had a glass in one hand and he was looking off toward the west.

Reckon he heard my footsteps, cause he turned his head and looked straight on at me. He lifted his glass. "I'm having a nightcap, Judas. Elderberry wine made by Virgil Ayers, my very own brother over to Mobile. He's a great one for elderberry wine. Suppose I like it well enough myself. Join me in a glass?"

"Oh, I wouldn't want to drink your good wine, Mr. Ayers," I said. Didn't seem natural, him offering me a drink, and I felt uncomfortable. Judging by his voice, he'd already had a glass or two, and in my experience once a man has a drink you can never tell what will happen. Drink takes everybody different. Some get sleepy and some get weepy and some just want to fight. Others develop a strong hankering for a woman. I belong to that last denomination.

"Don't worry about that, Judas. I've got a dozen bottles down in the cellar. Pull you up a chair and have a glass with me."

Sure enough he'd had a couple. I could tell that clear. Should have noticed before, but I reckon I was too wore down. At the edge of the drive there was another of their wrought-iron lawn chairs, the kind that naturally rocks a little when you sit in it, and I drug it over and sat down. I heard a gurgling as he poured and then I felt the smooth coolness of glass pressing against my hand.

"Thank you muchly, Mr. Ayers. My throat is right parched."

"Expect it is," he said, "and you have a long walk home still ahead of you."

"Yes sir," I said, "I sure do."

"Well then, we'd best drink up, Judas." He lifted his glass. I could see that much in the light spilling out the screen door. He lifted his glass like he aimed to make a toast.

"Here's to peace," he said.

"To peace," I replied and then we both drank.

For homemade, it wasn't bad wine. For some time we set there sipping, watching the lightning bugs go on and off, listening to dance music from the radio Mrs. Ayers had turned on. Once my mind got to wandering and I started wondering what it would be like to dance with a woman like Mrs. Ayers. But I shook that image out of my mind and took another sip of elderberry wine.

"You reckon you'd have to go, Mr. Ayers? To the army, I mean, if there is a war."

"No," he said, after a minute. "I'm too old and fat. But as for Lenny, well, I just don't know. He's nineteen now and I hate to say it, but that's the age the army likes their men, especially those that don't have families."

"That'd be bad," I said.

"Yes, it surely would," he said. "War is not much good. My dad went to the last one and he never was the same man after he got back. War changes everything, Judas, everything and everybody. Usually not for the better, either."

Not knowing much about war, except what I'd heard and read, I didn't know what to say in response. So I only sipped and kept my thoughts to myself.

Mr. Ayers went real quiet for a moment. Then he chuckled and said, "Drink up, Judas, the night is warm and young and we are blessed with good wine. We can worry about tomorrow, tomorrow."

Then I heard him drinking, so I drank, too. And when my glass was empty, he filled it up and we sat there sipping and listening to the night breathing like we were two old friends.

Only we weren't friends and I couldn't see any way we ever could be. So after I finished my second glass, I set it down on the back step and pushed up out of my chair.

"Guess I'd best be going, Mr. Ayers," I said, real soft and slow like, so as not to startle him. It was that sort of evening. "Thank you for the wine."

He looked up then and nodded, but his face was closed in on itself and I knew he was thinking hard thoughts, so I nodded back, stepped out of the light and trudged on down the drive into the blackening night.

Nine

"I used to play down here when I was a kid, you know?"

His voice startled me and I jerked like I'd been bee stung. I'd been bent over pulling crabgrass out of that damn flower bed in the swale, mumbling to myself, listening to the wind that had been up since daylight ruffling the tops of the locust and birches, so I hadn't heard him coming. I took a deep breath before I turned around.

I'd never seen the young man before, but right off I could tell who he was. He had his mother's cheeks plus his father's way of standing at attention yet slouching all at the same time.

"Looks different now, what with the fence and the honeysuckle gone, but I can still make out where my friends and I used to play cowboys and Indians over in the woods. Although the way they're building houses these days I look for those trees to be cut down any day now."

As though he felt some urge to see them again before they were gone, the boy walked over to the line of trees and stepped into the shadows. For some reason, I sorta expected him to keep walking until he disappeared in the cool, dark shadows. He struck me as that sort of guy.

But he only took a few steps into the woods, and it was a stretch to call them that, especially after you've seen the forests of North Carolina and Kentucky and West Virginia. Then he turned around and stepped back into the sunlight, blinking a little.

"Looks like you must be the new yard man," he said.

"Yes, sir," I said, "and you must be Mr. Lenny."

He laughed. "Suppose so. Although nobody calls me that."

"The other yard man passed," I said, just for something to say.

"I know," the boy said, "Mom wrote and told me. Tell the truth, I wasn't all that surprised. He was awful old, especially to be trying to work. My folks only kept him on because he'd been around almost forever and they felt sorry for him."

The boy walked over to the flower bed. I went back to pulling crabgrass. Better to be busy was the way I saw it. Besides, there was the Bible parable about the talents.

"Place got kind of rundown looking the last few years. You've been busy."

"Yes, sir."

"Getting rid of that old fence was something Mom has wanted to do for the longest time. Honeysuckle being gone, now I miss that. Smelled sweet, you know. Summer before I went off to college I used to walk the girls down here. That honeysuckle smelled so sweet and southern and familiar that I could almost always get a kiss. At least a peck on the cheek."

I didn't have anything to say to that and he went quiet for a moment. Bees hummed among the clover and a mockingbird was carrying on near the top of a sweet gum. Traffic had died off and the street looked white hot in the sunlight.

"Awfully hot for so late in the year, isn't it?"

"Mighty hot," I said. "You been going to school this summer?" He'd been away to Ole Miss down to Oxford ever since I'd started working.

"Actually, I did take a couple of courses this summer, but they were correspondence. Most of the time I've been up to New York. I'm majoring in Finance and a friend of my father's works on Wall Street. He got me an internship there this summer. McNamara and Sons. Don't suppose you've heard of them?"

"No, sir."

"Oh, you don't have to sir me."

I nodded and wiped the sweat off my face, looking closer at the boy than I had before. He seemed nice enough, and he was going to make a good looking man. Standing there in the sunlight with the wind ruffling his fine, light brown hair, he looked like a kid who could go anywhere in the world and do whatever he wanted. But then I recalled that when I was still wet behind the ears and as foolish as only young men can be, I'd fancied I could do the same. Then I'd gone off to school, too. Yep, the old College of Hard Knocks. Life was a kind of college, the way I saw things. Only you never got to graduate. You only quit going to class when you quit breathing.

"Big news in the paper today."

"Oh, what was that?" Maybe the Detroit Tigers had traded Hank Greenburg. Or maybe Roosevelt had tried to appoint anther fossil to the Supreme Court.

"German and Russia just signed a non-aggression pact. Means they won't be going to war against each other. According to the columnist, the French are really uneasy."

"Reckon there'll be war, Mr. Lenny?"

He looked off toward the northwest. He appeared to be looking beyond the house and beyond the street, staring off into places so distant and different that I couldn't even pretend to see them. I tried to mirror his line of sight, but all I saw was Mrs. Ayers taking sheets off the line and a flock of starlings pecking on the lawn. Beyond all that was a line of dark clouds curving along the western horizon.

"Oh, I don't think so," he said finally. "Surely Hitler wouldn't be so crazy." Then he turned his face back toward me and grinned. "Anyway, all that's in Europe. We've got the whole Atlantic Ocean between us and them, so I don't see how it bothers us much. At least not for a long time."

He glanced down at his watch. "Almost lunch time. Think I'll go wash up. I'm taking Betty Jo Curtsinger to the movies later, so I'll probably take a nap after lunch."

I don't think he was really talking to me, merely speaking his drifting thoughts. So I didn't say anything. Wasn't my place anyway. After a moment, he nodded and started walking toward the house, moving easily like the heat meant nothing to him and he didn't have a single care in the world.

Ten

I came out of the picture show stretching and blinking my eyes, my mind still filled with cowboys and horses, six-shooters and mountains that rose up until they kissed the sky.

It was Saturday, late in the afternoon, and it was one of those days which mark changes. When I'd gone inside, shortly after noon, the day had been warm and sunny. The calendar said it was getting on for fall, but for two weeks the sky had been high and bright and blue. The day had been sunny and sultry, and I was expecting more of the same.

Only when I opened the door, I could feel the change. The air had gone cool and there was a bite to it. Out in the street a mist had rolled in. It wasn't rain, but your face grew damp as you walked along. It had been so warm when I left the house that I'd never dreamed of needing a jacket. I shivered, bent my neck and stepped out at a good pace.

Most of the farmers had done their shopping and headed home. I didn't own a watch, but it felt like it was getting on for five o'clock. What with a double feature, an intermission and assorted previews that would be about right. A few people still milled around on the sidewalks or peered in shop windows. I kept my head down and stepped around them. I still had the walk home and was starting to get hungry.

I hiked down Main Street until it came against the railroad tracks. Then I turned south and started down Jackson. On one side of Jackson were the Mobile and Memphis tracks, on the other dives and greasy spoons and cheap hotels. An old dog lay sleeping in front of the Beauregard Hotel and half a block away a skinny man who needed a haircut was sitting with his back against a wall with his eyes shut. A rattletrap rolled down Jackson and I caught a whiff of hamburger frying.

The aroma came from a little café on the corner. *Pete's Place* it said on the sign and I sure wanted me a hamburger bad. I paused and took a look inside. Twelve men sat at the counter or stood alongside of it and there was a cook wearing a tall white hat behind. First thing that came to mind was Jesus and the disciples, but all the men in Pete's were hard-eyed and closed-faced.

They looked like dirt farmers who sold produce out of the backs of pickup trucks, railroad men between shifts, and old men who'd retired from the mill or the lumberyard or the little shop they had nursed along for forty years. I was trying to make up my mind whether to spend my money or eat leftovers at the shack when warm air brushed across the back of my neck and I caught a whiff of perfume. I went tight all over and turned slow.

"Thought that was you," the woman said. "Recognized the line of your neck. That's the way I recognize men, the line of their necks, or the shape of their hands, maybe their way of walking." She grinned. "Remember me?"

I took a deep breath, let it out, and said, "How you doing, Jessie?"

"You're the man with the funny name," she said. "Now don't tell me. Had something to do with the Bible. Sort of like Jehoshaphat, only that isn't it."

"Nope."

"Jonah?"

"Nope."

"Well, it sure as hell ain't Goliath."

"It's Judas," I said and grinned.

She shook her hair out and arched her back like a prideful cat. "Well, just cause you got an unusual name that don't make you a smart man."

"Nope."

"What you are is a smart-aleck, yes sir, a pure smart-aleck."

"What does that make you then, Jessie?"

"Don't you worry none about me, mister. Jessie's been taking care of herself for a right smart time, and doing all right, too."

"Okay," I said. "Guess I'd better be moving. They won't want us standing out in front of their establishment. Might be bad for business."

"And for their appetites. Speaking of which, I saw you staring through the window like a hungry hound dog." She put a hand on my shoulder. "And talking about being hungry, how about you buying a girl something to eat?"

"I don't eat much in town."

"I know a place over in Slabtown. Abe's, it's called. Good home cooking, and the prices are real reasonable. They serve all trade. I've been hankering for a mess of fried taters and soup beans. You maybe want to buy me some supper?"

I felt in my pockets. Two dollar bills in there, along with a handful of change. Plus, I had a five dollar bill stuffed down in my right boot and two more fives hidden at home. I might not have spent it on myself, but for Jessie… "All right," I said. "Show me the way."

Halfway down the block, she slipped an arm through mine and we strolled on through the mist, keeping close to the buildings and shivering in the biting wind.

~ * ~

She sat back in her chair and dabbed at her lips with a paper napkin. "Um, that was some kinda good. I'm so full, now. Think I could lie down and sleep for a week."

She did look tired, not that you'd notice at first, and not the way a woman might look tired if she'd spent all day cooking or cleaning house or washing clothes, but a deep down tiredness like it had settled in her bones. It was there all right, but the only place you could see it was in her eyes and then only when she turned her head a certain way and the light caught her just right.

I knew where to look because I'd seen it in my own face. No matter how hard you try, after a while you get to where it gets harder and harder to take people and their attitudes and their pure meanness. Finally, at some point you have to decide. Some people let their anger bubble over and strike out, others cry and wail and finally give in, or go crazy. Then there are those like me; I move on down the line. I wondered which kind she was. Maybe she wasn't at the breaking point, but she wasn't far away.

We were both through eating, but I wasn't ready to say good-bye. It had been a long time since I'd eaten supper with a woman. A helluva long time since I'd done that with a woman as pretty as Jessie.

Yeah, there were dark circles under her eyes and fine lines grooving her face and her hands shook a little because she was tired. Then when she turned you could see the skin sagging along her throat. But she was still a beautiful woman, and I was no movie star. Wasn't a Romeo either. Small talk was what was needed now and that came hard for me.

"You lived in this town long?" I asked, to get some conversation started. Most women only need a chance and they'll take care of the talking. I hoped Jessie was that way. Except for yard work, hopping freight trains, fishing, and being able to recite a smattering of Bible verses, I wasn't much a hand at conversation.

She didn't answer right off. Instead, she stared out the window. It was going dark and the mist looked thicker. Autumn was coming in with the night, and I hated to see summer go. For after autumn comes winter, and then the nights sure get cold and long.

She turned back reluctantly, as though she wished she were out in the mist. Or at least somewhere besides Abe's. "Been here a little over a year, I guess." She smiled, a softer smile than usual. "I'm from Macon originally. Ever been there?"

"Passed through once."

"It's a nice town. When I was kid, I thought there was no place like Macon."

"Why'd you leave then?"

She made a funny sound in the back of her throat. "I grew up and life came along. Thought it would be fun to hitch a ride." She stopped talking then and smiled again, more to herself than me, though. "You pays your money and you makes your choices and you takes your chances," she said. "And sometimes you win and sometimes you lose."

I nodded. I didn't know what to say after that. Her words sounded like somebody confessing a crime, but, when you get right down to it, we're all guilty of something.

She didn't say anything either and after a bit other sounds began to drift in. Back in the kitchen somebody was clanging pans, a car whooshed by on the street and then I could hear somebody blowing low on a harmonica. I looked over and a skinny kid was sitting in a booth in the corner with his eyes closed, and he was blowing the blues. That music made me think of freight trains and rain and gravestones shimmering under a cold moon.

"Want a cup of coffee, Jessie?"

She looked out the window again, then back at me. "No, this place is getting on my nerves. I thought it was nice, but it's lonely like the rest."

I couldn't see that, but I said, "Okay, if you want to walk over to my place I'll put a pot on."

She pushed her chair back and stood up. "Naw," she said, "not tonight, Judas. I got to work. Night falls and duty calls. You can walk with me a ways if you want. I'm working Forsythe tonight."

"All right," I said and stood up and laid the supper money on top of the bill. Then I quickstepped around the table and she took my arm and we styled it out into the night like an old married couple. By then the mist had turned to rain and the wind was hard out of the northwest. You could smell change in the air.

We walked along together, clinging close to the buildings when we could and getting under the trees when we couldn't. Anybody simply looking and not knowing might have figured us for a couple out for a stroll who'd got caught by the rain.

"You're going to get wet tonight," I said as we crossed Poindexter.

She nodded. "That's for sure."

"Don't you have an umbrella or a slicker?"

"Nope."

"You have to work tonight?"

"If I want to eat."

"I could cook you some breakfast if you'd like."

She reached up and pressed the palm of one hand against my cheek. "You're sweet, mister, real sweet, but you're dumber than dirt. I've got to work to survive. If I don't work I don't eat. And you know how scarce jobs are these days."

"I've got a little money saved back."

She laughed then. The rain started to come down harder. "I've got to go," she said. "Find me a doorway to stand in. You'd better get going, too. Hear you tell, you got a long walk home. Don't worry about me. Jessie knows what she's doing. Been taking care of myself since I was fourteen."

I started to say something, but she put a finger against my lips. "Now, hush. I've got somebody who looks out for me. Ain't nothing bad gonna happen to Jessie. Not as long as Brad Menifee is around. I'm too valuable to him for anything to happen to me."

Thunder rumbled then, off to the south, over toward Benson Crossing. "Go now," she said and gave me a shove. I took a step back into the street.

"Wait," I said. But she had already turned and was walking away, moving toward a row of houses rising up out of the rain. For a long time I stood in the street, raindrops peppering against my face.

Eleven

A block away, you could smell turkey roasting. To lots of folks Thanksgiving means turkey and dressing, sweet potato casserole and pumpkin pie, or maybe pecan. To me, it was another chance to make a little money.

It was a chilly, raw day, with a sharp wind out of the west that carried a threat of rain. That wind was blowing falling leaves across yards and down the street and rattling the ones still clinging to the branches. The grass had quit growing and gone to seed. A long line of geese was winging its way south, headed for Lake Natacoma or on down to the Gulf. I was going to the Ayers for the big Thanksgiving Day meal, only I wasn't going to be eating. Least not with the family. I was there to clean up and wash dishes. Still, I hoped to nibble on leftovers while the family was visiting.

Cars lined one side of the street in front of the house and I hunched against the wind, crossed the street and trudged up the driveway. Feeling that cold wind against my neck put me in the mood to hop the next freight headed south. But I needed the money and lately I'd been feeling my age, so I walked under the carport and slipped in the kitchen door.

The Ayers had hired a couple of Negro girls to serve as maids and old Granny Washburn was standing at the stove. Tales of her cooking were legendary. Just smelling that turkey roasting in the oven made my mouth go to watering.

Granny turned as I stepped into the kitchen and I winked at her and walked to the laundry room and hung my coat on one of the pegs. Then, I eased back into the kitchen. The room was warm and full of good smells and I was glad to be there, even if I did have to work. Beat walking down the road in that cold wind, or staying hunkered down in my shack.

The maids were fixing a tray of celery and carrots and crackers with little slabs of cheese on them. I picked a cracker off the tray and popped it into my mouth. I'd read once that kings and dukes and such back in the Dark Ages had a hired man to taste their food first, to make sure they weren't being poisoned. Besides, I hadn't had any breakfast.

"You're here to work, not to eat, Mr. Cain."

I turned and looked at Mrs. Ayers. She was standing in the doorway that led to the dining room, with her face puckered up like she'd bit down on a green persimmon. I almost said something smart, but thought better of it and only nodded. Mrs. Ayers started giving orders then and we all got busy. My main job was carrying food into the dining room.

The guests weren't gathered around the table yet. From the sound of the talk and the laughter, they were all in the living room, and it sounded like some of them had already been celebrating. I could hear Mr. Ayers above the crowd. He was telling his favorite joke. The one about the Baptist preacher, the Catholic priest, and the Jewish rabbi. I'd heard it enough times to tell it.

The table was already set and pies and cakes lined the sideboard like rows of soldiers. There was a big bowl of cracked walnuts and pecans all mixed up and I scooped up a handful when no one was looking. Still, by the time I carried the turkey in, my gut was growling.

"Set it down there, Judas. Right in the middle of the table. And be careful. I hope not to get any stains on my tablecloth. It's a family heirloom. I got it from my mother, who got it from her mother. If the story has come down correctly, it originally came from Ireland."

I took a look at the gravy and the cranberries and thought to myself, good luck. I didn't say that, of course. Mrs. Ayers liked her servants to be both humble and silent, certainly when there were guests. Some days, the woman purely got on my nerves, but I didn't want to embarrass her in front of her guests, so I only eased the turkey down dead center of the pure white tablecloth.

She called them all to dinner then and I hustled back into the kitchen. Just the help was in there now, and we kept one eye out for Mrs. Ayers, who kept popping in to tell one of us to bring more rolls or silverware or butter. When she finally sat down and started eating, we picked around on what hors d'oeuvres and rolls and scraps of the fudge that hadn't made it out to the table. We all took turns watching the table.

By the time it was my turn they had said the blessing and gotten the first helping out of the way. Some of the ladies, at least those who were watching their figures, had already pushed back and were giving everybody the onceover with eyes as cool and smooth and hard-looking as glass marbles.

Mr. Ayers, though, was leaning in and sawing away on big hunk of turkey. When he got it cut, he stuffed a big bite in his mouth. Then he jammed in mashed potatoes dripping gravy, followed by a forkful of green beans. Already, he'd got gravy on his tie and his face was flushed. His cheeks and eyes both bulged and I marveled that his stomach didn't burst the way he wolfed his food.

I hadn't been standing there long till the table was out of green beans. I went in and got the serving bowl then carried it back to the kitchen. Maria, one of the maids, filled it up and I carried it back. Before I could get back to the kitchen, Mrs. Ayers called out, "Judas, I've forgotten to set the dessert plates out. Will you get them from the corner cupboard and bring them in here?"

"Yes, ma'am," I called back. Knew she liked that kind of talk. It was easy to make people happy. Just give them what they want. Maybe I'd get an extra dollar or two.

I went and found the dessert plates and brought them back and stacked them on the sideboard by the pies. As I turned, Mr. Ayers caught my eye. "Fetch me the whiskey, Judas. You know where I keep it. Oh, and bring some glasses, too. Who all wants whiskey? How about you, Joe? Sam? I know you do, Bill." He went around the room. I wasn't paying much attention. Fact was, I felt silly standing there on the fringe of their big dinner. Thanksgiving didn't mean much to me, but seeing all the family gathered there, talking and laughing and eating and soon to be drinking whiskey made me feel hollow inside. When Mr. Ayers told me, "Six glasses, Judas please," I nodded and hustled out of the room.

The two maids were seated at the kitchen table eating turkey with their fingers. Granny was chewing on a piece of cake. My guts were growling. The few nibbles I'd had weren't doing much to control my hunger.

"What do they want now?" the youngest maid asked. Her name was Francine.

"Mr. Ayers wants his whiskey."

"They are having a party."

"Doing it up right."

Granny chuckled. "Been cooking for the Ayers for a long time. They always knows how to have a good time."

"Well, can't say I'm having much of a good time. I'd better get the whiskey back in there." I had six glasses and the whiskey bottle on the tray by then so I turned and headed for the table.

Mr. Ayers waved me over as soon as I stepped into the dining room. The women were starting to get up to serve the dessert. One of the nieces was a tall slender woman with legs that didn't want to quit. She had her hair up like I liked it. Looking at her made me remember how long it had been since I'd been with a woman. She gave me a smile and I could feel my heart start pounding a little harder.

"Set the tray down there, Judas. Here, let me pour. Sam, I'll start with you."

Everybody seemed like they were set for the moment so I started easing back toward the kitchen. Then, out of the corner of my eye, I caught a glimpse of Mrs. Ayers' face. She was looking at her husband. I couldn't quite read her expression. It sort of looked like she was worried and it sort of looked like she was mad. And maybe she looked just the least bit afraid. Well, none of that was my business. I kept on moving. Turkey and giblet gravy were on my mind. As I left the room I heard Mr. Ayers starting in on what he called the coming conflict. "Now you take Germany, boys," he said. I quit listening. Germany was nothing more to me than Jupiter or Grant's tomb. I lived a hard, narrow life. It worked better that way.

The maids had finished eating so Granny Washburn was starting to move the leftovers into lidded bowls and jars and cover plates with clean dishtowels. I snatched up a chunk of dark meat and a yeast roll. I'd hardly swallowed the last bite before Mrs. Ayers stepped into the room.

"All right," she said, "let's quit feeding our faces and get started on the clean-up. You girls get started on bringing the desserts back in and Judas you can bring it what's left of the turkey and dressing. Oh, and bring in the green beans and sweet potato casserole, too." She turned and walked over toward the stove. "How you holding up, Granny?'

"Tolerable, I reckon."

"Everything was so good."

"Thank you muchly. I do the best I can. Course I ain't as young as I used to be neither."

Mrs. Ayers laughed. "None of us are, Granny."

One of the maids had a left a deviled egg on a plate and I casually picked it up as I walked by. Couldn't remember the last time I'd eaten a deviled egg.

"Get a move on, Judas. You act like you're plumb worn out and you haven't struck a lick at a snake." Mrs. Ayers snorted, putting me in mind of a horse. "If a body didn't know better they'd swear the dead lice were dropping off of you."

I kept walking. When I stepped out of sight, I popped the deviled egg in my mouth. It was a tad mustardy for my taste, but I swallowed it just the same.

The dining room was empty. From the sound of things, the men had gone to the room Mr. Ayers called his study and the women seemed to have moved to the living room. Laughter was coming from both rooms. I picked up the platter with what was left of the turkey. Not a lot of meat remained on the carcass. I guessed Mrs. Ayers could make turkey soup out of it.

I took the turkey to the kitchen and then went back and got the dressing and the casserole. I was headed for the green bean bowl when I heard Mr. Ayers calling. His office was down a short hallway. Smoke was drifting out the door and I knew from the smell the men had been at his Cuban cigars.

Over the years, all sorts of furniture had made its way to Mr. Ayers' office. Mismatched chairs and sagging couches, an old rocking chair in need of fresh paint, along with a nice armchair with the stuffing coming out of one arm. He always said his office was the elephant graveyard for the Ayers family furniture.

I stopped in the doorway. They were talking about the war in Europe and if it would come to America. War was what Mr. Ayers talked about most every day. It was like his mind had fixed on it so hard it couldn't let go. In that way he reminded me of an old snapping turtle. Talk about dive bombers and tanks and *blitzkrieg* swirled around the room like angry wasps swarming out of a damaged nest.

Mr. Ayers waved me in. As I stepped into the study, I caught a glimpse of the bottle. They'd been hitting it hard. Mr. Ayers' face was flushed. An older man, I think they called him Uncle Ned, was dozing on a swayback davenport. All the men in the room stared at me with glassy eyes. Even Lenny had been drinking. I could tell by the boy's eyes. They glittered like hot polished stones. His face was flushed.

"This here's Judas Cain. Judas is my yard man." Mr. Ayers sat up a little straighter and reached for the whiskey bottle. He picked it up. There was one empty glass on the tray and he poured whiskey in it until it was half-full. He put the bottle down and picked up the glass and handed it to me. As he did I couldn't help but notice how red his face was. It looked like he had been sitting in front of a fire.

"Have a drink, Judas. It's Thanksgiving. You need to have some of the good stuff. Give you something to be extra thankful for. Go on, now."

"All right," I said. "Thank you, Mr. Ayers."

"You're welcome. Now take a drink and tell us when and if you think this war in Europe will come to America."

I took a sip. Right off I noticed that it was good stuff. Noticed that even though I was trying to think of what to say. Oh, I'd heard about the war, all right. Who hadn't? What with news of the battles splashed on all the newspapers and reports of it on all the radio newscasts it was hard not to be aware of it. But, to tell the truth, I really hadn't concerned myself with it very much. It wasn't that I didn't realize what an event it was; it was more that I just couldn't see how it was ever going to affect me much. I was probably too old to serve, and besides the government didn't even know where I lived. I never voted or paid taxes or got any mail. Look at things a certain way and I was almost invisible.

The whiskey burned a little going down and I could feel it warming my insides. I grinned and said, "Well, Mr. Ayers, like you said, I'm a yard man, not a newsman."

"But you've heard about Germany and the Nazis and that crazy Hitler, haven't you?"

"Sure."

"Do you think they're coming over here?'

"Sure hope not, boss. But maybe they will. First, though, from what I hear they've got to deal with England. All their planes couldn't do the job. Beating England will take men. Beating the United States will take a lot more men."

Mr. Ayers nodded like I was a pupil at school who had gotten a test question correct. He took a draw of his cigar and leaned forward. "See, Sam, I told you old Judas was a smart fellow."

A man wearing glasses nodded. His head was too big for his body and it made him look lopsided. His eyes were sharp enough, though. I could feel them going over every inch of me. "Sure enough, Arthur, for a yard man, Judas is right well spoken."

"Yes, indeed, and for a yard man he sure does spend a lot of time eating turkey and drinking up our good whiskey."

I didn't need to turn around to know Mrs. Ayers was standing behind me, looking down her big, long nose." Now Judas," she continued, "I need you to quit gabbing and get back to the kitchen and start washing dishes. At the rate you're going it will take you till midnight."

Mr. Ayers smiled and shrugged. "Better go on. No use getting Marilee all upset. That won't be good for any of us." All the men started laughing then and I drained off the rest of the whiskey, eased the glass down on the tray, turned and followed Mrs. Ayers down the hall. She was wearing her good shoes, the ones with heels, and they made her bottom wobble. I could feel the whiskey in me, smoothing out my innards and sending out heat like it was smoldering fire.

~ * ~

One thing I had to say for Mrs. Ayers, she was a good hand at estimating how long it took to clean up after Thanksgiving dinner.

It wasn't midnight, but it sure was hard dark by the time I dried the last serving spoon and put it away. I yawned, stretched and looked around the kitchen.

I'd been pushing, trying to get finished and hadn't paid attention to how quiet the room had become. In fact, the whole house had fallen so silent I could hear a light wind worrying up under the eaves as well as the mantle clock ticking from the living room. Somebody had been playing the radio earlier, but it was off now.

I was the last one in the kitchen and I hung my towel over the back of one of the kitchen chairs, walked to the back porch and got my coat off the rack. The room wasn't heated, except by what warm air drifted there from another room, and I could tell a deeper chill had come with the night. I slipped my coat on, wishing I had a cap. Then I turned and walked back across the kitchen.

I stepped out into the hallway and stopped, trying to figure out where Mr. and Mrs. Ayers had gone. All the guests had left an hour before and the boy had taken off with some friends. The maids had been gone a good ten minutes, but both the Ayers ought to be somewhere.

There was no one in the hall, but I could see a light back toward his study. Walking as quietly as I could, I headed that way. I hadn't quite made the final turn when I heard the snoring. I eased on and peeked in through the door. He was still in his chair, but his head was thrown back and his mouth hung open. His cigar was still smoldering in the ashtray so I tiptoed over and ground it out. Then I tiptoed back out of the room.

Out in the hall, I stood and listened hard and it seemed like I could hear voices coming from the vestibule by the front door. I walked down the hall and through the empty living room. Every pillow was neatly in place and the doilies were straight on the arms of the sofa. I could hear the voices clear now. They sounded like Granny and Mrs. Ayers.

A matching pair of Charleston chairs were by the door and they were each sitting in one. Granny was telling some story about a preacher she knew who swore that the rapture was coming on December 7. My shadow fell across their feet and Mrs. Ayers looked up at me and then turned back to Granny and said something along the lines of well then it wouldn't be long now.

Granny Washburn mumbled something, but I wasn't paying attention. Ought to have been used to Mrs. Ayers and her snubbing ways, but reckon I'm one who can't ever get used to snubbing. Bible verses sang through my head, *Do unto others...* and *an eye for an eye...* and *judge not lest ye be judged...* I suppose they were all good, but sometimes the Bible messed with my mind. In the end the one that stuck was *Let he who is without sin cast the first stone.* Now, I surely was not without sin, so I followed the example of Jesus before the Pharisees and the elders and held my silence. Silence can be a heavy stone. Heavy on those it strikes. Heavy on those who hold it.

The foyer grew so quiet I could faintly hear Mr. Ayers' snores. The sound brought my father to mind and I shuffled my feet to drive out that image. After a few seconds, Mrs. Ayers turned and looked up at me and someway the angle gave her a different look. The shape of her head seemed different, the structure of her face appeared different, even her eyes were different. I tried to name the difference, but couldn't. It was like I was seeing another woman, or a separate version of the same woman. In some way I couldn't define, she looked younger.

"It's late, Judas. Granny needs to get home. I told her you would walk her to her house. It's not far."

In any number of ways it had been a long day. I glanced at the old woman. The day had taken its toll on her, too. Her body sagged on her bones and a nerve twitched in her cheek. I wasn't at all sure she could walk.

"She looks awfully tired. Maybe I could borrow the car and drive her. I'd bring it right back."

Mrs. Ayers' eyes got real wide and she opened her mouth, but nothing came out.

"Oh no," Granny mumbled and started pushing out of her chair. "It's not far. I can make it, Mrs. Ayers. Don't you worry now. And we don't need to bother with no car."

After that, there was nothing for it. I could see Mrs. Ayers was fixing to let loose with some smart remark and I wasn't anywhere near sure I could put up with that right then. So I slipped around Mrs. Ayers right quick, got Granny by the arm with one hand while I opened the front door with the other.

"All right, Granny," I said, "here we go." I stepped out on the stoop and sorta tugged her along. Without looking back, I said, "See you Saturday morning, Mrs. Ayers. I'll pick up my pay then."

Granny mumbled something under her breath that was probably good-night and Mrs. Ayers was starting to say something, but I pulled that door to with a vigor that made the closing pop in the night like a handgun. I wasn't about to give that woman an ounce more satisfaction. Not this night. No sir.

The rain had turned to mist and the wind was down low, worrying the shrubs and rustling the fallen leaves. Lights were on in houses across the street, but they were pale and smeary, the way a lighthouse beacon looks on a foggy night. As we went down the steps, the night train to Memphis blew its whistle down at the station and I knew people were going home on the steel rails.

At that moment, it surely seemed like a fine idea to be riding in the club car on the night train headed to Memphis. A fellow could sit back and relax, read a book or watch the people, or simply sit and look out the window at the lights flickering in that darkness that covered everything.

But I wasn't on a train and all that was just my imagination. Which that along with a nickel would get you a cup of coffee. I'd ridden trains before, all right. Only they were all freights, and I'd hopped every one. Never had ridden on a passenger train; I couldn't go the fare.

So I wasn't going to Memphis tonight. I was walking Granny Washburn home, and then I was walking myself home. Except home was maybe too pleasant a name for my shack. Home made it sound like there would be somebody waiting for you and there would be lights burning with a fire in the hearth. But there was nobody waiting for me—not a wife, nor a child, not even an old hound dog. And the place would be as dark as the night and the hearth would be stone cold.

Thinking all that didn't help a thing. Every man and every woman made their own bed. And I'd made mine, and I'd jolly well have to lie in it. So I got a good grip on Granny's arm as we walked down the drive. Then we turned onto the street toward what the locals called Slabtown. Usually Granny was a talker, but I guess she was purely worn out as she didn't hardly say a word, just mumbled under her breath and put one foot in front of the other. By the time we got to Mulberry Street she was leaning heavy on me along with moaning about every other step. I was sure glad when one of her granddaughters stepped out on the porch and called to her. The sound of that girl's voice perked Granny up enough so that she climbed the three stairs like a younger woman. Somebody called "Thanks" out of the dark, and I lifted a hand. Then I turned and bent to it. The wind was rising again and now it felt like veins of ice were running through it.

Twelve

I was walking down Main Street looking for a barbershop. A block past the post office there was a drugstore, and I walked in to warm up. Ever since Thanksgiving the weather had been raw and damp. I tried to remember the last time I'd seen the sun.

Inside the drugstore it was warm and the air was thick with smells. Coffee was brewing and the scent was strong, mingling with the perfumes some of the ladies were testing and you could smell damp wool, unwashed bodies, plus mediciny scents like Mentholatum and witch hazel. The smell I liked best came from over by the candy counter. They had one of those machines that heated rotating trays of nuts. The scent of roasting cashews made my mouth water.

If I'd had any spare change I'd have bought me a sack of them, but since I didn't I walked on over to the other side of the store and looked at the notions, fountain pens, and handkerchiefs. I wasn't buying any of them either, but at least they didn't smell so good.

I looked around until I started warming up and I was getting ready to leave when I saw a calendar hanging on the wall. It was one of those big calendars that railroad companies give and somebody had X'ed through the days. I'd lost track of exactly what day it was and I wandered over and looked at the calendar. If you could believe the X's it was the middle of the first week of December. Christmas was less than a month away. I wondered if the Ayers would give me a little something extra for Christmas. I thought about that for a minute. In the end, I decided they probably wouldn't. Mr. Ayers wouldn't think of it, while Mrs. Ayers would and decide against it, convinced she'd made a virtuous decision. Guess that all worked out fine, cause I sure wasn't planning on getting them a present. Sure, I knew it was more blessed to give than to receive, but dangerously close to flat broke just didn't feel particularly blessed.

I maneuvered around a pudgy woman in a checked cloth coat and strolled down the aisle and out the door. The wind snatched your breath away and I shivered inside my jacket and wished for a heavier coat. The barber shop was down a block and across the street. I could see the pole. A Buick was rolling east and I waited and crossed in its wake.

~ * ~

There was a wait in the barber shop, but I thumbed through a newspaper somebody had left and back issues of *Field and Stream* and *National Geographic.* I learned that Cordell Hull was in frequent contact with the Japanese ambassador, the best way to catch crappie was by jig fishing, and the ancient pharaohs had been buried with gold and silver. The radio in the shop was on and the station was playing Christmas carols. After forty minutes, the barber motioned me into his chair.

While he cut my hair, we talked about the weather, Roosevelt, and when hard times were going to end. He said he been born two blocks over and never been any further from home than Louisville, where he went to barber school. I allowed as how I had been born in Platte County, Missouri and had at least passed through every state west of the Mississippi and all of them south of the Mason-Dixon Line. He gave me a good trimming and a close shave and I felt like a new man when I walked out of the shop. The wind was still straight off an ice flow, but I was humming "Silent Night."

Maybe I should have gone home, and if I had a whole lot of lives might have turned out different, but since I felt so sharp I thought I'd walk over a few blocks and see if Jessie was out in the wind.

By the time I spied her, standing in front of a joint over on Claxton Street, daylight was starting to go and I was chilled clear down to the bone. But I put a smile on my face and stepped lively down the sidewalk. She was half-turned so that I caught her face in profile. If she caught a glimpse of me coming she never gave any indication. I came up on her quiet like and studied her face, or at least one side of it for a minute. She appeared lost in thought, and I wondered what she was concentrating on.

"Hullo, Jessie," I said, soft like so as not to startle her.

She flinched, but not much. If I hadn't been watching for it, I'd have missed the movement, it was that quick and that slight. For a woman, she had pretty steady nerves.

She turned her head and looked at me. The last of the daylight lighted her face, putting me in mind of one of those Madonna paintings this old professor had always been talking about. He was some retired college professor down on his luck, lugging around a bag full of books and hopping trains in Georgia, when our paths crossed. For a couple of months, we'd hoboed around together, working our way along the Gulf and on in to Texas. He caught pneumonia that fall and I'd had to leave him at the relief in Brownsville.

Anyway, one of the books in his bag was an art book and he'd shown me the pictures of famous paintings and statues and tried to teach me all about them. He was a good teacher, too, except when he started hitting the bottle, which he did whenever he could get a few bits together. Most of what he'd tried to tell me I'd forgotten. But the Madonna painting stuck with me because of a picture in that art book.

"Well, look what the west wind blew in. If it ain't Judas Cain himself." She leaned in and studied me closer. "And look there, he's all barbered up and smelling like talcum powder and pomade. You looking for a big night on the town, Judas? Maybe aiming to celebrate Christmas early?"

"Nope, was looking for you."

"And why were you looking for me, big boy?"

"Does it matter?"

She shrugged. "Not so much, I guess. It's just that most men do for a particular reason."

"Maybe I'm not most men."

Her eyebrows went up and down while her eyes gave me a good going over. "No," she said finally, "don't guess you are."

Down at the station, a freight train was starting to roll. You could tell it was a freight by how long it was taking to get up to speed. I stood and listened to it rumble, thinking, as I always did when I heard one, about where it was going and what I was missing by not swinging up into a boxcar.

A car rolled down the street, its headlights painting us for a second, then moving on. In that moment, I caught a glimpse of her face and it wore an expression I couldn't read. I wondered what mine looked like. The wind flared up, whirling dead leaves down the sidewalk. Jessie shivered and I hunched up tighter inside my jacket.

"Come on," I said, "let me buy you some supper."

She shook her head. There was only enough light left to let me get a sense of the swing of her hair. "Can't, honey, I'm working."

"How about a drink then? Surely you've got time for a drink."

"Can't. There's no bars close."

"Sure there are. I know a nice little one downtown. It's only a ten minute walk. Come on."

"No can do. There's not a bar in my territory. Menifee wouldn't like it."

"What do you mean your territory? And who in hell is Menifee?" She'd mentioned that name before, but it was only another name to me. At least it was then.

She went still. So quiet I could hear the sound of my own breathing, and very faintly, as though it came from far away, the crying of a baby.

Then a light went on in an upstairs room across the street and she gave out a long sigh and spoke into the coming night. "We all have our territories. The streets we work, see. Menifee is the guy who assigns the territories. He sorta watches over us. Understand?"

I didn't say anything. There are times when it's all a man can do to choke down the truth, or at least the truth as he understands it. I finally got it down. Even managed to arrange a smile on my face.

I reached out and took her hand. "Come then," I said, "walk me to the end of your territory. Now I know Menifee can't object to that. Besides, he's probably not out tonight."

"All right," she said. "But you never know about him. He can turn up in the least likely places and you never even know he's there until all at once he's in your face. Some nights I truly believe that he's a natural devil."

I started to laugh then, only I could feel her hand trembling. Instead, I gave it a squeeze and started walking. She hesitated, turning her head and looking both ways like she was crossing a busy street, but she took my arm and we stepped out, strolling down the sidewalk like we were lovers, or maybe even husband and wife.

For three blocks we walked together and the only living thing I saw was a calico cat that crossed our path without even a glance. The cat was moving fast, looking straight ahead. Heading home, I figured, and I wished we were going home, or at least someplace warmer.

Without saying a word, she stopped at the corner where Claxton crossed Washburn. "This is as far as I go, baby."

"All right," I said. "All right for tonight. But let me tell you where I live if you ever need a hot meal or a place to stay. I'm working regular now and there's plenty of room."

She leaned in and kissed me on the cheek. "You're sweet, Judas, and I already know where you live. So, thanks for the invitation. And who knows, I may show up unannounced some night. Never tell with me. I move in and out of people's lives like a spirit."

She squeezed my hand and then let go. "Don't expect too much out of me, Judas. I am what I am and nothing you or any other man can do will change me."

I didn't necessarily buy that, but now wasn't the time to argue. "How do you know where I live?" I asked.

She laughed. "I asked around. This is a small town, in lots of ways. Folks know your business. Sometimes better than you do."

Jessie squeezed my arm. "Gotta go now. Not out in this for my health, you know?" She kissed me on the cheek again. Then she brushed her lips across mine. She tasted of tobacco and whiskey and life. "You're sweet, Judas, but watch out. There's some ornery people in this town."

"You take good care of yourself, Jessie. I'm a big boy," I said. But I was only talking to the dark. Jessie had already turned and was walking back the way we had come. The wind painted my face with cold. I whirled and started the long walk home. Once, I turned back, but all I could see were shadows shifting in the night wind.

Thirteen

"I tried to tell you, Merilee. I tried I don't how many times, but you wouldn't listen. Now they've done it. The damn Japs have done it."

"I know, Arthur. I know already. I heard it on the radio and I read about it in the newspaper. And I've heard you all morning. What good does it do to keep on talking about it? I can't do a d-a-m-n thing about it, and neither can you."

"Damn Japs! This is going to be hell. Pure hell, I tell you. I wrote the old senator, but of course he didn't listen. Nobody listens to me."

"Calm down, Arthur, you're going to have a stroke."

"I'd like to stroke some Japs up the side of the head with a baseball bat. I tell you that, Merilee."

"Honey, your face is all red."

"So my face is red, so what?"

"Why the veins in your neck are popping out."

"What the hell does the state of my neck have to do with the Japanese bombing Pearl Harbor? There will be war. I tell you there will be war."

"Honey, calm down, you're going to have a stroke. You get too upset about things. Just like my Uncle Fred. He got in a big argument with Uncle Jack one Thanksgiving and got all red in the face, then the veins in his neck popped right out and the next thing anybody knew poor Uncle Fred was face first in the candied yams." Mrs. Ayers sighed. "Dead before they could get him to the hospital. All over an argument over the League of Nations. Dead."

"Well, too bad about old Uncle Fred, but I'm telling you there are hundreds, maybe thousands of American boys, soldiers and sailors, lying dead over in Hawaii, and the question is what the hell are Roosevelt and the Congress going to do about it. Well? Answer me that, Marilee. You and your oh don't worry attitude. Answer me that."

"Oh, Arthur, you get so upset. And over something you can't do anything about."

"What! What did you say?"

"I only meant..."

"Pacifist!"

I was standing outside the back door, waiting for them to calm down. Walking in on an argument never struck me as a good idea. Family arguments are the worst. I'd heard them all the way up the driveway. Already it was looking like a long week. They both said something at the same time and then fell silent. I opened the door into that silence.

Mr. Ayers was seated at the kitchen table. A cup of coffee steamed in front of him and he had his newspaper spread in front of him. His face was red and his hands trembled enough to rustle the pages. I glanced at Mrs. Ayers. She was standing at the sink, with a dishtowel in one hand and a plate in the other. Her hair was wild and her eyes looked like they wanted to cry.

I cleared my throat and Mr. Ayers whipped his head around. His eyes were open real wide and they looked like they were burning. A vein throbbed on one side of his head. He hadn't shaved and I wondered if he was sick. By this time, he was usually getting ready to go down to his bank.

He took a deep breath and let it out. Then he managed to grin a little. "You got to quit sneaking up on a man, Judas. For a second I thought you were a Jap."

I must have looked at him funny, cause he said, "You haven't heard, have you?"

I didn't know what he was talking about. He must have figured that out pretty quick, cause he turned and picked up the paper and shoved it at me. "Here," he said, "read it for yourself."

I took the paper. It was open to the front page. A huge headline took up most of the paper above the fold. It said *Japs Bomb Pearl Harbor.* I turned the paper over and read a few lines. Hundreds dead, ships sunk. According to the article, the Japanese were running wild all over the Pacific. I'd known they had been fighting the British over there, so I wasn't totally surprised. Especially the way Mr. Ayers had been ranting and raving for weeks about war. Well, it looked like the boss was right. Not that it mattered much to me, or if it did I couldn't see it.

"Well," he said, "what about those horse apples?"

"Real bad about all those men getting killed."

"You're damn straight. But the really rough thing is Pearl Harbor is only going to be the beginning. Mark my words, Judas, a helluva a lot of Americans are going to die before this is all settled."

"Arthur, I do wish you'd watch your language, especially in front of the help."

There were times when I wanted to smack that woman. Right when she said that about the help was one of them. Maybe I was a yard man, but even a yard man doesn't need his face rubbed in the dirt.

If I could have thought up the right words quick enough I'd have said them. However, whenever I get mad I can't seem to think what to say. Not then, anyway. Later, after I've calmed down, sure I think of some absolutely corking responses. Anyway, it didn't matter cause right then Mr. Ayers turned around and looked dead on at his wife and said, "Just shut up, Marilee." He shook his head slowly, as though it was heavy or he was tired. "Sometimes you amaze me. You know that. Sometimes you absolutely amaze me."

It was one of those moments that was embarrassing for everyone. I wished I'd been a few minutes later. Mrs. Ayers was crying. Not that she was making any noise, or that I could see her tears. She'd turned her back on us and was facing the window that framed the backyard. But her shoulders were going up and down, and then her back jerked and it was easy to see that she had her face buried in her hands. Funny, but in a way I felt sorry for her, yet glad at the same time to see her cut down a notch.

He turned and looked at me and I shrugged. I didn't know what to say. Yeah, it was bad, all those boys being killed and all. I mean I sure didn't want to die. But I couldn't do anything to help the dead.

Mr. Ayers took a deep breath and let it out. "It's going to get bad, Judas. Real bad. I can feel it in my bones."

I thought he was going to say something more. He opened his mouth like he planned to talk, but shut it again, pushed back and stood. "I'm going to go to work. I won't be home for lunch." He stared at her until she nodded, then he turned and walked out.

For a minute I stood quietly and studied her back, wondering. Then, I eased out the back door and walked down the slope. The week before I'd cut down a handful of smaller, trashy trees that had been growing along the edge of the property. Today suddenly seemed like a good time for a fire.

Fourteen

Spring had finally come. The winter had been long, full of raw days and bad war news. The day before there had been rain, driven by a vicious west wind and peppered with sleet. Even this day had dawned cold and overcast. It was a Saturday and the Ayers hadn't needed me, so I'd walked to town to see a cowboy picture and drink a beer. As the apostle Paul said, take a little wine for thy stomach's sake. At least that's the way I remembered that verse.

While I'd been in the picture show a front must have moved in, because when I came out the clouds had disappeared and the sun had warmed the air so I didn't need my jacket. By the time I came out of the bar the thermometer was pushing seventy. Before I could get out of town I'd started to sweat.

As if they had been waiting for the first warm day, crocus had pushed their purple and white heads through the dead leaves and still brown grasses. Robins hopped about on lawns, and spring peepers had begun to call. I took my jacket off, slung it over my shoulder and strolled along like I didn't have a care in the world. With a belly full of popcorn and beer and the first warm sun of the year toasting my back, I felt like a new man. All the bad news in the Philippines and the worries the Ayers had about their boy vanished. At least temporarily.

Between one step and the next, a notion came on me to sit by the tracks and watch the trains pass. I hadn't been there five minutes before a passenger train chugged by, headed for the coast. The faces in the windows were mostly those of young men and I wondered what camp they were headed to. So far the Ayers boy hadn't enlisted. I'd heard them talking though, and he'd only promised to finish the semester.

Guess it was a combination of beer and sunshine and a restless night, but sometime after that train passed I dozed off. The whistle of a southbound freight woke me.

I sat up and looked around. Judging by the shadows, it was late afternoon. The sun hung low on the horizon. In a quarter of an hour it would start to drop behind the tops of the tallest trees. The air had turned cooler and I pushed up, brushed off the seat of my pants, put on my jacket, and started for home.

By the time I made the cutoff, dusk had started to settle in amongst the trees and there was a chill in the air. My hands were cool so I stuffed them into my pockets and picked up the pace.

At first I thought it was an old dog that was sick or hurt and had crawled off into the milkweeds to die. Then the sound came again and something in it made me stop, cock my head and listen. For a minute, there was silence. Then it came again, a low moan. I stepped off the road, jumped the shallow ditch and pushed into the weed patch.

Daylight was gone now, but the afterglow was enough to light the way. Weeds were thick and there were brambles in them and I had to pick my way. With every step it was getting harder to see and in the end I stumbled over his boot.

I fell forward, going down to my hands and knees. Then I could see the face real clear. Right off I knew I'd seen it before and after a moment I figured out who it was. It was the old man I'd fished with back in the summer. The name wouldn't come until I recalled his comment that we both had Biblical names. Then I remember it. Moses, Moses Jurand. He groaned again and I crawled over to him.

In the poor light, it took me a few seconds to see the blood. It was trickling down his face from a gash above the hair line. He was curled up like his stomach hurt and his eyes were closed. His mouth hung open like a sprung door. His shirt was ripped along one shoulder and when I bent down I could see welts. I touched one gently with the tip of a finger and he jerked and moaned. One eye opened very slowly and he mouthed "Don't."

"Hey, Moses, don't be afraid. I'm not going to hurt you. It's me, Judas Cain, your fishing buddy. What happened?"

He blinked and I could see him trying to rouse himself. His open eye glazed over and he blinked and then it went clear and he murmured, "They jumped me. Three of 'em."

I drug my handkerchief out of my hip pocket and dabbed at the gash. The blood seemed to be flowing slower now and I pressed against the wound and got an arm in under his shoulders and lifted his head. He moaned and I think for a second he passed out, but then he groaned and sat up a little straighter.

"Come on, let's get you up."

"No man, I can't make it. Just let me be."

"No way, old man, I'm going to get you home."

"No doctor."

"Nah, no doctor, but let's get you up and over to my place. It's not far and I need to get you in the light where I can see how to patch you up."

"Can't walk, man."

"Don't worry, I'll help you." I began to tug and push up off the ground. He moaned, louder than before.

"Watch the ribs. Think a couple of them are cracked. Bruised for sure. Ouch. Umph. Ohhhh. Damn, man, take it easy."

"I am," I said, and I was. As easy as I could be. Seemed to take a long time, but in the end I got him standing. By then he was cussing me like I was a mangy dog under his breath and I was sweating good. His warm blood was sticky on the side of my neck and I could smell that coppery scent that smells like nothing else in the world.

"All right, Moses, we've got you upright. Now let's start walking."

"Damn you, Judas. You're fixin' to finish what those white bastards started."

"No way, old man. Only planning to get you to my place where I can see what the hell I'm doing and then see how much of my hobo medicine I recall."

"You're probably nothing more than a witch doctor. Damn, man, watch those ribs."

"Hush, you old varmint and start walking."

"I can't. My legs ain't cooperating so good at the moment."

"That's all right. I'm going to help you. Now here we go. Step."

"Ouch."

"Step."

"Um."

"Almost to the road now. We're going to make it."

"Maybe. If you don't kill me first with this Good Samaritan act."

"Hush and keep moving."

"Damn, oh damn. You're killing me, Judas Cain. Purely killing me."

~ * ~

"You live hard, Judas."

He'd been quiet and still so long I thought he'd dozed off. For sure, I must have been dozing, for when I blinked and looked around I could see that daylight was trying to burn through the morning mist. It was very early because the light was still chancy. I could make out the line of trees and the sand road curving through it like a scar. But I couldn't make out more than that, and the lone bird that chirped did so sleepily.

I turned from the window and looked across the room at the old man lying in my bed. He had raised himself up and propped his head against the wall. In the dim light, his skin looked lined and wrinkled and folded in on itself like a poorly tanned hide.

"I've lived harder. Lots of people live harder now."

"Reckon so," he said, "but I allowed how you'd be doing better. I mean working for the Ayers and all."

"They live high on the hog, but pay bottom of the barrel."

He started to laugh at that, but then winced and wrapped his arms around his chest.

"Hurting?"

"Some."

I pushed out of the chair I'd spent the night in and crossed the room. "What hurts worse, the head or the ribs?"

He studied on that one a moment, then said, "Head, I reckon. Ribs hurt like hell when I move or laugh, but if I'm still they're not so bad. Head, though, it hurts all the time. Throbs."

I leaned and gently plucked at the homemade bandage until I could see the wound. It was a long slash, running from almost the crown of his head at an angle until it crossed the hair line and slid on along his forehead. It looked nasty, but the good thing was that it wasn't very deep. Had it been, I doubted there was much I could have done. He'd have probably bled out, either before I stumbled across him or after. I'd had the devil's own time getting the bleeding stopped as it was. In that pale early light the wound looked raw and alive. My stomach churned and my head felt woozy just looking at it, but I swallowed hard, took a deep breath and felt considerable better. Thing now was to keep it clean and covered.

"I'm going to get some water heating, so we can wash that out."

He turned his eyes up and peered into my face. "You ain't fixin' to use no boiling water on that cut are you, Judas?"

"No, we'll let it cool down first. It's only that the water out here isn't strictly sanitary, and we sure don't want infection to set up."

"No, don't reckon we do."

I went then and lit a fire under a pan of river water. I put some more on for coffee. My eyes felt heavy, gritty.

While the water was heating, I walked over to the window and looked out. The light was stronger and the sun was burning off the mist. A robin hopped about in the scraggly grass and a squirrel chattered from a low branch of a hickory. "Want to tell me what happened?"

He didn't say anything. Not right away. I stood there and listened to a wren start chirping from under the eaves. After a bit, I heard Moses shift in the bed. Then he grunted. Finally, he said, "There was three of them. Jumped me as I was coming home."

I turned and looked at him. "Who were they?"

"Don't rightly know their names, but I sure enough know their faces. Sure won't never forget them." He closed his eyes. Then he opened them. They looked like small stones that had been heated and polished.

"Two of them were some of the Cox boys. The ones that live over toward Mayking. The other one I'd not seen before, but he had that long-headed look that lots of them Bennett men have."

"Why would they jump you? Think you had money?"

"No way. Everybody know I'm straight from poverty row. No sir, they jumped me on account of my niece, Sissy Greenlee."

I didn't understand where Moses was going with this. I walked over to the stove. Tiny bubbles were popping to the surface. I spooned coffee into one pot. "What's your niece got to do with anything?"

Moses started to laugh again, then choked it off. "That's right," he said, "you ain't from around here. I keep forgetting. My niece is one of those girls what's always had a hard time knowing right from wrong. That comes from no daddy in the house and a momma who likes her wine."

He looked away from me then, staring out the window. His eyes looked like they were focusing on something miles away.

"She's run hard ever since she come into her womanhood. I tried to step in and be some kind of a daddy for her, but I'm an old man and young girls don't pay no nevermind to old men."

He sighed and his eyes came back in the room. "Soon as she was able, she went to hanging around with boys, and from there she graduated to men. Sissy was always one of those kids who wasn't very good in school, but she sure was fine at pleasing the men."

I didn't see anything particularly wrong with that and I guess what I thought showed through on my face. He lifted one hand and pushed it at me.

"Yeah, I know what you're thinkin', Judas, and if she'd ever have settled down with one of those fellas and had some babies and raised a family, well, I'd say all right. A few wild oats ain't too bad. Most young people sew a few before they learn. Only Sissy, she never learned. I tried a dozen times to tell her, reason with her, you might say. But..." He paused and shook his head slowly, gently.

I could hear the bubbles starting to pop in the pan and I crossed the room, took the one off the fire and poured water out in my wash pan. Then I carried it and a clean cloth over to the bed. I set the pan down on the floor and dipped the cloth in the water, let it soak a minute, then pulled it out, wrung some of the water out of it and let it cool. When I pressed the damp cloth to the puckered skin around the wound Moses grimaced and sucked air in between his teeth.

"About two, maybe three years ago now she quit giving it away and started selling it. Went to work for Brad Menifee, who happens to be about the worst excuse for a human being I ever did see. He controls all the prostitutes around here. Took over when Leroy Artis went swimmin' in the river wearing a logging chain around both legs. Brad Menifee don't brook no competition, nor no interference from friends or family. It was his enforcers jumped me."

I dabbed at the wound, soaking off dried blood. The light had grown better and the wound looked worse. "You're going to need stitches. Guess close to twenty. Once you get your strength up, you'd better catch a ride into town and see a doctor. You know one?"

"Actually, I know three doctors. But one of 'em purely hates Negroes and I wouldn't trust him one inch further than I could throw him. Of the other two, one won't doctor on credit, at least not for Negroes. Which leaves only Doc Blevins, and he drinks right smart. But I guess if he's sober, or not too bad hungover, he'd sew a fellow's head up for him and let him pay along as he could."

"Know anybody that will give you a ride?"

"My sister's boy, Eudell, he's got a truck. He'll be glad to take me. I cured his wife of the dropsy a year or so back."

As gently as I could I patted the old man's head dry. "Didn't know you were a doctor, Moses."

"No, no, don't misunderstand me. I ain't no doctor. Only learned a few ancient remedies and medicines from my grandmother and some of the other old timers. Certain diseases and spells I can sure enough cure. But I'm not a real doctor, not one with a diploma and one of them x-ray machines and a nurse and all such."

I laughed and laid the wet cloth across the back of my chair to dry. Then I bandaged his head again. I was no doctor, either, but the wound was covered and I'd stopped the bleeding. I wondered about something the old man had said. It reminded me of a conversation I'd had. "You say this Menifee guy has all the prostitutes in this town on a string?"

"That's right, every dang one. And if some other man tries to start a string or some woman figures to go into business for herself, well, let's just say that they don't last very long. No, it's either Brad Menifee's way or the highway."

"You know for sure if he's got a woman named Jessie working for him?"

Moses gave me a quick hard look from under his bandages. "Tall woman, big old dark eyes, and cheekbones fixing to poke right through the skin?"

"That's the one."

He nodded. "Yeah, she's one of his. At first, he kept her to himself, but I heard they had a fallin' out. Never did hear why, but I've heard she's a high-spirited woman with an independent streak. Old Brad, now he wouldn't appreciate such as that, specially in a woman. Still, I'd go real careful around Miss Jessie. Hear tell, Brad Menifee is one jealous man."

I'd sort of had an inkling and tried not to let my face show anything. The room went quiet as we fell silent, watching the light change, listening to each other breathe, thinking our own thoughts.

Finally, the old man fingered the bandage gently. He smiled. "You ain't too bad a witch doctor yourself, Judas."

"Just a little hobo doctoring I learned along my travels."

"You've seen a lot of this country then?"

"Fair amount."

The old man eased his head back on the bed. "Which part would you say is your favorite?"

I thought about his question for a moment. "Hard to say, Moses. Guess I like something about most of them, but not everything about any of them."

"Sort of like women, eh?"

"Sure enough," I said, and then we both laughed.

"Let's have a cup of coffee," I said and pushed off the side of the bed.

"Sounds mighty fine," the old man said. "Mighty fine."

Fifteen

Daylight was going fast by the time I finished mowing the bottom and I rested for a few minutes on a large rock that always made me think of a buffalo. The air faded to blue, then slashes of purple filtered in and then it went a smoky gray. Finally all the light left and there was only darkness.

The evening was a quiet one. I could hear a bird or two twittering sleepily and tired-sounding mothers calling their children home for the night. Tree frogs started up and then a whippoorwill began singing across the road. When I heard the night train to Birmingham start up down at the station, I got off the rock and started pushing the mower back up the slope. My sweat had dried and I felt sticky all over. Mosquitoes whined like electricity gone bad and the air was so humid it felt like invisible rain.

A tiny red light was glowing in the deep shadows beneath the big elm that stood by the tool shed. It wasn't until I got to the flat part of the back yard that I figured out it was the hot end of a cigarette. Mr. Ayers smoked cigars and Mrs. Ayers didn't smoke, so I had a pretty good idea who was standing there
. Now why he was sitting in the shadows, well I didn't know.

Inside the house somebody had the radio on and they were listening to dance music. The music made me think about Jessie and right then I wanted to be with her so bad it hurt like somebody had stabbed me in the guts with an ice pick.

Whoever was smoking in the shadows must have been listening to the music, or else their mind was miles away, cause they let out a small surprised sound when I pushed the mower into the tool shed.

"Damn, but you scared me, Judas. Didn't have any idea you were around."

"Wondered if that was you, Mr. Lenny. Saw the glow of your cigarette."

He chuckled. "Thought for a second you were Mom. She hates to hear about young people smoking. Started last semester and now I smoke about every day. After Pearl Harbor it didn't seem to matter so much. Still, I haven't told her."

"Don't you think she'll find out?"

"Yeah, probably. But I'd rather not stir her up right now. She's so upset about the war."

"What's got her so upset?"

"Well, it's that...Hey, you want a smoke?"

"Sure," I said. Smoking wasn't something I did a lot of, but it usually wasn't good practice for the hired help to turn down the boss's son. He handed me the pack and I tapped one out and stuck it in my mouth and bent over. He fired up a match and I drew in smoke.

"You were saying."

"Well, she's all upset cause the paper has been listing the local soldiers who have been wounded or killed. We knew a couple of them. One of them was Eddie Tutt. He was in my high school class. Stayed home after graduation and worked out to the Burdine Plant. Joined up right after Pearl Harbor. Japs killed him somewhere in the Pacific. Hit her pretty hard."

He paused and drew in smoke, then blew it out. The night seemed to be settling gently around us. The air was fragrant with the scent of mimosa blossoms and the dance music was soft and sweet. The only other sound was the faintest whisper of leaves as the night breeze ruffled them.

If a stranger had passed by and seen us smoking he might have thought that we were simply a couple of friends having an after-dinner smoke. Out here, in the shadows, the only light came from the glowing cigarette ends. Beyond the shadows, lamps had come on in houses and light spilled from the windows. That light looked soft and warm and homey. Hard to believe that halfway around the world young men were getting killed and maimed. I wasn't particularly scared of the Japs or the Germans, but I also wasn't sure I much liked the world the way it was. I took a drag off the cigarette and blew smoke into the soft darkness.

"Judas?"

"Yeah?"

"You ever been in the army or the navy?"

"Army, a long time ago."

Lenny coughed and spit. "I've been thinking about joining."

I leaned against the tool shed. My legs ached and my throat was dry and my stomach was growling. I wanted to go home, not stand around smoking and jawing with a college kid. But he was the boss's boy and, besides, there was something about him tonight that made me think he wanted to talk, needed to talk. Over the past few months we'd said a few words whenever he was home, but I couldn't claim we done any real talking. Tonight felt different. I took another drag off my cigarette.

"Thought you promised your mother you wouldn't do that."

"What I promised my mother was that I wouldn't do anything before the end of the semester. Been home over a week now."

"Aren't you worried about being killed?"

"Don't you think there are more important things in this world than dying, Judas? Why, if we don't stop the Japanese and the Germans, who will?"

"Reckon that's a good question, Lenny. But there are lots of other ways to serve than being a soldier or a sailor. A fellow could work in one of those aircraft plants or raise money for the war effort or go to school and learn to be a doctor. Before this war is over, the country's going to need a whole lot of doctors."

"Oh, Judas, that's plain goofy. What do I know about building airplanes? And movie stars are who go on War Bond drives. And as for being a doctor, well, no thank you. No, I'm going to join up. Since I'm not sure about riding in a boat, think I'll join the army. I'm in great shape, you know?"

I looked out across the night. The sky was clear and the stars were coming out and a big moon hung lopsided and orange above the horizon. "You realize, Lenny, that no matter how good shape you are in, you're no match for a bullet."

The kid didn't say anything and I wondered if I had made him mad. Well, all I had done was tell him the truth. And sometimes, maybe most of the time, the truth hurt. I took a final drag and ground out the cigarette against the sole of a boot. I heard Lenny stand up. He must have put his cigarette out, too. There was no light in the shadows.

"Yes," Lenny said, "there is that, I suppose." He turned then. I could tell by his voice that he was facing me. "But then I've always been the luckiest kid I know." He laughed and then I saw him step out into the moonlight and stride across the yard, moving in and out of the shadows like a wild animal on the prowl. For a moment his face would be lighted with moonbeams and then he would step into a shadow and simply disappear, a man-shadow swallowed by a larger one in the thickening night.

"Good luck, kid," I whispered as his shadow disappeared for the final time in the blackness that clung tight against the house. "You're going to need it." Then I pushed the mower into the shed and locked it against the night.

Sixteen

I came awake out of deep sleep with all my nerves jangling. Pale silver light filled the room as though some stars had been melted down and poured in through the window. The moon was up and low and full. I'd never seen such a moonlit night. Back when I was a kid, I'd heard tales from my Uncle Johnny of cutting corn by moonlight, but I'd figured he was pulling my leg. Now, I knew better.

A scratching sound drifted on that moonlight. At first I thought a breeze had sprung up. But then I noticed the remnants of the curtains at the sides of the open window. They hung straight down, unmoving.

I sat up and listened. The sound came again. It sounded like a cat scratching. I got up and slipped on my pants. Something was scratching at the door. Cats ran wild all along the river and I figured it was one of them, hungry. Or maybe a hurt dog. I walked across the room, wishing that I had a good stick, or a knife.

As I reached the door there was another sound. It sounded like a fussy baby. I cocked my fist and opened the door.

She was propped up against the wall next to the door. Blood was on her face and her dress was torn. She looked up at me. Her eyes were glass. Pain wriggled across her face. I knelt.

"Where you hurt, Jessie?"

"All over, baby, all over."

"Let's get you inside," I said, sliding one arm under her. "See if we can't doctor you up."

"Be easy," she said, and a long low moan slipped out and hung there in the night.

"Sorry."

"Go on. Get me inside."

I twisted up on one knee and then pushed off. She came up in my arms, lighter than I'd expected. I carried her across the room like she was a child and eased her down on the narrow bed. She moaned again and the sound made me wonder if she was broken inside.

I lit the lamp and filled a bowl with water. Then I dug out a clean white handkerchief and began to wipe away the blood. Her eyes were closed and my heart jumped. Then her eyes fluttered open and she smiled. It wasn't much of a smile, but I was glad to see it anyway.

"Anything broken?"

"Naw. They know how to hurt without breaking. They're experts."

"Who did it, Jessie?"

"Nobody you'd know."

"Some of Brad Menifee's men?"

Her eyes widened. I could sense them searching my face. Then she closed them. "You do get around don't you, Judas?"

"I try."

Her face looked like a punching bag. She'd have a shiner for sure in the morning, along with a bruise was already turning blue along her jaw line.

"What did you do to make him so mad?"

Her eyes opened again. For a moment she stared at my face. Then she said: "None of your business. Got any whiskey?"

I kept a little for the Spanish flu and I crossed the room and found the bottle and carried it back over along with a dainty looking teacup a prior resident had left.

"You sure you should be drinking? Way you're holding your stomach you're all beat up inside."

"Shut up and pour."

Against my better judgment, I poured. Never had been any account at talking a woman into much of anything. I lifted her head and held the teacup to her lips. She got it all down in two swallows.

"There," she said, "that's better." I eased her head back on the pillow and she gave me a rather wilted smile. "Thanks, baby."

I nodded. "Feel like something to eat?"

"Right now, I don't think I'll ever want to eat again." She shifted her body and made a face. "My insides feel all mashed up."

"They worked you over pretty good."

"Don't think I don't know it."

"Why don't you go ahead and tell me who they are?"

"No way. You're a nice guy, Judas. Those guys don't play nice."

"Maybe I'm not as nice as you think."

She had closed her eyes, but she opened them again and gave me a long cool look. "Maybe not, but you're not the man to take them down. No one man is."

"They need to be stopped, though."

She made another face. "Maybe the Japs will, or the Germans."

I'm sure she meant to be funny, but the way things were going in the Pacific and Europe I didn't feel much like laughing. I thought about Lenny then, wondering if he would really enlist and if he did what his mother would say. She was one woman I sure didn't understand. Not that I truly understood any woman. Maybe she was simply more of a pain than most.

Jessie sighed then, a soft sound that evaporated as quickly as it had entered the room. Her eyes were open, but they were filled with that faraway look. Her bruise was purpling up quickly and she winced as the pain bit. Tiredness was settling on my shoulders. It felt old and heavy and mean. I stood up.

"You better get some sleep. Always heard that sleep was nature's cure."

"What about you? You don't look so fresh yourself."

"It's late, that's all. Way after midnight. I'll just lay a blanket on the floor and stretch out."

"Hate to take your bed."

"Don't worry about it. Slept in worse places plenty of times."

She smiled and sighed and closed her eyes. Lying there, she looked real peaceful. Like a little girl. Only those marks on her face told another story. I went and got a blanket off the shelf I'd nailed up back in the winter and spread it out across the doorway. I'd didn't have any idea how Jessie had gotten out to my place and I half-expected Menifee's goons to show up. Wasn't sure what I could do if they did. One thing I didn't aim to be, however, was surprised.

All the trees and the ground were bathed in moonlight. Don't think I ever saw a brighter night. If a man had a newspaper he could have read it by that light. Small creatures rustled through the underbrush and an engineer laid on his whistle down where the tracks bend to the south. I closed my eyes and listened to that old lonesome sound and a part of me sure wanted to be rolling on down the line. But I had business to tend to here. Just wasn't at all sure how any of it was going to play out.

My eyes felt heavy, but my mind was spinning like a child's top. Jessie's breathing was ragged for a bit, then it smoothed out and my mind started to still. Last thing I remember was hearing an owl hooting down in the timber and that made me think of an old slave saying about an owl being a sign of death coming in the family. I'd read that down in New Mexico in the Tucson Public Library. A hobo sure leads an interesting life.

~ * ~

I blinked and came awake. Outside a dog was barking. I pushed off the floor and eased over to the window. Judging by the light, it was mid-morning. I couldn't see the dog, but he sounded close. I was still looking for him when I heard the sheets rustle. I turned around.

Jessie was sitting up in bed. A purple bruise covered one side of her jaw, she had a shiner under her right eye, and her lips were swollen. Other than that, she was gorgeous. She stretched and dredged up a smile. I felt my face smile back.

"I'll say this, Judas, you've got a nice face to wake up to."

"That can be arranged," I said, then felt my face grow warm.

Jessie laughed. "Why, Judas Cain, you're blushing."

I shrugged and tried to focus my mind on something else. "You hungry? I can fix us some breakfast."

"Um, let me remember when I ate last. Yeah, maybe I ought to eat a little something. Only not too heavy. My tummy is pretty sore."

"You feel all right? I mean, inside? Not like you're bleeding in there, is it?

"Don't think so. Just sore. I'll sit here awhile, though, okay?"

"Sure. What would you like to eat?"

"Got any eggs?"

"One."

She nodded. "Okay, one egg, soft-boiled, and toast."

"Best I can do there is cornbread. Don't have any light bread."

"All right, but how's about a cup of tea. A cup of tea always cheers a girl up."

I shrugged again. Until that moment, I don't guess I'd done much thinking about how poor I really was. "Sorry, Jessie. All I got is coffee."

"Really?" She twisted up her face until she managed to look halfway ugly. "Okay, then. What's the old saying? Beggars can't be choosers. Oh, and while you're at it, I guess I'll need some clothes. I realize it's too much to hope that you've got a dress my size lying around, but what about an old sweater or a shirt?"

"Okay," I said, "I'll see what I can do. First, let me get started on the cooking. Oh, and while I'm doing that do, you mind to tell me how you ended up at my place last night? This shack is not exactly downtown."

She eased back on the bed and pulled the sheet up to her chin. "They dumped me at the end of the road. I knew where you lived from asking around and, since I wasn't going to go far anyway, I thought I'd take a chance. Now enough questions, mister. I'm not going to talk about it anymore." She eased onto her side and shut her eyes. "Wake me when breakfast is ready."

There were a lot more questions I wanted to ask. Questions I felt needed answering. But even a moron could see that she wasn't in the mood to talk right now. I got a fire going under some water and dropped the egg in. Then I went to hunt up an old shirt.

Her breathing had changed. It was soft and low and rhythmic. For a moment, I stood quietly and watched her breasts rise and fall. Out in the woods the dog was still barking. He sounded every bit as lost as I felt.

Seventeen

It wasn't much past ten o'clock, but already it was hotter than three shades of hell. At least, it felt that way to me as I trudged up the driveway. Usually, I was at work by eight, but today I'd had to swing by the hardware store and pick up nails I needed for a job Mrs. Ayers wanted done. The man who ran the hardware store, I think his name was Perkins, had been late and then he'd left his keys at home and had to go back. One way and another it had taken a hunk out of the morning to buy a sack of nails. According to the calendar, it was only late June, but a front had swung up out of South Texas and heated up the entire south. The air felt like it was straight from the bowels of Mexico.

I was sweating like a big hairy dog by the time I was halfway up the drive, so I tucked the sack under one arm, pulled out my handkerchief and started mopping my face. The morning was still and quiet. Only the high, dry hum of locusts broke the silence.

"Hot enough for you, Judas?"

I hadn't known anybody was close by and my body jerked as I turned toward the voice. Mr. Ayers was sitting in a lawn chair in the shade of the biggest sugar maple I'd ever seen. Gorgeous when the leaves turned, but a pain in the butt when they started to drop. A bottle of beer was in one hand and a cigar was drifting smoke in the other.

"Yes, sir, it sure enough is," I said and started wandering over his way. What he had in his hand wasn't wine like the apostle Paul said we should drink for the stomach's sake, but all of a sudden a cool beer seemed like a mighty fine way to break up the morning. Experience had taught that if Mr. Ayers had one beer, he was likely to have more nearby.

Even in the shade of the maple, the air was warm and sticky. Seemed like the wind had plumb forgot how to blow. Still, it was some better to not have sunlight pouring directly onto your head.

Although he was sitting quietly, the boss had unbuttoned his shirt and sweat coated his hairy chest. Probably at one time he had taken care of his body. Maybe he had even been an athlete. But now his chest was sagging and his stomach pushed out so much it looked like he'd swallowed an inflated basketball. I mopped at my face some more and studied him out of the corners of my eyes. His skin looked flushed, yet doughy. His eyes had that bulgy look some dogs' eyes have.

He lifted his beer bottle and inclined it in my direction. "Want one? Or is it too early for you?"

"Not in this heat."

"Awful, isn't it?"

"Brutal."

"Beer's in the tub under the tree. Help yourself. But try not to let Mrs. Ayers see you. Bring it back over here to drink it. That way, she can't see us out the window. Angle's no good. She's on the warpath and I don't need any more grief. Every day she's upset about something. Of course, it's really because Lenny enlisted."

He twisted his neck and peered up at me. His eyes seemed to be trying to focus. Looked to me like he was already half loaded. "You know he'd enlisted?"

I shook my head. "We talked about it, but at that point he hadn't made up his mind."

"I don't blame him. Enlisted myself back in the Great War. That's what they called it then. Claimed it was the war to end all wars. Bull shit, as usual." He jerked his head. "Go get your beer."

"Okay," I said and moseyed over to the bucket, which was really an old tin tub that had held flowers at one time. Now it was about half full of melting ice. Four or five full beer bottles stood in the ice. I pulled a bottle out and carried it back over to where Mr. Ayers was sitting. Two empty bottles stood at attention beside his chair.

"Sorry, Judas, don't have a chair for you. Wasn't expecting company."

"That's okay," I said, easing down to the ground. "This will do mighty fine." I flipped the cap off with a thumbnail and took a long drink. It had been a while between beers and it tasted good.

Mr. Ayers titled his head and winked. "Good stuff, eh?"

"Sure enough."

He nodded and for a couple of minutes we sat quietly, drinking beer and looking out across the sun-soaked grass. I don't know what he was seeing. I was simply looking, glazing over everything, not really thinking of anything. All that heat made me stupid. Hated to think about having to get up and work.

"This war is bad news, Judas. They're starting to draft boys now."

"I heard."

"Draft means almost every blessed family in America is going to be affected. Lots of boys who are called up aren't ever going to come back."

"Things aren't going so hot for us, are they, Mr. Ayers?"

He took a puff off his cigar, held the smoke for a moment, then blew it out. "Nope. Japs and Germans are rolling up the Pacific and Europe. Hard to see how they can be stopped, but somebody will have to do it sometime."

"What about the British?'

"They're good fighters, sure enough. Just not enough of them and they can't hold out forever. Damn French collapsed like wet tissue paper." He took another drink, a big one. "Worthless bastards. Never did like the French."

He drained his beer and tossed the bottle over by the other empties. "Grab me another one, will you, Judas? Get yourself another, too, while you're at it."

I got up and walked over to the tub and snagged him another one. Not that I wouldn't have liked another one, but I had to work and Mrs. Ayers would surely notice if I was too loaded. I carried the beer back to the boss.

"Thanks, but what about you?"

"Thanks anyway, but I've got to work. Mrs. Ayers has got a special job for me." I shook the sack of nails. "You know how she is."

"Don't I though. She's been on a rampage all week. Always on my case about something, moaning and griping and generally raising hell. All that bitching makes my head hurt. Doesn't do my blood pressure a damn bit of good either." He belched and grinned and I nodded and drained my beer. I set the empty down by the others and started up the driveway again.

At the top, I turned and looked back. Mr. Ayers was still sitting under the maple. He lifted his bottle to me as though he was making a toast.

~ * ~

Mrs. Ayers was sitting at the kitchen table. Her back was to the door and she was facing the window. Only she wasn't looking out of it. Her arms were folded on the table and her head was pressed down on them. Her shoulders trembled and I stopped outside the door.

Didn't seem right intruding when she was like that. She wasn't crying now, at least not that I could hear, but something in the way her body had arranged itself made me think maybe she had been.

That was a strange thought; Mrs. Ayers had never struck me as the crying kind.

I shifted my feet and must have made more noise than I intended because she jerked her head up and cleared her throat.

"Is that you, Arthur?"

"No ma'am, it's me, Judas."

She sniffed and cleared her throat. "I see," she said, although she never turned around. I stepped into the kitchen and could see her dabbing at her eyes.

I walked over to the table. She never even twitched. I put my hand on the back of her chair. Something in me wanted to touch her, pat her on the back and tell her everything was going to be all right. Course, I knew better than to do something stupid like that. Still, I thought I ought to make some sort of an effort. It was clear as Sunday morning she was suffering over something.

I knew I'd probably catch grief over it, but I asked anyway, "Anything wrong, Mrs. Ayers?"

She sighed and for a moment I thought she was going to answer me. But then her back straightened and she pushed away from the table and whirled away from me, headed for the pantry. Over her shoulder, she said in her clear, calm voice. "Time to get started on the shelves, Judas. You did get the nails, I trust."

"I got 'em," I said and started for the coat room. I could feel the back of my neck turning red. "Bitch," I muttered under my breath.

I can't say whether she heard me or not, but her whole back twitched like it was one jumping nerve and she came to a dead stop. But she didn't say anything. After a minute, she started walking again. Mrs. Ayers had always struck me as a hard woman, a woman who was soft on the outside but with a core like a shaft of oak on the inside. All the way to the shelves I kept thinking about that. I'd shake the sack of nails and think about that hard core. It was like some thought related to that hardness was trying to poke out, but couldn't quite make it.

It was on up in the day, after lunch, when it came to me. A memory of a time, four or five years earlier, when I'd been on-the-bum in Florida, sleeping in town squares or on the beaches, catching rides on the fruit trains and existing mainly on oranges and strawberries. That October one of those hurricanes blew in out of the Gulf. It was supposed to hit at least fifty miles from where about a dozen of us were gathered in a hobo camp on the beach. None of us had ever been though a hurricane and fifty miles was a long way to men who most usually had to walk if they were going anywhere. So we stayed.

The forecasters must have missed the mark on the landfall, or maybe the storm veered at the last minute. In any case, it smashed into our little camp right after daybreak. Don't let anybody kid you, being in a hurricane, even if you not in the dead center, is pretty damn close to hell on earth. Three of the guys in the camp were killed. Four or five more simply vanished.

What I remember most, even more than the dead bodies and the surging water and the sand that was everywhere, was the trees. That wind smashed into them like a cannonade. Funny thing was that all the big strong trees, like the oaks, broke in two and splintered like balsa wood, while the palms swayed like Hawaiian hula girls but rode out the storm in pretty good shape. Oh, they'd dropped a few fronds and damn near all their coconuts, but they survived, while those hard-ribbed oaks were only good for firewood. I wasn't predicting, now, only remembering.

Eighteen

It was that time of the afternoon when stillness holds. Most afternoons you'll find, if you study them the way a man out on the road does, have a quiet period, a time when the wind dies down, the birds go quiet, and bees float off to other pastures. The entire landscape goes silent for a spell. Happens all over the country—Tennessee, Texas, Missouri, Kansas, Kentucky, California—you name a state and I promise you the days there will have their quiet time.

I was having a quiet time, too. It was a Saturday and the Ayers had gone to see Lenny, so I had the day off. He had been sent to Fort Knox, up in Kentucky, for training and had a weekend pass—the last one before he shipped out. Mrs. Ayers had been teary-eyed all week thinking about that. Mr. Ayers had been quiet, hitting the bottle in the evenings and puffing like a fiend on his fat cigars.

One afternoon I'd happened on him sitting quietly at his desk, writing what looked like a letter. He saw me standing in the hall and lifted his head. Think he aimed to say something—he even opened his mouth—but he never spoke. Only shrugged and shook his head and went back to his letter. Later, I wondered if he'd been writing his son. As I never had any kids, at least not any I knew about, I couldn't truly put myself in his shoes. Still, I figured it had to be a sorry sort of hell to see your only son go off to war. Every day the paper listed the boys who had died or been wounded or captured, or gone missing-in-action. Some people the Ayers knew had already gotten telegrams from the War Department.

But, to tell the truth, I didn't think too awful much about the war. Some days I thought about Jessie and some days my mind drifted back to my travels, to the men I'd met riding the rails, or picking peaches, or drinking rotgut around a campfire in the night on the wrong side of the tracks deep in the poor side of town.

Then there were days I spent wondering about what was going to become of me. Oh, what with the work at the Ayers I was getting by, but what about tomorrow, or the day after, or the day I woke up and found my body had grown old without my permission. That happened. Witnessed it with my own eyes. People's bodies betrayed them all the time. Sometimes it was the cancer, other times a heart attack, or TB. In the end, even if you managed to avoid the killing diseases, old age got you. Yeah, the Grim Reaper was out there and somewhere down the line he was sure to get you.

Anyway, like I said, the afternoon had gone quiet. I was shaving, getting ready for Saturday night, sipping coffee and not thinking about anything of importance to anybody else. I was scraping my jawline when I heard a faint whistling.

At first, I didn't think anything of it. Some kids had been playing under the hickories earlier and lots of people walked to town and back on Saturday. In all the months I'd lived in the shack the only people besides me who'd crossed my threshold had been Jessie and old Moses, and both of them had been hurt bad. Neither one had come back. I wasn't figuring on that to change.

In a minute I heard a shift in the whistling sound. Now, it sounded like whoever was whistling was coming down the path that lead to my door. I laid my razor down, picked up my coffee cup, and walked to the door.

On account of the heat it was standing open, and I leaned against the frame and looked out across what passed for my yard. Under the stand of oaks I could see a man walking. He was deep in the shade and I couldn't make out his face. Then, he stepped out into the sunlight and I saw it was old Moses of the river.

He looked up and must have seen me standing in the doorway, because he stopped and waved. I waved back and he came on. I sipped coffee and watched him tromp across the yard, his boots bending the weeds down and stirring up dust.

He slowed as he came up to the shack and I wondered whether he wanted to come in. Like I said, I wasn't used to visitors. Maybe ten yards away he stopped and pulled a handkerchief out of a back pocket and swiped at his face.

"Hot, ain't it?"

"Considerable."

"And you drinking coffee, too. In this heat. What's up with that?"

"Trick I learned down in Mexico. Tampico. Got to wondering how the Mexicans stayed so cool in all that awful heat and I studied them for a while and figured out why they ate so much hot spicy foods."

"Now, tell me, why do they do that?"

"Well, a buddy of mine, name of Howard Vandergrift, and I decided that what those Mexicans were doing was getting the insides of their bodies hotter than the air outside, so that air naturally felt cooler."

The old man took off the straw hat he was wearing and rubbed at his wooly head. "Got to admit that's an interesting theory."

"Drunk a heck of a lot of coffee ever since," I said. Then I grinned and winked. "Course that could be cause coffee is only a nickel a cup and lots of places a man can get a free refill."

Moses let his head fall back then and he laughed. Sweat stood out on his face like he had walked through a waterfall. There wasn't even a hint of a breeze and the afternoon was so still you felt like it might crack solely from his laughing. Then, way off, I heard the grumble of a tractor and I took a sip of coffee and said, "Want to come inside? Get out of that heat."

"Sounds good to me," he said and I turned and went back inside.

He paused inside the door, blinking as he adjusted to the light.

"Have a seat," I said, nodding at my only chair. "Looks like you've been walking a ways."

"Thanks," he said. "Think I will." He sighed deep as he eased down on the chair and I wondered how old he really was.

"Want some coffee? Or maybe a sip of whiskey? Just to cut the dust."

"Little dust cutter surely sounds fine."

I drug the bottle out from under the bed. There were about three good swallows left. I poured him one in a coffee cup and carried it over. He swallowed it whole, blinking and clearing his throat.

"There, that's better." He gave me a look up and down, lingering on my face, and I figured I had lather clinging. I reached up and wiped it off with my towel.

"Looks like you getting ready for a big time."

I nodded. "Saturday night, you know."

"Sure enough," he said. Then he handed me the coffee cup and stood.

"Thanks for the whiskey. It naturally eases a man's mind. Now, I see you're getting ready to head to town, so I won't keep you long." He looked away and then back. "Ain't really aiming to get in your business, and I hope you don't mind me asking, but have you got a date?"

I put the cup down. "Might say that."

"With a woman named Jessie?"

I wondered what was going on and how he knew my business. "You get around," I said.

"Not really. You recall my niece I mentioned?"

I nodded.

"Well, I seen her the other night and she said there was a lot of talk in certain circles about you and Miss Jessie. She didn't know your name, but she had your description down real good. Didn't take me anytime to figure out who she was talking about. According to her, you and Miss Jessie been seeing a lot of each other."

"I've bought her a couple of drinks and supper a time or two. No harm in that, is there?"

"Not normally."

I studied his face. It was full of lines and wrinkles that told me nothing. "I'm supposed to see her tonight. Buy her supper and maybe take a stroll. You got a problem with that?"

"Not me, brother. But I don't count for a hill of beans. Who does count, at least in this, is a man I know too damn well. You recall what I told you about Mr. Brad Menifee?"

I nodded. I was beginning to see where this was headed.

"Well, according to my niece, and I know she's not always in touch with the truth, but I believe her this time, Mr. Brad Menifee considers himself to, let's say, have a special place in Miss Jessie's life, sohe don't like another man messing with her, leastwise on no regular basis. Know what I mean? For sure, we both know how rough Mr. Brad can play."

He quit talking then and looked at me like he was expecting me to say something. Only, I didn't know what to say. Sure, I'd been aware of Brad Menifee, but Jessie hadn't mentioned him lately and I'd figured maybe he'd lost interest.

"Well," Moses said, "after all the doctoring you did for me, figured I at least owed you a warning. Now that I've said what I came to say, guess I'll be going. You a busy man, Judas Cain, working for a banker and dating Miss Jessie. Bet nobody else in the whole county can say that." He nodded then, real formal like, and started for the door.

I reached out and touched his arm. He stopped and stared at me. His face might have been carved from burled walnut.

I put out my hand and he took it. There were calluses on his old palm. "Thanks," I said. "Thanks for coming, and thanks for the warning. I'll keep an eye out."

"You do that now, you hear." We shook hands and he grinned. "Hard to find a good doctor like you. Least one who don't charge a passel of money and yet had a drop of the good stuff for a thirsty man."

"Take care of your own self, old man. I might need you down the road."

He chuckled and nodded and let go of my hand. "See you down to the river," he said as he started walking.

"See you," I said. I watched him walk across the yard and slip into the deep shade. Then I went and put on a splash of bay rum and my best shirt. By the time I started for town a breeze had come up and was worrying the tops of the trees and a cardinal was cutting loose from a big cedar on the back side of the shack. As I swung out, I tried not to worry about Mr. Brad Menifee, but I have to admit he was on my mind.

Nineteen

"You've got a dab of gravy on your chin,' she said, grinning at me in that way she had of making you feel foolish and happy at the same time.

"Damn." I wiped my chin with my napkin. "Did I get it?"

"You got it," she said, although I wasn't sure how she could tell. Her eyes were drifting around the restaurant, lingering on a face for a moment, then moving on.

"See anybody you know?"

She smiled and smoothed down her hair on the right side. "Recognize a face or two. How about you?"

"Nope. They're all out of my league." All the men were in suits, or at least dress shirts and tailored slacks. Most wore a tie. I had a tie on, too, but it was an old one Mrs. Ayers had given me. Said Mr. Ayers didn't wear it anymore. I could see that now that he didn't wear it because it was out of style. However, it didn't have any stains on it. At least it hadn't before we'd sat down.

"What is this, the nicest restaurant in town?"

"The second nicest," she said, and laughed. "Or maybe the third, depending on your taste."

I drained the last of my coffee and wiped my mouth and eased back in my chair. My plate was as clean as if I'd licked it. I glanced at hers. "You didn't eat much."

"Girl's got to watch her figure, you know?"

"Nothing wrong with yours," I said. "Nothing at all."

"Why thank you, Mr. Judas Cain," she said in a southern-belle voice straight out of Hollywood. "You do say the nicest things. Why, you're liable to turn my head any minute now." She giggled, and I grinned along with her. A couple of faces at other tables turned and stared at us, but she never paid them a bit of attention.

Instead, she kept looking around the room, gazing at the chandelier, staring at the waiters in their white shirts and pomaded hair, and cocking an ear when the lady at the piano started in on a tune. I sensed she was listening for a certain song, or looking for a certain face. But maybe that was true of everybody.

When I wasn't looking, she reached over and ran her fingers across the top of my hand and sighed. "Geez, this is a nice place, Judas. You sure are spending some cash tonight, baby."

I turned my hand over and squeezed her fingers. "Long as you're happy."

"Oh, I am, I am."

Over her shoulder, I could see the maître d' giving us the eye. I didn't own a watch, but there was no arguing we'd been here awhile. Beyond the maître d', there were people standing around the hostess station. From what I could see of their faces, they looked impatient. One woman caught me staring at her, arched her thin eyebrows and scowled. I glanced down at my hands then up at Jessie's face.

"You want some dessert?"

"No, but you go ahead. I know how a man likes to eat."

I shook my head. "I've had enough. Not used to eating this much. You want to take a stroll?"

"Sure," she said, "only not too long."

I must have let something show in my face because she shrugged and twisted up her face. "You know how it is, baby."

I looked away, took a deep breath, and turned back. "But I thought—"

"On Saturday night, come on now, you're a big boy."

"Yeah," I said. And big boys don't cry, I thought. Only I sort of wanted to. Actually I didn't really want to cry. What I really wanted was to smash something. I signaled for the check.

~ * ~

We walked along a line of old, abandoned warehouses. Enough light drifted in from the buildings across the street so you could see the machinery that had been left behind. In the dimness they looked like nothing so much as the pictures of dinosaurs I'd seen in a library book one time.

At the end of the block I stopped and leaned against the brick wall. Warmth still oozed from the bricks. A bird chirped sleepily on the rooftop. I eased back into a doorway and pulled Jessie to me. She came willingly and I pressed my mouth to hers. She tasted of lemons and butter and sugar and something indescribably delicious. Thick, heavy darkness surrounded us. The air smelled faintly of used motor oil and old grease and mold.

Her breasts were soft against me and her hands suddenly grew busy. I felt myself grow hard and I got one hand on her dress and lifted it. She leaned back and tugged at her underwear and stepped out of them. I bent and entered her without thinking. She was warm and wet and I could feel the sweat popping out on my body. I heard her moan once, softly as if the sound was only for herself, and then I could hear the breath rattle through my throat. Then there was only a rushing in my ears as though a west wind was rising.

~ * ~

From three or four streets away came the shushing sound of traffic moving in the night. I wondered where all the people in the cars had been and where they were going. For the first time in a very long time I didn't wish I was going with them.

We had wandered down to the end of the street. It didn't stop at a river or the railroad tracks. It simply died in a patch of crumbling asphalt. Weeds and grass were coming up through the cracks and off in the undergrowth what looked like a possum made the leaves rustle.

No streetlight or lamplight reached here, only a faint shimmering of moonlight. Except for the subdued hum of traffic and a few possums, coons and feral cats, the world had gone quiet. Jessie and I might have been the only people left in the world. In a way, I wished we were.

At the end of the asphalt we stopped and she turned her face up to me and I kissed her again.

"I've got to go, baby," she whispered against the side of my face.

"Don't," I said. "Just for tonight, don't go."

She stepped back and smoothed out her dress. Then she reshaped her hair with her fingers. "Sorry, baby, but I've got to. I told you how it was."

"Tell him you were sick."

"You don't know Brad Menifee. He never believes anything anybody tells him and only about half of what he sees."

"We could leave. Slip out of town. There'll be a freight train pulling out before daylight. We can be long gone before he ever wakes up."

"You don't know Brad Menifee."

I was tired of hearing that line. "I know he's watching us," I said.

Jessie gasped a little, coughing to try and cover the sound. She took a step back. Don't think she realized she was doing it. "How do you know?"

"People tell me things."

"People you can trust?"

"I think so," I said without thinking. A second later I realized I did trust old Moses.

"Are they sure?"

"Very."

"How would they know?"

"Let's just say some of their family works for Brad Menifee."

Her head swayed in the pale light. She stretched out one hand and her fingertips brushed my face. They felt like dry kisses.

"Baby, you don't know what you're getting into. I'm warning you plain, don't mess with that man. He doesn't fool around and he plays mean, real mean."

"Yeah," I said, trying to sound bolder than I felt, "well maybe he ought not to mess with me. I can be right ornery my own self."

Jessie didn't say anything then, simply made a soft clucking sound and shook her head. Then she stepped in close and brushed her lips across mine.

Before I could respond she was turning. "Got to go, baby," she said over her shoulder and waved.

I wanted to go after her and shake her and make her see that the best plan was to catch that freight train to Biloxi. But I only stood there and watched her walk away into the soft, shimmering shadows. From far away came the midnight hum of Saturday night traffic.

Twenty

"Arthur, Arthur?"

Mr. Ayers closed his eyes. "Damn," he said. "Damn it all to hell." He opened his eyes and looked at me. "Why can't that woman ever show me even a little mercy?"

I shook my head. Sure didn't have the answer to that question. Women in general, and that woman in particular, tended to confound me. "Sorry," I said, "can't help you there, Cap'n."

Mr. Ayers lifted the bottle and took another slug. I glanced at the sun. Near as I could tell, it was about three o'clock. Mr. Ayers had come down the slope right before lunch time to where I'd been whacking on a patch of horse weeds. He'd sat down in the patchy shade of a stand of honey locusts and started sipping. Not ten minutes had passed before he asked me to join him. We been at it, on and off, ever since. Between us there was barely a swallow left in the bottle. He sloshed it around and eyed it. I could hear Mrs. Ayers coming down the hill. She was muttering under her breath and I wished I were somewhere else.

"Arthur, Arthur, where are you? It's time for my library meeting and I need you to drive me. Arthur?"

I could tell by her voice that she was close. We were in under the trees, but that was no real cover. Besides, Mr. Ayers had both legs sprawled out in front of him and his shoes were in the sunlight.

Another couple of steps and she'd see us. Our only hope was if she turned around. Her shadow fell onto the open ground.

"We're in for it now, Judas," he whispered.

There wasn't anything for me to say.

Her shadow came across his feet. He sighed.

"So, there you are. And what, if I may ask, are you doing down here in this miserable heat?"

"Visiting with Judas."

"For over three hours? Surely you don't expect me to believe that?" She sniffed. Her eyes open wider. "Whiskey. So that's the reason. You're down here drinking. Drinking with the hired help in the middle of the day. Now don't try to deny it, Arthur. I can smell that nasty stuff, and look at you. Just look at you."

He'd been leaning on one elbow and he roused himself up then and stared her square in the eye. I'll give him that. I was mostly looking at the ground, only glancing up now and then. Mrs. Ayers was so mad she was trembling. How he remained so calm was more than I could understand.

"Okay, I had a drink or two. So what?"

"You promised me."

"Sure, and you promised me a lot. Don't even think about claiming you've kept all your promises."

"I've never lounged around in the middle of the day, drinking with the hired help, I tell you that."

"No, that would be beneath you. Seeing how you think you're so much better than the rest of us."

"I do not."

"Bull."

"Arthur Ayers, you are drunk."

He shrugged. "A man's got to find some peace of mind somewhere."

She pursed her lips and for a second her body shook like a wet dog's. "Peace of mind can be found in the home, or, if you prefer, in church."

The boss snorted. "Not in my home you can't. And as far as church is concerned, best I can tell it's a home for hypocrites. Frankly, Marilee, I prefer to sit in the shade and drink whiskey with old Judas here."

She snorted like a bee-stung cow, and he added: "Besides, it's Saturday afternoon. I don't have to work and it's way too damn hot for Judas to mow the grass. I work hard all week and need to unwind." He closed his eyes and smiled. It was a nice enough smile. "Now, my dear, why don't you go and call Mary Edna and have her come pick you up. Tell her I've got a yard project going."

"Oh," she said, her voice rising and cracking like a dropped light bulb, "oh, you jerk." She turned and glared at me. "And look at you, Mr. High and Mighty Yard Man, drinking right along with him. Probably encouraging him. Why you're just as bad. Maybe worse." Her nostrils flared. "You and your Bible verses. What happened to all that religion? Huh, mister? Well?"

I looked up and gave her a smile of my own. She was still trembling. Her eyes seemed to throb in her face. No wonder the boss drank. "'Judge not, that ye be not judged,' Matthew, chapter seven, verse one."

"Oh, oh, oh," she stamped her foot. "Oh, I hate you. I hate you both." She kicked at me like I was a one-eyed alley cat. "I absolutely hate you."

"'Hated stirreth up strife: but love covers all sins.' Proverbs ten, twelve."

"Oh you, you, you, you—"

I'm not sure what she aimed to say, cause all of a sudden she burst into tears and turned and ran up the slope, her big body moving awkwardly across the uneven ground. I turned and looked at Mr. Ayers. "Didn't mean to upset her so," I said.

He sighed and shook his head and said: "Don't worry, she's just turned that way. Don't think she can help it, but you can see why I have to sip a little on occasion."

I nodded and he passed me the bottle. "Here, finish this rascal off, Judas, and tell me about the fishing down your way."

I lifted the bottle to my lips. The air was hot and heavy and still. Bees buzzed in the lilac bush. Over on Rosemont, a car engine fired to life. From the house came the faint sound of a woman sobbing. The whiskey burned all the way down.

Twenty-one

The moon was up, but so was the wind and it was pushing clouds across the sky. Shadows crossed the sandy road and passed on into the night. Sycamores and live oaks lined the road and you could smell honeysuckle and fresh manure. Judging by the moon, it must have been getting on for eleven o'clock.

I'd worked that afternoon on Mrs. Ayers' shrubs and had stopped off for a beer on my way home. I'd drunk three. Now it was late and I was tired and cutting cross-country on the old Washoe Road. It hadn't rained in better than a week and the sand was hard packed, except where the wind had whirled it into small drifts. I slipped a couple of times in the loose sand, but I wasn't sure if that was due to the drifting sand or the beer.

As the crow flies, I wasn't more than a half-mile from the house, but Washoe Road twisted down in the bottom like a snake and I probably still had twenty minutes to walk. If it hadn't have been for the wind and the clouds I'd have cut across the fields. But old barbed-wire fences sliced across the ground in this part of the county, and there were a couple of sinkholes big enough to swallow a cow. Better to plod on.

Like I said, I was pretty tired, just plodding along, only once in a while a thought of Jessie would drift across my mind, or I would think about the Ayers boy and wondered how he was doing. Some boys take to army life, others don't. Last word was that he was shipping out for the west coast and then on to the Pacific. Then I got to thinking about how long I'd been living at the old shack and how that was the longest I'd lived any one place since I was a kid. After I studied on that for a few minutes, I began to wonder why I was staying there so long. The Bible said that God had a purpose for everybody and it crossed my mind there on that sandy road that maybe he was causing me to stay there for some reason that was beyond me at the moment. But then I told myself that was the thinking of a fatigued brain and I started to whistle, to keep my spirits up, you see.

I was climbing the slope up out of the bottom and I'd worked my through "Yankee Doodle" and "Dixie" and was halfway through "When Johnny Comes Marching Home" when I heard a motor whine off down the road.

At first I thought it was a trucker making a night run to Memphis or Birmingham. As it got closer I could tell that it was a car motor and figured it was one of the Gleason boys hauling a load of shine out of the county, back roads generally being better for that sort of thing.

I crested the rise and started down the other side, looking for a clear place to step off, in case whoever was driving the load had been taste testing. The car was coming up the slope, but only making fair time. I wondered why they were going so slow. Then the headlights popped over the crest and poked at the blackness and I heard the car start down the hill. I stepped off into a ditch choked with weeds.

As soon as the car crested the rise it began to slow even more. I couldn't figure out what was going on. The car stopped and the doors swung open. My first thought was that if whoever was inside aimed to rob me they were sure in for a big disappointment.

I stepped back and up and out of the ditch as four men piled out of the car. One of them had a gun in his hand. Moonlight glittered off the barrel and I felt my insides chill as the skin on the back of my neck puckered up.

"Don't even think about running, buddy." The man with the gun waggled it in my general direction. "You ain't got a prayer. Besides, Mr. Menifee here just wants to have a talk with you." He nodded at a taller man coming around the car. The other two men eased out of his way, but they kept their eyes on me. I kept mine on the black hole at the end of the gun barrel.

Menifee came on around the front of the car until he stood directly in front of me. He was bareheaded and when he turned his head moonlight showed his face. I couldn't see details, but his jaw jutted out and his nose poked at the darkness.

"Know who I am?" he asked.

"Judging from what the man said, I figure you must be Mr. Brad Menifee."

"You've heard of me then?"

"Who hasn't?"

He nodded like I'd answered that question all right. "And I figure you're a yard man who goes by the name Judas Cain. That right?"

"Correct." I swept my eyes along the four men. The man holding the gun leaned against the side of the Chevy. Menifee hadn't moved. The other two men had worked their way across the ditch and one of them stood on either side of me about ten feet away. In a field some distance away a cow mooed. The hair on the back of my neck was standing up. The sandy road was empty in the moonlight.

"What can I do for you fellas?" I asked, and eased back another step from the ditchline. I didn't like the way the scene was playing out and wanted to get space between me and the gun. Not that one step mattered much. Not at this distance.

"For starters, you can step back over that ditch. I need to talk to you," Menifee said.

"We can talk from where we stand," I said, and eased back one more step. At the edges of vision, I could see the two men on my side of the ditch move a step closer.

The man with the gun pushed off the car and pointed the business end of the pistol at me. "Mr. Menifee said for you to come back across that ditch. I think maybe you ought to do what he says."

"I can hear him fine from right here," I said, and backed off another step, trying to make the movement real casual.

"Now, that's not really the point is it," Menifee said and nodded his head.

I heard the men moving and I turned to face the one coming in on my left. He was a big, rawboned looking thing and I cut loose with a looping right that smashed him flush on the mouth and sent his hat tumbling. I only had time to notice that he was bald before the other man smashed into me like a football player making a tackle.

I'd half-twisted toward him and he didn't hit me solid. Still, the blow was solid enough to send me staggering back. He had a grip on my legs I couldn't break and I bent over and smashed a fist into the middle of this back. I heard him grunt and then about a hundred and seventy-five pounds of dead weight smashed onto my back and I went down hard.

I tried to fight back, but all I could do was swing wild and half blind with my one free arm. I landed one good blow, but the next one missed and then their fists started finding my face and neck and chest and I saw stars and tasted hot blood. Then the night swirled and everything went black.

~ * ~

I couldn't have been out more than a few seconds. Menifee was still stepping across the ditch. Lying flat on my back in the weeds and peering up at him, he looked like a giant. My head was woozy and Menifee seemed to sway like a palm tree in a rising gale. The giant bent down and pushed his face so close to mine that I could smell the whiskey and onions on his breath.

"Cain, can you hear me?"

"Yeah," I said. The word came out thickly between lips starting to puff. The taste of blood was in my mouth and I wanted to spit it out; only right then I couldn't raise my head.

"Good. Cause this is three warnings in one. Your first, your last, and your only."

His head swirled closer. In the paltry light it looked lopsided and misshapen. But then I wasn't seeing so good at the moment.

"Jessie Monday is taken. She belongs to me. Not to you, not to the Baptist preacher, and not to Franklin D. Roosevelt. Now, I know that she's got loose hips and a wild way of talking, and that's why I'm giving you this warning instead of plugging your sorry ass with a deer slug. But I don't chew my cornbread twice, so you'd better listen real good. I catch you even looking at her cross-eyed again and I kill you hard dead before the next daylight. You hear me?"

I took a deep breath, blinked and I could see his face in a swatch of moonlight. It was all snarled up, with his eyes bulging like they were coming out of his head. He was sweating and a drop of his sweat fell off his chin and splattered on my forehead and my guts knotted up. A sudden urge to get up and carve his heart out surged through me.

Only right then my legs felt far away, or like they belonged to someone else. So I made myself a promise and mumbled, "I hear you, Menifee."

He nodded and his lips twisted into a painful smile and he looked off toward town and then out of the corner of one eye I saw his head swivel back and one arm draw back. I saw the fist coming and tried to move my head. But my reactions were still slow and the fist smashed into my face. I felt the bridge of my nose go and blood squirted like I was a stuck hog and I screamed against the pain.

More fists smashed against my face, chest and the side of my neck. They were only blurs and then there was only pain. After a while the blows ended and someone started kicking me in the ribs. Whoever was kicking me knew their business. They kicked me hard and rhythmically, first one side and then the other. They were wearing steel-toed brogans and they kept on kicking until there was only blackness.

~ * ~

Something warm and wet kept sloshing across my face. I tried to open my eyes but they weren't working right. Whatever it was dampened my face again and I got one arm up and waved feebly until I heard something moving away. I lay still then, not quite unconscious, but not really conscious either. Maybe I slept a little, or maybe I drifted out of this world but not quite into the next.

I came back and felt the pain. For a minute I didn't know who I was or where I was or why I hurt like hell. Then I remembered and got one eye open. The light was changing and it would be daylight soon. My head felt like it was broken and so did half my ribs. I figured it would be about all I could do to sit up.

A faint mist shimmered inchesabove the ground and I could hear thunder rumbling off to the west. The smell of rain was in the air. I was lying face up in a ditch. Birds were starting to come awake and off toward town a train whistle moaned. I moaned in response and started working my way out of the ditch. All the time I had the sense that something was watching me.

After what seemed like a long time, but could only have been a couple of minutes, I got back on the road. I could feel dried blood on my face, my ribs ached, and my head throbbed, but my legs worked. They were wobbly, but they worked. I started for the shack.

It wasn't pretty, just put one foot down and lift the other, but I kept moving. After a few minutes I heard something padding along beside me and I looked down. A tan and black hound looked back up at me. His ribs were showing. Well, mine ached, so maybe we were even. I kept moving and he trotted along. The light was better and I could see the road and the trees that lined it. I was glad not to have to look at myself.

Thunder rolled again, closer this time, and then I could hear raindrops peppering against the leaves. A crow flew across the road and landed in a black gum tree. Rain dotted the road and then I could feel it on my face. It felt cool and good and I kept moving.

My legs found a rhythm and I plodded along in the rain, bent over a little and holding my ribs, but making progress. The hound trotted along, pausing a couple of times to sniff and then hurrying on after me. And the rain came down, washing away the shimmering mist and the blood on my face, but not the memories of the night before. Those I'd never forget.

Twenty-two

Next morning I couldn't get out of the bed. Every time I raised my head it felt like somebody was splitting it open with a meat cleaver. My ribs ached and it was painful to draw a deep breath. Around noon, the throbbing in my brain eased enough for me to get up and get a drink of water. Then I drug my chair over to the open doorway and sat down and tried to do some thinking.

For a while my thoughts wandered along some Bible passages I'd read over the years. Ones about the lilies of the field and God looking out for the sparrows. Those, and the twenty-third Psalm. That valley of the shadow of darkness seemed to cover a lot of ground. Then I got to wondering where God had been when Menifee and his henchmen had been beating me. For a few minutes that bothered me. Then I recalled some of my actions and got to thinking that maybe God had decided I needed a good lesson. I'll admit that maybe I did need a lesson, but surely not such a tough one.

Reflecting on my owns sins wasn't making me feel any better, so I started thinking some about Jessie and a helluva lot about Mr. Brad Menifee. Then I thought about catching a freight out of town when I got back to feeling halfway decent. Leaving had been on my mind for some time. One thing for sure, I was a man who never left a town owing anybody anything. By any standards, I was a poor man. But I did have my pride. And I surely did owe Menifee a little something.

Thinking about leaving got me to thinking about the Ayers. I wondered some about what they would say when I didn't show up, but mostly I wondered about the kid and how he was doing in the army. Lately, the radio had been full of news about a big offensive in the Pacific and I knew he was out there somewhere. Both his parents were worried, even though Mr. Ayers tried not to show it. Couldn't blame them. Western Union kept delivering telegrams and the newspapers kept printing pictures of boys who looked far too young to die. Made me glad I didn't have any family.

When the shadows had grown blue and long, I got up and ate some cornbread and a handful of walnuts. I washed that down with lukewarm water and hobbled out into the yard. For some reason, being inside the shack that day was like being in jail.

The rain had passed and it was cooler under the trees. I wondered where Jessie was and what she was doing. Then I wondered where Menifee was and pondered the best way to pay him back. Jesus had said we were to love our enemies. Looked like I never was going to make a first class Christian.

When dusk started to fall, I slow walked back to the shack and took my clothes off and looked at my body. My chest was splotched with yellow and purple bruises. Even my arms were bruised. I drug the bottle out from under the bed and finished it. Just to ease the pain. Sleep came as a soft blessing.

Twenty-three

Monday morning came and went and I really didn't want to go to work on Tuesday, but as I was already a day late and a dollar short and Mrs. Ayers didn't strike me as a particularly understanding woman, I gave myself a good lecture and got dressed and eased out into the morning. Even then I was running late and moving slow and figured I'd get the evil eye when I made it.

By the time I trudged up the drive, the boss man was already gone. Judging by the sun, I was better than an hour late. That morning sun was strong and my head felt like it was cracking open. Sweat covered my chest and back. I hurried into the shade under the carport.

I tapped lightly on the screen door and walked into the kitchen. Mrs. Ayers was sitting in her rocker in front of the window, looking out across the yard. One side of her face was visible. It looked waxen, so that, for a moment, you could almost believe she was a statue. I eased into the room, unwilling, for some reason I couldn't explain right then, to disturb her.

Dirty breakfast dishes sat on the table and she was still in her robe and slippers. Under the material you could tell the slopes and curves of her body. They looked as though they had fallen in on themselves, the way old buildings do. The one eye I could see looked wet. I felt awkward standing there looking at her. The kitchen was so quiet I could hear the hands moving on the clock on the wall. For some time I stood quietly, watching the lights change in her eyes, hearing time mark off the seconds of my life. Then I cleared my throat.

She jerked, the way a person will when they're startled but are trying not to show it. In that moment she looked vulnerable, and she wasn't a woman to like that.

"You okay?" I asked.

I expected her to say something sharp. Instead, she sniffed and took a deep breath. Then she let it out and said: "It's awful, you know."

"What's awful?"

She turned then and looked straight at me. There wasn't any question now, there were tears in her eyes. "This war, Mr. Cain, this war."

Right off I thought the worst and looked around for the telegram.

"Oh, it's not that. He's okay. In fact, he's only just shipped out. No, it's Mrs. Pettigrew. She lives down the street. In the red brick on the corner, the one with the day lilies along the walk. You know her?"

"Know the house."

"I see. Well, her son was killed last month. In Africa. He was a tank gunner. She got the telegram yesterday."

"That's rough."

"It was the third one this month somebody in town has received."

I shook my head. It was hard to know what to say. "I hope you never get one," I said.

She looked at me funny then. I'd never seen an expression quite like it and didn't know how to interpret it. For a minute or so we simply stared at each other. A car rolled by, going toward town. Outside the window, a blue jay started up. I felt funny standing there looking at her and having her look at me. I wondered what she was thinking. Probably about the telegram that might come someday.

Of course, not every family got one, but it seemed like they came far too often. Made my head hurt to think about all those young men lying in a jungle or out in the desert or in the rubble of a bombed building with their guts shot out or the tops of their heads blown off. Sons of barbers and bus drivers and mayors and preachers were dying. Old Man Death was no respecter of persons.

Football stars were coming home with a leg or an arm blown off. College kids who had made straight A's lay in hospital beds unable to speak or even remember their names. And here I stood, a lousy yardman. Only one step above a bum. A man who had nothing or nobody. Yeah, it all made my head hurt.

She was still looking at me. Her eyes looked different. I couldn't figure out exactly what was different, but something definitely was. After a moment I quit trying to figure out what had changed. Women are a mystery to me. I wondered if she was looking at my bruises.

Off toward McCormick, a train whistle moaned. She turned to the sound and cocked her head as though she was trying to decipher a message out of it, the way Indians do with smoke signals.

I looked out across the yard. Sunlight covered everything. There had been no rain for a couple of days and in the heat the grass was starting to brown. Some of the tree leaves looked wilted. Summers were brutal down here. All the heat made me remember cool Wyoming ridges at the edge of the timber line. One summer, I'd helped a man build a hunting cabin there. The scent of the pines had been sweet. I could almost taste the cold water that flowed over the rocks.

A sudden sob brought me back into the room. Mrs. Ayers had buried her face in her hands. I watched her shoulders jerk. Her sobs grew louder. It hurts me inside to hear a woman crying. I walked over and put a hand on her shoulder. Part of me was afraid to touch her. I'd never done it before. But I felt like I ought to do something.

Tell the truth, I expected her to smack my hand away, but she only kept on crying. After a little bit, she covered my hand with one of hers. Slowly her sobbing faded.

"I'm sorry," she said, still looking down. "It's this awful war. The war and the worry. It's all too much."

She lifted her head then and studied me out of the corner of one eye. "Not being a parent you can't understand, but it's awful. Hell, pure hell."

She got up then and walked over to the window and pressed her face close to the glass. "It's hell and we all respond differently. Arthur drinks and I cry." Without turning around, she said: "And how do you respond, Judas Cain?"

I didn't have any answers for her. Far as I could see there weren't any answers, at least not good ones. For a minute, I stared at her broad back. Then I turned and walked outside. As I walked toward the shed I wondered if we had connected at all, or if we had simply occupied the same room at the same time.

Something in that thought made me remember an old man I'd ridden with across Georgia in a boxcar years ago. He'd lost three fingers on his left hand and had been a real motor mouth. Most of his palaver was long gone, but I did remember one thing he'd said. It was along of the lines of nobody ever really understands anybody else, which made me wonder what I'd been missing.

Twenty-four

"You took an awful chance, you know."

Her voice was soft in the darkness. We were lying in bed in the corner room of the Dufrene Hotel. Under the sheets we were naked. I rolled over and searched for her mouth and kissed her. Her lips were soft and yielding. I curled an arm around her and pulled her to me. "You're worth it," I murmured against her throat. I felt myself grow hard. She moaned softly as I entered. I don't think she realized she made the sound.

~ * ~

The night had that after midnight feel. Traffic had died on the street. I could tell Jessie was awake by her breathing. "We could go away, you know."

She was silent for so long that I didn't think she was going to respond. Then she sighed. "And where would we go?"

"Aaway. Doesn't matter where. Simply get out of town and go wherever the wind blows us. As long as we're together it wouldn't matter."

Her lips brushed against the side of my face. They were the softest lips I'd ever felt. "You say it wouldn't matter, but trust me honey, it does. This girl is not going to Canada or North Dakota or some cold place like that. Besides, we don't have a car and I don't have the price of a bus ticket. Bet you don't either. How do think we're going to go anywhere?"

"We could hop a freight. It's not hard. I've done it dozens of times."

"Not me."

"Oh, come on. It's not as bad as you think, and yes I've seen women riding the rails."

"Well, you won't see this girl riding no old freight train. No sir, no boxcars for me. When Jessie leaves, she is going out in a Cadillac limousine."

I sighed and pushed up against the headboard until I was more sitting than lying. "So, you're going to stay here in this nowhere town working for a lowlife like Brad Menifee? Tell me, Jessie, how that is better than riding a freight train for a couple of hundred miles?"

"I've got a certain style, I want you to know," she said as she rolled over. Enough light drifted in from the street so that I could see a smooth, bare shoulder. "A woman has to have style or she's nothing."

I sure didn't understand that. Couldn't see where style was so important. What did that matter when we could be together? Besides, how was hooking for Brad Menifee a style anybody would want?

"But you said you loved me."

"I do, but I'm not leaving town on a freight train. Not for you or anybody else."

"How is life any good staying here working for that bum?"

"Sometimes he's not so bad."

"When is he ever not so bad?" I tried to keep my voice calm, but I didn't feel calm. Inside I felt mad as hell. After all he had done to her, and she was giving him a pass.

She rolled over and ran her fingers down my arms. Her nails were sharp. "Oh, he's not so bad when he gives me money or buys me clothes. Sometimes we even get dressed up and he takes me to a fancy restaurant. Like a date, you know. He's real nice then."

"Yeah, well what about when he beats the hell out of you?"

Jessie jerked the sheet up over her shoulder and turned away from me. "You're a real jerk yourself sometimes, you know?"

I didn't answer. I was afraid of what I might say. For a minute I lay there trying to calm down. Then I rolled out of bed and crossed the floor and stood by the window.

Outside, it had grown dark. Across the street, a security light still burned in Dawson's Furniture Store and down the block the marquee for the town's picture show flashed yellow and blue. A car rolled by, its headlights stabbing the night.

In the wake of the car's passing the room grew quiet. Across the street, a man came out of a darkened building and fired up a cigarette. In the arc of light from the furniture store his silhouette was barely visible. The glowing end of his cigarette reminded me of the light at the top of a distant lighthouse. Next door somebody coughed. Slowly, the room grew quiet again.

Bedsprings squeaked and Jessie cleared her throat. "Sorry," she said. "Didn't mean to make you mad. It's only that I don't want to talk about him."

"I gathered that. But he is a part of what this is all about."

"Can't we forget about him for a few minutes and enjoy ourselves?"

"I thought we were."

She sighed and I turned from the window to look at her. Only one small lamp burned in the room and her face was wreathed in shadows. "Come on back to bed, baby."

Part of me wanted to and part of me was still angry and part of me didn't know what to do or say. For a moment I didn't say anything. Then I said: "Maybe later."

She tilted her head, but didn't say a word. Now her face was all in shadows and I couldn't read her eyes. "This is a nice room, Judas."

"It should be. I washed dishes and scrubbed floors for six hours to pay for it."

"Be a shame to waste it, don't you think?"

I didn't say anything. Way it looked to me, we needed to catch the next freight out of town and leave Brad Menifee behind. In a way, I hated to leave the Ayers and old Moses behind, but these days a man had to keep moving, no matter how good people were to him. Down the hall somebody turned on a radio. For a minute there was news and I listened to hear what the announcer said about the war, but somebody turned the knob and suddenly a man was selling soap powders. Then there was static and then dance music floated in under the door. It was a song that I'd never heard and it rose and fell and swirled like it had a life of its own. I heard the bedsprings squeak again and then her footsteps as she crossed the floor. Her lips brushed mine and then they wandered down my throat and chest and then they worked their way lower. Her lips were soft and warm, but we hadn't solved anything. Maybe I should have said something, but I didn't. I'm weak in my way, like any other man.

Twenty-five

Dusk was coming on as I slogged back to the shed. Even in the hot weather the weeds had kept growing, especially along the backside of the swale where whatever rain fell had run off. All afternoon I'd been whacking away and now I stank with sweat, and grass and leaves spotted my clothes. I hadn't shaved that morning and coming out of the brush I must have looked a sight.

I hung up the sickle and locked the shed. Light spilled out of the back door and then the screen door thudded shut. Somebody started walking across the yard. I stood where I was.

Mr. Ayers stepped out of the shadows. He had a glass in each hand. He thrust one at me. "Have a drink," he said.

"Don't mind if I do," I said, although what I really wanted then was a glass of cold water. Still it didn't seem polite, or a good idea, to turn down a drink from the man who bankrolled your payday.

"Cheers," he said and we clinked glasses. I sipped, deeper than I meant to and coughed a little. The whiskey burnt all the way down.

"Hard day, Judas?"

"Pretty hot out there."

"Yeah, it's been brutal. About the hottest summer I can remember."

"I've sure been sweating a lot," I said and sipped again. The whiskey wasn't easing my thirst, but I figured it wouldn't hurt my aching back.

Mr. Ayers touched my elbow and said, "Come on, let's take a stroll."

I was glad it was dark. At least he couldn't see the surprise on my face. "All right," I mumbled, and followed him down the driveway. Figured we might wander down into the swale. He'd drifted down there a few times and chatted with me when he got home from work or when he needed some air on a Saturday. For the past few weeks he'd been working late and I hadn't seen much of him. I'd sensed that he wanted to talk about something, although what was beyond me.

Instead of going down the back slope, he turned in the other direction and we meandered down the driveway, turned left at the end and started strolling toward town. Just two buddies taking an evening constitutional, only one of them looked nasty and smelled worse, and they both were carrying shots of whiskey. Just when I thought I'd seen it all.

There was no breeze and only a scattering of clouds off to the west. The moon was starting to rise and it was huge and amber, tinged with red. It looked like it had been snared in the tops of the sycamores. The frogs started up in Simpson's Pond and I could feel sweat trickling down the crack of my ass. That was when old Roy Burke, who lived on up around the bend when I was a kid, said it was time to quit work. I wouldn't argue with that corn patch philosophy.

We'd come to the bridge that crossed Holcomb Creek, and Mr. Ayers stopped walking and leaned over the low concrete wall. Down among the willows and cattails the air was still. It felt like almost all of the oxygen had been sucked out of that air. My mouth hung open the way a fish's does when it winds up on the creek bank.

"Damn, it's hot," Mr. Ayers said. "I'm sweating like a big pig." He turned his head away from the river. A shaft of moonlight sliced through the willows and painted his face, but it was too pale for me to read his expression.

"I know a place that's a helluva lot hotter than this," he said. "Know where I'm talking about?"

"Mexico?"

"Nope, but you're right it's west of here. Only it's a damn long way further than Mexico. It's thousands of miles away. Way across the Pacific Ocean. Bunch of islands out there. Full of snakes and monkeys and Japs with machine guns. My boy's out there, but you know that."

"I knew he'd shipped out."

The boss lifted his glass and took a sip. "They're there now. Had a letter from a buddy of mine, we went to school together at State and we've stayed friends. Our families have vacationed together." He shrugged. "Not sure what that signifies. George, that's my friend, he's a colonel now, in charge of an artillery bridgade. Wrote he'd seen Lenny and that the boy looked good. But he also said they were going into action. Oh, not in so many words. Censors, you know, but I got the drift."

He lowered his glass and stared into my eyes. His eyes were so intense they made me nervous, but I tried not to let it show. "Sounds dangerous."

"Oh, it will be. Not a doubt in my mind but that a helluva lot of those boys won't come home. At least not in one piece." He shook his head. "Makes my stomach hurt thinking about it."

"Hear that," I said, because I didn't know what else to say. A fish flopped in the shallows and I turned and watched the ripples.

"Got a bad feeling, Judas."

"What's that?"

He made a funny sound in the back of his throat. "It's about Lenny. I know it's awful, but I got a bad feeling about him. Makes me want to puke to say it, and I hope to hell and back that I'm wrong, but I've got this feeling that he isn't coming home."

"Oh, he'll surely be all right. All those big ships and guns, why they ought to blow the Japs right off those islands."

"Don't think it'll be so easy as that, Judas. Japs are damned good fighters. Never surrender, either."

"We've got all those planes—"

"Oh, hell, damn Japs hide in caves until they're gone and then come out and kill our boys. Trevathan kid from over to Bradfordville got killed last month. Sniper got him. Damn Japs. I know his father from Rotary. Bastards."

"Sorry, Mr. Ayers," I said, "but I think you're borrowing trouble. I mean I know anything can happen, but Lenny could as easily come home without a scratch. Lots of guys do. Thousands."

"Sure, sure, I know that. Only this time I got a bad feeling." He paused and turned and spat into the water. A bird started singing on the far bank and we both cocked our heads and listened. Then he curled his body and leaned toward me.

"Another thing, Judas." His voice wasn't much more than a whisper. I wondered why he was being secretive. Except for a few birds, some fish, and maybe a raccoon or two, there wasn't a creature anywhere close.

"Now keep this to yourself, for God's sake, okay?"

"Sure."

"Promise?"

"Yes."

"Well, it's like this, see. Lately I haven't been feeling so good, but I figured it was the heat and the stress from being so busy down to the bank. But I kept feeling like crap and last week I gave in and went to see Doc Fister. He ran a bunch of tests and today he called me with the results."

From the tone of his voice, I knew this wasn't going to be good, but I asked anyway. "What did the doc say?"

"I'm thirty pounds overweight, my blood pressure is sky high, and my heart's not real good." His teeth were white against the darkness. "Sort of makes a little gout and a touchy back seem like paper cuts."

"Hear they've got lots of new medicines and I reckon Doc Fister is supposed to be good."

"Oh, he's good all right. Only I'm supposed to take it easy and not worry and all that shit. What with the bank and the boy and Marilee carrying on, taking it easy isn't in the cards."

"That's rough."

"No kidding. But you know about tough, I figure."

"How's that," I said.

"Have you seen your face in the mirror lately, Judas? Looks a herd of wild horses ran right over the top of you."

I didn't say anything. What was there to say? I sipped on the boss's whiskey and stared at the water. Moonlight glittered on the dark surface. The water looked cool and I wished for a swim.

"Want to talk about it?"

"Reckon not," I said.

"All right by me. Man doesn't want to talk about something, he doesn't want to talk about it. Tell me one thing, Judas."

"What's that?"

"Was it woman trouble?"

"Might say that."

Mr. Ayers grunted. "Figured as much. Ninety percent of the trouble in the world is traceable, one way or another, to women." He turned and leaned against the side of the bridge. A car rolled by a street or two to the north. I followed its headlights until they disappeared.

"That's the other thing I wanted to talk to you about."

"I don't follow."

"Women," he said, "or more specifically a woman. My wife."

"Afraid I don't follow you," I said and eased a step away from Mr. Ayers. He'd been drinking. No doubt about that and who knows what crazy thoughts a drunk man can think.

If Mr. Ayers noticed he didn't let on. Just kept talking like he had been. Like we were the best of buddies and had been for years. "Last few years I've lost track of most of our friends. That's what comes of working too hard, and maybe from drinking a little too much. My dad died four years ago and last year my brother keeled over dead from a heart attack on the number seventeen green. Marilee doesn't have any family left here in town. Only me and Lenny. If something was to happen to both of us I'm afraid of what might happen to her. She's a good woman, but too emotional, if you know what I mean."

"She does have a bit of a temper."

He laughed at that and then he nodded and sipped his whiskey. The moon was up over the sycamores, a pale alabaster face in the night. Moonlight covered the bridge until I figured a man could almost read his paper by it.

"You're right there, Judas. Marilee does have a temper, but she also goes on crying jags and gets all down in the dumps until I wonder sometimes if she's ever going to get back to normal. Been worse since the boy joined up. Cries herself to sleep about every night. If something happened to me, why I don't know what she would do. Then if something happens to the boy, well that would be a real bad time. I'd like for you to do what you can for her, if it comes to that."

"Ah, nothing is going to happen, boss. You just need to quit working so hard. Relax some. You ever go fishing?"

He rubbed at his jaw. From the way he held his head I figured his mind was traveling back across the years. When you see a man holding his head at that angle you can count on him remembering something that happened a long time ago.

"Used to fish when I was a boy. My old man would take me down to the creek. No poles, just a line and a little hook with maybe half a worm on it. We caught redears and bluegill and rock bass. Never anything big, but for a kid it was really fun."

"I fish down to the river some. You're welcome to join me anytime."

Mr. Ayers chuckled. Then he stretched out a hand and put it on my shoulder. "I meant what I said about taking care of Marilee. Can I count on you?"

For a bit I didn't say anything. I sure didn't want to agree to such, but I didn't see how I could turn him down. Not with him paying my wages and being decent to me on top of that.

"Nothing's going to happen," is what I finally said.

"But if it does?"

A whippoorwill started up in the meadow across the road and I cocked my head and listened to it. Way far off a woman was singing what sounded like a lullaby. Maybe she was trying to get her baby to sleep. Vaguely, I could remember my mom singing "Rock-A-Bye-Baby" to the younger kids. Fireflies flickered in the tall grass.

"If it does," I said, "I'll do what I can."

"Thanks," Mr. Ayers said. "Knew I could count on you, Judas. Most people are all talk, but you're a man who does what he says. Admire that about you." He gave my right shoulder a squeeze. After a bit, as though by common consent, we turned and started walking back to the house.

Twenty-six

The wind had died and the night sounds drifted across the darkness. I was standing in the doorway sipping on a last cup of coffee, watching moonlight paint the ground. Some animal, probably a groundhog, was rustling in last year's leaves under the biggest hickory. Down the road a dog barked, while off to the south, toward Timmonsville, church bells tolled. In their wake came a new sound, the sound of someone walking. The hound picked up his ears.

It took a minute, but I caught movement along the edge of the oak shadows. An old path ran there, sand mostly, half-choked with weeds. I'd discovered it by accident, then wandered down for a few dozen yards, but had no idea where it began or ended. Figured it either led to the river or to some cabin that had burnt or blown down years ago. I sipped coffee and watched a figure emerge from the shadows.

Right off, I could tell it was a man from the way he walked. Women and men move so differently that and even from a distance you can tell. The man stepped out of the last shadow and I could see it was old Moses from the river. I sipped more coffee and wondered why he was coming to my shack at this time of night.

He lifted a hand and kept walking. About ten yards away he started slowing. "Come on in," I said and he nodded. The hound sniffed at his trousers, then padded off into the yard.

"Want some coffee?"

"Cup of coffee sounds good," he said and eased down on my chair.

"You've come a long way."

"Fair piece."

I poured coffee into my other cup and handed it to him. "Don't have any cream. Might have a little sugar."

"Don't take either. Strong and black is the way I like my coffee." He snorted. "Used to like my women that way, too." He grinned. "Back when I was a younger man."

I grinned at him and sat on the bed. The springs creaked and, as if in response, an owl started up deep in the oaks. Old Moses blew on his coffee and sipped. Then he nodded in my general direction.

"Good coffee, just the way I like it."

It was my turn to nod.

For a few minutes, we simply sat there, sipping coffee, listening to the owl, each man thinking his thoughts. I drank the last of my coffee and got off the bed and walked over to the dishpan and eased the cup down. I didn't have a clock and wasn't sure what time it was, but there was an aged feeling to the night. Not having anything better to do, I stood there and watched the old man sip on his coffee.

The owl went quiet and Moses peered down at the coffee remaining in his cup. His head lifted. "Guess you're wondering why I came."

I shrugged. "Maybe a little curious."

"Would be, too, so I'll get to the point."

But he didn't. Instead his eyes took a long slow lap around the little room. Not that the trip took long. He closed his eyes and rubbed the back of his neck while I wondered how old he was. Then he opened his eyes and rubbed a hand across his mouth.

"Was recalling the last time I was here. Wasn't doing so good that night. Appreciate all you did for me then."

I shrugged. "No big deal. You'd have done the same for me."

"Hope I would, cause that's what the good book teaches." He twitched his shoulders. "Anyway, I'm a man who likes to repay favors." He winked. "Don't like to be beholden, you see."

"I understand."

He punched himself lightly on the thigh. "Well, enough palaver. Better get to it. Reason I came was that I heard that maybe you ain't exactly on Brad Menifee's Christmas list and that maybe some of his knuckleheads paid you a visit."

"Yeah, so what?"

"So, word is they gave you a beating and a warning, as in you better stay away from a certain party." He squinched up his eyes and studied me out of the slits. I stared back at him, wondering where all this was headed.

"A warning, I hear, you haven't been paying much attention to."

"Everybody seems to be paying a lot of attention to me all of a sudden."

"You're the talk of the town."

"Bull."

Moses opened his eyes wide and laughed. The old fellow had an infectious laugh and I couldn't help but grin.

"Well, maybe not the talk of the town, but there are people keeping their eyes open for you."

"Why would they do that?"

He cocked his head and rubbed his jaw with one hand. Stubble rustled. "I'd say some of them want to get on Brad Menifee's good side and others want to put a stick in his spokes."

I wondered who had it in for Menifee, but I didn't ask. The old man was already talking again.

"I've got friends in this town and they let me know what going on. Some of them is white, too. See them on the street, or at work, or in church, you'd never guess they was friends of old Moses, but they are. They're in the know on lots of things and they pass some of it along. Also, got a lot of Negro friends. Brothers and sisters who have known me for thirty, forty years. Many of them work in the big houses and they hear things. Lots of white folks don't pay no nevermind to what they say around a Negro. Treat them like they're nothing more than another piece of furniture." He leaned forward and grinned. He was missing a tooth, or two. "Couple of my friends even work for Mr. Brad, himself."

"And they tell you things?"

"Oh yes, lots of things. Lots of bad things going on in that house. That man has got a mean streak in him that won't quit." The old man stretched out a hand and tapped me on the knee. "And one area where he's pure mean is his girls. Now, since you're messing with one of his very favorites and since he knows about it, well, that don't bode too good for you. Understand?"

"I hear you."

"Good, cause what he's got planned for you ain't pretty." He cocked his head and licked his lips and managed to look like a cross between one of those mad scientists you see in the picture shows and Franklin D. Roosevelt, only black. It was hard to take the old fellow seriously. I bit my lower lip to keep from laughing.

"What's Menifee got up his sleeve?"

Moses shook his head. "Hard to say, hard to say. Nobody quite knows. Least not the people who talk with me. All they been hearing is rumors. Real vague, see?" He looked away from me and his eyes seemed to peer into the darkness beyond the cabin. After a moment, he turned back.

"Think of it this way, Judas. Bet you've seen some powerful thick fogs in your day?"

"Sure."

"Well, you members how hard it is to try and see, I mean really see, something clear through that fog. Like a tree stump might look like a bear, or you don't see a ditch till it's too late. Know what I mean?"

I nodded.

"Now that's the way it is with old Brad's plans. My people know there is something sure enough going on, but hard as they try, theycan't make out plain what it's going to be." Moses shook his head slowly. "After a few days of hearing rumors, I says to myself, 'Moses, you can't let your friend down like this.' I studied right smart on the problem, but couldn't think of a thing. Then two nights ago, in the dead of the night, I woke up with my head as clear and cool as ice and right away I figured I had it."

"Had what?"

"The way to find out Menifee's plans."

"So what are they?"

He smiled and nodded and kept on nodding. "Hold on now, friend. I'm a gettin' there. But gotta tell it my way."

I pushed my lips together and nodded. No use hurrying the old man. He'd get there in his own time. I wasn't going anywhere anyway. Something rustled in the grass beyond the light. I wondered what Jessie was doing. Then I wished she was here with me. Or I was somewhere far away with her.

"Mama Tyree." The old man's voice jerked me back into the room.

"Who in the world is Mama Tyree?" I asked, wondering if Moses' mind had slipped a cog.

"You don't know Mama Tyree? Thought everybody knew her." He shook his head like I was a prize pupil who had missed an easy question on a test. "But then, you ain't really from around here. Least ways you've not been here your whole life. That do make some difference."

"Good," I said, feeling slightly aggravated over all his carrying on over some old woman I'd never heard of. "Now, tell me about Mama Tyree."

He nodded and rubbed his nose and eased into a more comfortable position. "Ah, yes, Mama Tyree. Let's see now, where should old Moses start?" He twisted his face up until it looked like an uncured leather hide that had been left out in the sun, the rain and the wind. "Guess I'll start by saying that she is surely about the oldest woman in the county, mayhaps the oldest in the whole state. She was a slave in her time, too. Just like me. She belonged to Mr. Samuel T. Gunderson. Big cotton man. Big. Fact is, most folks back in those days called him Big Cotton Gunderson. And that big worked two ways. First, he raised more cotton than anybody. Second, Samuel T. Gunderson was a big man. Way over six foot tall and had to weigh three hundred pounds if he weighed an ounce."

"Was Mama Tyree a field slave?"

"No sir, no indeed. She was a house slave. Lived in the big house from the time she was a baby girl. Was companion to Ethel Gunderson, Big Cotton's daughter, till that girl growed up enough to go away to finishing school clear up to Vicksburg. Think that might have been after the war.

"Course Mama Tyree, she got freed when it was all over and she was up some in age then. She dusted and cleaned for some white folks and later she was a maid for Big Cotton's wife. Don't recall her name at the moment. Kind of a sickly creature, as I recall. She died early and Mama Tyree stayed on and more or less ran the household after her mistress passed. Made sure the cook got the food on the table at the right time and the maids cleaned to suit. That sort of thing. She was still doing that when Big Cotton passed. Died of a heart attack right in the middle of supper one night. Had a mouth plumb full of butter beans."

"What did Mama Tyree do then?"

"Oh, not sure I rightly know the all of it. For a couple of years she stayed on at the home place. Then it started going down and the heirs sold it. If I recalls rightly, he had a couple of sons. Might have been twins. Don't think they ever amounted to much. Anyways, they sold the place and Mama Tyree had to move on. Think she worked for old Doc Wheeler awhile and then he died. By then she was getting old and she moved into Shacktown and she's been there ever since. Used to take in washing, but since she got her real age on her she only reads the bones and tells prophesy."

"Can she really tell the future?"

Moses straightened his leg and grimaced. "Old bones ache right smart these days, but then I'm an old man." He laughed a little and then he swallowed the rest of his coffee.

"Now, strictly speaking, Mama Tyree don't claim to tell the future. She only casts the bones and reads 'em."

"Okay," I said, "how accurate are those bones?"

Moses nodded. His expression was quite solemn. About as solemn as the judge in Joplin, Missouri who gave me ten days for vagrancy a few years back.

"You asking the right question, Judas. That's for durn sure. They's crystal balls, plus the cards and tea leaves, and I guess they all right. Onlys sometimes they wrong. But I ain't never in all my born put-togethers known the bones to be wrong. No sir, never."

Wasn't sure I believed the old man, but something in his words made the hair on the back of my neck stand up and the fleshy part of my arms pucker. I sat up straighter and stared into Moses' black eyes. They had a depth to them that made you wonder if you'd ever see to the bottom of them.

"Well then, tell me what they said."

He nodded and poked his stomach with a finger. "Right there," he said. "Right there is where your trouble is going to come. They didn't say how it would come, only where. So you better watch yourself sure, Judas. Brad Menifee might come at you with a gun or a knife, or a baseball bat for all I know. Just be careful and guard your stomach," he said.

"All right," I said and stood up. Simply hearing the old man's words had turned my blood icy. It was like a fever chill had come on me between one heartbeat and the next. I was cold to the bone. Voodoo, I told myself. I'd heard stories.

"Going to fire me up another cup of coffee," I said. "Want one?"

Moses licked his lips and sighed. "Believe I will join you, brother. I got a goodish walk home and a cup of coffee surely would do me good."

I picked up the water bucket and started filling the saucepan. Way off I heard the engineer leaning on the whistle and that rambling fever rolled through me like a high tide.

Twenty-seven

"Quieter down here than I remembered." Mr. Ayers stretched and jiggled his pole. Twenty feet from the bank a bobber twitched.

"Usually is here in the bend. This is backwater to most people, plus it's hard to get to from this side. Never have seen anybody on the other bank. Only a cow once in a while."

Mr. Ayers laughed. "If I've got the layout straight, that land belongs to Boyd Weaver. He runs a big herd and raises soybeans on the side. Don't guess he wants people tromping through his fields or stirring up his cattle."

"Don't spect he does. Those people would be messing with his cash flow."

"Yeah, and speaking of cash flow, think I owe you for last week."

I pulled my line in and checked my bait. "No hurry."

"Remind me when we get back to the house."

"Okay," I said. Something had got my bait and I started threading another worm on the hook.

"Want a snort?"

I glanced over at the boss. He was tugging a bottle out of his pocket. Not that I could say a lot—I liked a drink of the good stuff as well as the next man—but he was really developing a habit.

"Don't mind if I do," I said. My turning down a drink wasn't going to keep him from drinking.

He handed me the bottle and I twisted the cap off and tilted it up. The whiskey burned all the way to my gut. I wiped the top of the bottle and handed it back to the boss. He took a healthy slug and screwed the cap on. Then he sat the bottle down between us. "Help yourself anytime."

I nodded and flicked my bait back into the river. We were fishing a swirl of backwater created by a pair of bends in the river. Here, the water was always deep in certain spots and usually the surface was like shimmering glass. The sun hovered just above the line of trees across the river, but I figured it was still a good hour till dark. Summer days had a way of lingering that made a fellow wonder if they were going to go on forever. Late sunlight shimmered on the surface like fire.

The boss was right; the afternoon had gone dead quiet. Not a dog barked, not a train whistle blew, not a fish flopped. The silence felt thick and heavy. As though he was reading my mind, Mr. Ayers said, "Quiet's so thick you can almost feel it and the sky's as clear as a looking glass. But it feels like the calm before the storm."

"We could use a break in the weather."

"Damn right," he said, and took a long slug from the bottle. "Messes with the fishing, doesn't it?" Then he tilted his head toward me and winked. "Got Marilee all hot and irritable, too," he whispered as though she was hiding in the bushes. "Makes her skin break out in a rash."

For some reason the thought of Mrs. Ayers' skin turning red and bumpy struck me as funny and a second later we both started laughing. When the laughter died, he reached over, picked up the bottle and took another long drink. Then he closed his eyes. I wondered what he was thinking. The still hot lay on my shoulders like a woolen shroud.

I sat quietly on the bank and watched the light begin to change. After a bit, I could hear Mr. Ayers snoring. Last light of the afternoon shimmered on the water and the heat began to ease. I checked my bait again, then flicked the line back out. A woodpecker started hammering in the timber on downstream. Mosquitoes whined on the banks while green and gold bottle flies crawled in the mud. A fish rippled the water and a bullfrog started chugging down the bank. Sitting there, I felt a sense of peace I hadn't felt since I was a kid. It seemed that if I squinted my eyes and held my breath the world would be exactly like it was in the beginning. Crazy thoughts flickered randomly across my mind. Like any minute God himself, or at least Jesus, might walk across the river and sit beside me. I could sure use a holy blessing.

Of course, neither one of them walked on the water. Although I wouldn't have bet against the Holy Spirit at least passing through. From the reeds off to my left, a blue heron rose silently, its large wings flapping slowly, making no sound at all. Mr. Ayers snored on. The air was the color of overripe grapes.

~ * ~

He came awake with a jerk, grunted and roused up. The boss stretched and rubbed the back of his neck and groaned in the back of his throat.

"Damn, Judas, what happened to the day? Did I nod off?"

"Yep."

He looked up. "Moon's up already. What time is it?"

I peered up at the moon and did some figuring. "Must be going on ten o'clock."

He snorted. "I was supposed to be home at nine. Marilee will flat out have a cow."

"We'd better head back."

"Naw, we'll stay awhile. Few more minutes won't make much difference. Besides, I sure want another taste or two of what's in the bottle. Any left?"

"Bottle's right there by you."

"Oh yeah. Damn, what happened to it? You been hitting it, Judas?"

167

"Only the one."

"You mean I did all that damage?"

"Yep."

"No wonder I went to sleep. Never could stay awake once I started hitting the hard stuff." He picked up the bottle and sipped.

"Been drinking a lot lately. Probably too much." He took in a deep breath, held it, then let it go. Across the river a bird cried out.

"So much on my mind, you know. Some loans I approved down at the bank have gone bad. And then there's Lenny. Did I tell you we had another letter from him?"

"Don't believe so. Hope he's doing all right."

I heard the bottle gurgle. "Sounded good in the letter. Happy, almost. Said he'd been through a bout of dysentery, but was better. Claimed he was as brown as an Indian and in the best shape of his life. Even better than when he was playing football."

"You sound proud of him."

"I am, Judas. Yes, sir, I'm proud of the boy. Worried, too, of course. Reading between the lines, it sounded to me like his outfit was getting ready to go into combat. Don't know any details. Probably on one of those damn islands out in the middle of the Pacific. Crazy Japs won't surrender. Banzai death charges, according to the paper. Willing to die just to take a few of our boys with them. Bastards."

"Sounds rough."

"Oh, it is. Not that Lenny lets on, but I know. I can tell from what he doesn't say, not to mention the pictures in the paper and the newsreels. Hell on earth, that's what it is."

I heard the bottle gurgle again and then I caught a blurry glimpse of something flying through the air. Then there was a splash.

"His mother drives me crazy. Cries every night and wants to talk about every awful thing under the sun that might happen. Talk, talk, talk. All that woman wants to do is talk."

He grunted then, and it wasn't a good sound. At least not to my ears. Sounded like a dog I had as a kid. He'd been a stray who wandered in off the road. He walked funny and his eyes were runny. Always figured somebody had dumped him out. He was sick, though. You could tell that right off and he'd made that same sort of a grunting sound, down deep in his chest.

"You okay, boss?"

"Yeah, only a shot of pain. It'll pass."

"Where does it hurt?"

"Down in my chest."

He was breathing fast and shallow. The moon was higher, but we were half in shadows and I couldn't see his face. I pushed off the ground and hustled over. His face was awash with sweat.

"Is it your heart?"

"Yeah," he said. "But it's not a bad attack. Starting to ease already. Help me up, will you? I'd better be getting home. Marilee can't stand being alone at night anymore. Goes crazy if I'm late. That's why she had Sally Holcomb come over for supper tonight. Told her we'd be late. Come on, give me a hand."

"Sure you can make it? I can go for help."

"No, no, I'm sure. Now help me get on my feet."

I knelt and got a shoulder under one arm. The sandy soil was loose, but I braced my feet. "On the count of three," I said.

On three, we both pushed hard and he came upright, staggering a bit with my legs going trembly. The boss was a heavy man and I wondered how we were going to make it up the bank, but he took a deep breath and said, "Let's get going while I'm still able."

We started walking then, if you can call it that. He was heavy and stinking with sweat and whiskey and I wondered if he'd pissed himself. What with having to stop and rest every few yards and maneuvering around fallen timbers and push through bramble patches, it took us ten minutes to go the hundred yards or so to the bottom of the bank. He tugged on my arm.

"Hold on a second. I've got to rest before I try that bank. I'm weak as a newborn kitten."

"Want to sit down?"

"Nope. I'd never get back up again. At least not tonight. Here, let me lean against that tree a minute."

I was glad to shift from under his weight. It took us two tries, but we got him propped up between the notch of a lower limb and the trunk of the tree. He wasn't quite sitting, but it was next thing to it. His face was in the moonlight and, though he was looking down, I could see enough to tell that he was still hurting bad inside. Had to admire him. He was gutting through the pain. Probably he should have swallowed his pride and let me go for help, but a man's got to hang on to something.

Tell the truth, I was plenty glad of a rest myself and wasn't quite ready when the boss said "Let's go."

Won't claim it was easy, or pretty, climbing that bank, although I guess it might have looked funny if anybody had been watching. But nobody saw us, except maybe a possum or an owl. Not sure how long it took us, but we were both sweating like we'd chopped wood for an hour at high noon on the Fourth of July by the time we leaned against the car. He was panting like a hard-run coon dog, and I was breathing right fierce, myself.

When I'd got my breath back, I looked over at him. His face was as pale as the moon itself, but he gave me what I figure was the best grin he could. "Well, we made it," I said.

"Yeah," he said, "but what about the poles and our fish?"

"I'll go get 'em," I said.

"Help me in the car first, will you?'

"Sure."

"Oh, and Judas?"

"Yeah."

"You'll have to drive."

"Okay," I said and headed down the bank. Moonlight was bright on the path and the crickets had started chirping.

~ * ~

All the way back to town he was real quiet. Once he got so quiet that I took my eyes off the road for a second to take a look. He was breathing all right. His chest rose and fell, but his face was all squinched up and his eyes were shut. I cut mine back to the road and took the Pontiac into a curve.

The town was deader than a hammer and we rolled right on through like we were on rails. His eyes were open now and out of the corners of my eyes I could see him glancing out the window. He mumbled something once, but I couldn't make it out and he didn't speak again. At the bottom of the driveway he put a hand on my right arm and I braked to a stop.

"Wanted to say thanks, Judas. Don't think I'd have made it without you."

"Glad to help," I said, grateful it was dark inside the car because I was afraid I was going to start blushing if the boss got all mushy.

"Appreciate more than you'll ever know," he said. "And you remember what I told you the other day?"

"What's that?" I asked, not sure I really wanted to know.

"That if something happens to me and the boy that you make sure Marilee is taken care of."

"Ah, now, quit that kind of talk. You just need to see the doc and get some medicine and the boy sounds like he's doing good."

"I meant what I said. Can I count on you, Judas?"

"Ah, boss—"

"It would mean a lot to me. Give me some comfort, you see."

I didn't want to do it. It would be like owing a dead man something, and I hate owing anybody. Still, he was a good man and, sitting there in the Pontiac, the odds of something happening to both of them seemed like a long shot.

I took a deep breath and let it out. "You got it, boss," I said, "you can count on me."

He squeezed my arm then. "Thanks," he said. "Thank you ever so much."

After a moment, he let go of my arm and said, "Let's go now and take our medicine," and I took my foot off the brake. As we started up the driveway he gasped and fell back against the seat.

Twenty-eight

A single light burned in the house. The street was dark and quiet. I had the windows down and warm wind blew across our faces. I glanced at Mr. Ayers. In the light from the dash, his face was pale and his lips were squeezed together. I wheeled the car onto the driveway and we chugged up the slope. Before I could turn the key, the kitchen door swung open.

She stood in the doorway, framed by the walls, backlight by a distant lamp. I tried to read her expression, but her face was wreathed in shadows. I cut the engine and sat studying her, listening to the cooling motor ping.

Her arms were folded across her chest and her hair was down. Best I could tell, she was wearing her robe. Her feet were bare. I popped the door and slid out.

"Well, Mr. Cain, you two are very late. What have you been doing with my husband?"

"Just fishing, only—"

"Only what? Do you think I'm stupid? I know what you two have been doing. Been drinking whiskey, haven't you? That's all he really likes to do on such excursions. Fishing. Ha."

Anger ran all over me, hot and cold, then hot again. The woman got on my nerves anyway and tonight was not a good night for her to be spouting off. I wasn't in any sort of a meek mood.

"Quit your bitching and go call his doctor," I said.

The words hit her like they'd been hammered against her head and she took a step back and grabbed the doorframe. She gasped for air and one hand fell across her heart.

"Is he—"

"No, but I think he's had a heart attack. I wanted to take him to the hospital, but he wanted his own doctor." I nodded in the boss's direction. "Condition he was in, I didn't think arguing was the thing to do."

"Oh," she said, "oh." And then she turned and ran into the house. I went up the steps and into the kitchen. I rumbled around in a drawer or two and found a clean dishtowel, ran water over it, and wrung it out. Then I went back to the car and mopped at the boss's face. His breathing wasn't good and his color looked off, but then the light was chancy. I heard her coming down the steps.

"Doctor Richards said to get him straight to the hospital. You should have taken him there right away."

Hard words formed in my mouth. I swallowed them and gave her a hard look instead.

"Well, in case you haven't noticed, he can be a tough man to convince."

She opened her mouth. Then closed it. She had a funny look on her face. In the light spilling out from the kitchen she might have been tearing up.

"I don't have time to discuss this with you right now, Mr. Cain. I've got to get my husband to the hospital."

"I understand."

"You've placed his life in grave danger."

"He wanted to come home. I brought him home."

"So I see. Well, straight thinking never has been your strong suit. If he dies, I'm holding you responsible."

I'd been considering offering to drive while she tended to Mr. Ayers, but after that comment I pressed my mouth shut and stepped away from the car. Her shoes clicked against the concrete as she hurried around the car. As she walked by she glanced at me. For a second our eyes met, but I couldn't read any expression in hers.

Then she was by and sliding behind the wheel. I took a quick look at the boss and started down the driveway. Honeysuckle was in bloom along the fence and the night air was thick with it. Music drifted through the darkness, floating from some unseen radio. Dance music, the old slow smooth kind that made a man want to dance real close with a pretty woman. Only I didn't have anybody to dance with. My footsteps were loud in the night. After a moment I noticed they were out of synch with the music.

"Mr. Cain, Mr. Cain."

Her voice cracked at the end of my name and I turned and peered back up the driveway. The door on the driver's side was still open, but I couldn't see either one of them. Part of me didn't want to, but I turned and started back.

She was sitting behind the wheel. She held out her hands. They were shaking. Her eyes came up and drifted across my face. "I hate to ask," she said, "but I don't think I can drive. Would you?"

Maybe that old anger still had a grip on me, but I didn't say a word. It sure wasn't very Christ-like, but then I wasn't Christ, or even a halfway good disciple. Sure, I'd read about the Good Samaritan plenty of times, but if it hadn't been the boss leaning white-faced against the car door I'd have turned and gone down the drive and headed for the shack. Just her and I'd have been long gone. But he'd been good to me. Treated me like a man and not some sort of glorified slave.

I closed my eyes and asked for strength. Then I opened them and said, "Scoot over." I slid behind the wheel. The scent of her perfume hung in the still air. All of a sudden I was conscious of the stench of my sweat.

She shifted against the seat. Her hair brushed against the side of my face. "You know the way?"

"Think so."

"You'd better be sure. He's not doing well. We can't waste any more time."

I shifted into reverse and gave it the gas. "Think I don't know that?"

She started to say something, then caught herself and stopped and turned toward her husband. I cut the wheel and we swung out onto the street. The boss shifted in his seat and moaned. She said something, but I didn't pay any attention. Maybe she sobbed once. I couldn't say for certain. I was too busy pushing the accelerator to the floor.

Twenty-nine

"Haven't seen you in a week. Where you been?" Her breath was soft and warm against my face. It smelled faintly of chewing gum, and more strongly of whiskey.

I nuzzled her neck. "Been busy over to the Ayers. Mr. Ayers had a bad spell with his heart. Only got out of the hospital yesterday. Been having to do a lot extra around the place. Plus, Mrs. Ayers claims with him being so sick and all that she's not able to drive. Makes her too nervous thinking about him being in the hospital. I've had to drive everywhere, hospital and the grocery, not to mention out to her sister's place, which is clear the other side of Prattville. Even had me drive her to church Sunday. Course I didn't go in, only sat out in the car and waited till services were over."

"Didn't that make you feel all funny? I mean having to drive some other man's wife to church is strange."

That was a question I hadn't thought about before and I lay there and considered the situation. "Nope, can't say it did. Just seemed like I was a chauffeur."

"You been a chauffeur before?"

"No, but I drove a milk truck in Atlanta for six months."

Jessie started to say something else, but I was tired of talking about the Ayers and I wanted her. Had wanted her for a week, make that a long week. I pressed my lips against hers and my hands and

177

some other body parts got real busy and for a while we didn't say much.

~ * ~

Afterwards, we lay as still as statues, sunk in the old mattress. Half asleep, I was only vaguely aware of the neon flickering on and off and on again outside the hotel as I listened to her breathing and tried to imagine all the people who had stretched out on that mattress before. The lonely ones who had tried to survive the night one swallow at a time, the happy ones who had lived out a fantasy, the businessmen who had made the sale and slept the sleep of the satisfied, the men and women who had been so tired of all the hard times that they didn't give a good hotdamn whether or not they woke up in the morning.

Time had drifted on and left us behind and I wasn't sure if it was ten o'clock, midnight, or two in the morning. Traffic still rolled on the street, so I figured it wasn't all that late. Lying in a hotel room in town seemed strange after all those nights alone in the shack. Neon and headlights and murmurs of street corner conversation were all right, but I'd rather have been hearing owls and tree frogs and small animals pushing through the weeds. Not that I was complaining, mind you. Wasn't much I wouldn't have done for Jessie and I wondered if she knew that. Probably did. Women always knew more than you thought they did. Way I saw things, women were a combination of mystery and miracle, only sometimes more one than the other.

A truck rumbled by, headed east, and I turned in time to catch a glimpse of its headlights penetrating the darkness.

"Are they nice?"

I jerked at the sound of her voice. I'd thought she had fallen asleep and my heart pounded hard for a few seconds. "Who are you talking about?" I said, my breath raggedy.

"Those people you work for. What's their name?"

"Ayers," I said. "They're all right. Especially him. He's always treated me like just another guy, not some servant or hired hand. She's not so bad, only she's got a temper and lots of the time she seems to take pleasure in making you feel small."

Jessie rolled over. Her breasts were soft against my chest. "Then why are you doing all this for her? Driving her around and such."

I kissed her forehead. Her hair tickled my face. "They pay me," I said. "Really, suppose I'm doing it more for him. It's what he would want. Owe him that much." Plus maybe a little more than that, I thought, but kept that to myself.

"I still say they're using you, Judas."

"People use each other."

She propped herself up on one elbow. Her face was very close. A wing of her hair brushed my shoulder. "Are you saying I use you?"

I was in a chancy mood. "Like I said, people use each other."

"So you admit you use me?"

In the next room a radio was playing just loudly enough so that every few seconds you caught a snatch of melody. I heard one then and it was from a song I'd heard before. Only I couldn't place it, couldn't give it the proper name. Then I heard another passage. Very short, six, maybe seven notes, but I knew then when I had heard it and where.

It had been in the fall, November seemed about right. A chilly raw day with on and off rain and a sharp biting northwest wind. I'd been hitching down along the Alabama state line without any luck. The gray afternoon had been growing darker and only a faint afterglow of daylight still lingered when a car crested a rise and headed down the slope toward me.

I'd been slogging along, hanging close to the pine trees that grew along the road, trying to keep out of some of the wind and rain. When I saw the car's headlights I'd hustled out of the woods and stuck out a thumb. Did that without a lot of hope. If it had been a pickup, or a timber truck, or even a grocery van I'd have felt better. Those were the sort of vehicles that I caught rides in. Dressed the way I was, with a three day growth of beard on my jawline and a damp bedroll slung across my back, I wasn't much of a candidate to get a ride in a car.

But that evening my luck was in. The car slowed, eased past me, then cut to the side of the road. I was running before the driver stopped or changed his mind. The car was a Chevrolet, only a year old and the interior was still in good shape. Remember that as clear as yesterday. Remember the song, too. The driver had whistled the same tune that was playing in the room next door, over and over, mile after mile. Don't remember much about him—think he wore glasses—and I don't remember much about the ride or the road. Only that tune. Funny how a man's mind works.

I bent and kissed Jessie on the mouth. "Yes," I whispered. "Expect I use you, too."

She made a small sound I couldn't interpret and shifted her body. She didn't move away, but she didn't come closer. "Don't you use me?" I asked.

She grunted and moved her body again in what might have been a shrug. A gust of wind fluttered the curtains and I caught a whiff of dust and motor oil and cooked cabbage. "I love you, you know."

"All men say that."

I scooted up to the end of the bed and sat up against the headboard. I hadn't had a drink in a week and all of a sudden I wanted one. Jessie had a way of getting on my nerves and making me want her all the more at the same time. "I mean it," I said. "Why don't you give me a chance to prove it?" I let my fingers slide across one of her bare shoulders.

"You're sweet," she said.

"That's no answer."

Jessie laughed. Then she repeated, "You're sweet."

I didn't have anything to say to that and I guess she was tired of talking, too. We lay there without speaking in that broken-backed bed, listening to the murmurings on the other side of the walls, watching the curtains shift in the evening breeze, thinking our own thoughts. I'd have given a dollar to know hers, but she wasn't telling.

I felt my eyelids growing heavy. Then, a loud metal clanging cracked the silence.

"They're coupling the train down at the yard. The midnight freight," I said. I bent and kissed her cheek. It was soft and warm. "If we hurry we can make it."

"Make what?"

"The freight train. We can hop it tonight before it even gets rolling. By morning we'll be down on the Gulf. What about it, Jessie? You and me catch that train and get out of this town. Start a new life. Just the two of us. The past will only be the past."

"What about your sick boss?"

"I told you, he's on the mend. He doesn't need me anymore."

"And what would we do for money, Judas? Answer me that."

"I'm not afraid of hard work."

"Yeah, and what sort of job could you get going to some town where nobody knows you? Sounds like a sure trip to Povertyville to me."

"I wouldn't care about being poor if I was with you."

"Well, here's some news for you, mister. I've been poor and it's no damn fun. I don't aim to ever be poor again. You can't ask that of me. Not if you love me like you say. No, you go ahead and catch that freight, but this girl is going to roll over and go to sleep."

Springs squeaked as her body moved. The music in the next room played on. After a bit, she began to snore. It was a very gentle, ladylike sound. I was tired myself, but there were emotions churning inside me. Sleep wouldn't come.

After some time, I eased out of the bed, then tiptoed to the window. The breeze was cool against my bare chest. For a long time, I stood peering out at the street, watching the neon flash on and off, like some forgotten signal. The engineer blew the whistle, then I heard the train jolt as it began to move. I watched its single bright eye poke at the darkness as it began to roll. Part of me surely did want to be sitting in one of those boxcars, staring out the open door at the night opening up before me like a gigantic ebony flower.

Thirty

She was smiling and I figured she must have gotten a letter from Lenny. I glanced down at the desk in front of her and there it was. V-mail. I was right; she'd heard from the boy. Her eyes were open, but unfocused. She didn't even realize I was in the room. Her mind was thousands of miles away, or maybe it had drifted back in time.

"Mizz Ayers?"

"What? Oh, yes, Judas. I see you're here at last. But you look awful. Dark circles under your eyes and your clothes all rumpled. Did you have a rough night?"

"Disappointing," I said.

"Well, I'm sorry to hear that. Still, you should always try to present yourself in the best light..." Her voice trailed off and she shook her head.

I nodded at the letter. "You heard from him?"

She smiled and her face opened so that in that moment she looked like a young girl. "Yes. We got a letter this morning. By now, he's on a big transport ship sailing for someplace he couldn't name. I'm sure it's one of those little islands they write about in the paper. Myrtle Evans says those transports are as safe as houses. What do you think, Mr. Cain?"

"I wouldn't know," I said and rubbed my chin. "What's on my list for today?"

"Lenny says he's meetings lots of nice boys from all over the country. His best friend is from Colorado. Imagine that, Colorado. I've never even been there. What about you, Judas?"

"Once. I was simply passing through."

"Did you like it?"

"Sure were some beautiful mountains there."

"Oh, I love mountains. When I was a girl my Uncle Lester used to take us all to the mountains in the summer. Up near Asheville, North Carolina. Oh, how green and cool they were. Were the mountains in Colorado cool and green, Mr. Cain?"

"Actually, when I was there they were covered with snow."

She smiled, then glanced down again at her letter. "I'm sure they were pretty," she murmured, "but I don't like cold weather."

Seeing as how I damn near froze to death riding through those mountains in an open boxcar, I couldn't disagree. That was about the most she'd ever talked to me, except about some job I was supposed to do, or had done wrong, and all her words took me by surprise so that I simply stood there. Guess I was waiting for her to say something else, but she was lost in the letter now and had no more words for the yardman. I didn't have any kids, but I could imagine how much hearing from your child might mean.

For some time I stood there, watching her lips move ever so slightly as she read the letter again. She hadn't told me what she wanted done, but I didn't have the heart to disturb her. I silently counted to two hundred; then I turned and walked back the way I'd come. There was always yard work to do; I'd find something. At the doorway, I turned and looked back.

She was still in her chair. Her eyes were open wide, but she wasn't seeing anything in that room. No, what she was seeing was thousands of miles away over the blue Pacific. She was smiling to herself and the late morning sunlight fell softly through the trees in the backyard and the open window and blessed her face. Have to say, at that moment she looked right pretty.

Thirty-one

Summer had come and gone and nobody was unhappy to see it go. It had been long and hot and so dry that the croaking of the frogs sounded like prayers for rain. All the little creeks had gone dry and the farm ponds had dwindled to little more than mud holes. Lightning had started a bad fire over toward Douglas Gap and more than a dozen people got burnt out of their homes. An elderly farmer by the name of McCabe had burned to death trying to save his barn.

Death had been a far too frequent visitor those long hot days. Western Union boys had become unwelcome sights. That's what happens when you deliver bad news to the front door.

Not that I kept count, but more than a dozen families showed gold stars in their front window. No telling how many servicemen had been wounded or gone missing in action. It had gotten so that every man who wasn't white-haired or a cripple received hard looks if he wasn't in uniform. Talk was, if the war went on long enough, they would start calling up men my age.

The rains hadn't come, but the winds had grown cooler and the leaves had turned and started to fall. The color hadn't been good this year, but big swatches of the yard were covered with dead leaves. Today, the sun was out and only a few white clouds drifted about, but there was a bite to the wind. I was raking leaves on the south side and in the shade I was glad for my jacket.

The boss was raking, too. Maybe not hard, but raking. He said the doctor had told him to get more exercise. So now he puttered around the house, doing odd jobs that didn't require a lot of effort, putting up a birdhouse for Mrs. Ayers, sweeping off the sidewalks, washing the Pontiac. A couple of weeks ago, he started going in to the bank a few hours most days. Not sure the doc wanted him to, and I know Mrs. Ayers didn't, but a man couldn't afford to give up a good job like that. That I understood. Besides, if a man wanted to keep his self-respect he needed to work. First hand was how I knew that.

A hawk was circling above, dipping his wings now and then to shift direction or keep level, but mostly drifting, riding the winds, a black speck against all that blue. Ever so often the boss leaned on his rake and watched the bird. I wondered if the bird was watching us.

Seemed like somebody was always watching somebody else. I knew Brad Menifee's henchmen still had orders to keep an eye on me. And for damn sure I was keeping an eye out for him. I'd survived one beating and didn't aim to take another,

A car wheezed down the street and I turned to watch. The motor sounded like it was seizing up. With the war on, parts were almost impossible to come by. A stub-tailed dog trotted in the car's wake. His head was up and he was padding steadily along like he had someplace to go with a time to be there. Mr. Ayers had been eyeing the street, too, and he turned, saw I was looking at the dog and smiled and waved. He said something, but the breeze caught enough of his words so that I couldn't understand them. I smiled as I waved back.

The dog was almost out of sight when a kid on a bicycle came into view. He was pedaling hard. Raking leaves wasn't much fun and I turned and watched him. When he got closer, I could see that he was wearing a Western Union cap and I was afraid he was going to turn into the drive. But he merely gave the house a passing glance and kept on pedaling. I watched him until he reached the end of the block and then went back to raking leaves.

~ * ~

I was raking on the far side of a sugar maple and not paying attention to much beyond the carpet of leaves that never seemed to get much smaller. Screeching metal caught my ear and I turned toward the noise.

Coming up the driveway was the kid on the bicycle, pedaling steady. I gave his face a look, but I couldn't read anything. I cut a quick glance down at the boss, then. He was leaning his rake against the trunk of a black gum and turning toward the house.

A few more clouds had drifted in and the drive was spotted with shadows. The kid pedaled into the shadows and out again. I glanced back at the boss. He had started walking toward the house.

The kid pedaled up to the front sidewalk and braked. He hopped off the bike and trotted up the steps. I tried to read him, but he was playing his cards tight to his chest. He rapped the door with his knuckles, then turned and glanced around the yard. I saw him look my way; then he turned back and knocked again. In his hand was a piece of yellow paper.

Mrs. Ayers came to the door. The boss was halfway up the drive. The kid nodded at Mrs. Ayers and handed her what looked like a telegram. I told myself not to panic…telegrams came for lots of reasons, but I dropped my rake and started after the boss.

Mrs. Ayers dropped whatever the kid had given her and he bent and picked it up and gave it to her again. Even from where I was, I could see her arm trembling. The boss was walking faster. She handed the kid a coin and he turned and headed for his bike. I was still watching him when I heard her scream. I started running.

The boss was running and I thought of his heart. She flung herself against his chest and I saw him grab the telegram from her. I put my head down and started running harder. The kid passed me going the other way, coasting.

I was almost to the top of the drive when I heard her scream again. My head jerked toward the sound and I saw the boss grab his chest. His face was the color of dirty cotton. He began to slowly turn. I started sprinting.

Halfway down the sidewalk, I saw him spin once and fall like a big tree going down. She tried to catch him, but all she did was sorta break his fall. The telegram slipped from his fingers and the wind caught it and whirled the paper toward the street. When I heard her scream again, I changed direction and started running for the telephone.

Thirty-two

The wind had been blowing all morning. It was a cold damp wind that seemed to gather strength as it whipped across the parking lot, as though it had come all the way from the Gulf and had been picking up steam since it made landfall. I bent against that wind and hustled across the parking lot. The sky was solid gray and I could smell rain.

After the grayness, the corridor was almost too bright. I blinked down the hallway until I came to the information stand. A moon-faced woman with shiny black hair sat behind the counter. She smiled up at me. "Yes."

"Can you tell me the room number for Arthur Ayers?"

She gave me a funny look, but then she flipped through a chart on a spindle. She lifted her face. "Number three twenty-six," she said. Her lips were smiling, but her eyes looked hard, like small blue stones. "The stairs are at the far end of the hall." She nodded, her head chopping like a hatchet.

"Thanks," I said and stepped around the counter. All the way down the hall I could feel her eyes on my back. I knew she was wondering why somebody like me was coming to visit a banker like Mr. Ayers. The woman wasn't anything special herself and her dyed hair looked silly, but she was staring down her nose at me and there wasn't anything I could do about it. It had happened before and it would happen again. I took the stairs two at a time.

~ * ~

The blinds were pulled and the lights were off. Only a little light seeped in around the bottom of the blinds and under the door. I sat on the hard chair by the side of the bed. A magazine lay on the bedside table, but the light was too dim to read. Under the covers, Mr. Ayers' chest rose and fell. His face was pale and a plastic tube was jabbed in his arm. I'd been there for some time and he hadn't moved. Only his chest shifted as he breathed. It was very quiet in the room. Now and then, I could hear the wind pressing against the windows and once I'd heard footsteps in the hallway.

I hadn't slept much the night before, what with thinking about the boss lying up in a hospital room and the kid lying dead somewhere on a lousy island in the Pacific. Even thought about Mrs. Ayers. Wondered how she was holding up. The doctor had given her a sedative and a friend from her book club had come over to stay the night. I'd tried to say a few words, but she had been crying and, anyway, my throat felt real tight.

Between the long night and the dim light I must have dozed. Or maybe I only daydreamed. Anyway, I woke up saying Jessie's name.

Something was different in the room. For a minute I couldn't name it. My first thought was that the boss had passed. I went real still and listened hard, but I couldn't tell his breathing had changed. I eased off the chair.

He looked the same and his chest still rose and his breathing sounded the same. Yet, there was something different about the room. I could feel a presence beyond mine and the boss's. I turned.

She was sitting in the corner in an arm chair that had the stuffing coming out of one arm. My guess was they'd drug that relic out of the doctor's lounge. In the poor light, her face was pale and indistinct. I took in a deep breath, let it out, and started walking.

Up close, I could see that her entire body was trembling ever so slightly. Her chin was quivering and her cheeks were wet. She lifted her face.

"What are you doing here?" Her voice was low and harsh, like her throat was sore.

"Just checking to see how he was doing."

Her lips came apart, but nothing came out. She sniffed and buried her face in her hands. Her shoulders jerked and her muffled sobs sounded loud in the quiet room.

Never could stand to hear a woman crying. Every one of those sobs was like a knife slicing. I stood it for as long as I could, then reached down and patted her on the shoulder. Probably, there were comforting words I could have said, but they wouldn't come.

After the sobbing eased, she reached a hand up and covered mine. She must not have had any words, either. If she had, she didn't say them. In the echo of her crying the room seemed hollow. Sound returned slowly, as if it were reluctant to enter the room.

First came the sound of her breathing. Her breaths had a labored sound. Gradually I became aware of a soft whooshing sound from one of the machines by the bed. Voices drifted in from the hallway. They sounded like nurses talking. A cart squeaked and I wondered if they were bringing a patient something to eat. All of a sudden I was hungry.

It was strange standing there with my hand on her shoulder and her hand on top of mine. I kept looking first at the boss and then at the top of her head. Down the hall a door slammed and as if in response her hand began rubbing across mine. Her hand was soft and felt nice, but I knew she wasn't thinking. It was only her hand moving on its own, the way a leg will bounce up and down or eyes will go to blinking. Still, it made me uncomfortable. But I didn't pull my hand away. If it was a comfort to her, well, maybe it was for the best.

After a while her hand quit moving. I took a look at her face. Her eyes were closed and her chest rose and fell gently. I wondered if she was asleep. I glanced at the boss. He looked small in the bed with all those tubes running from the machines and into his arms. In a way he looked like a little boy overwhelmed with all the medical equipment.

I'd never been in a hospital. Hobos and hospitals didn't mix. If a man got hurt out on the road, or jumping off a train, or in a fight in a hobo jungle, he had to hope that a buddy or a Good Samaritan took care of him. Injuries had happened a couple of times to me. Down in Georgia, I'd sprained my ankle bad and a railroad guard had smashed my head for me outside Biloxi. Both times somebody had taken care of me.

In Georgia, I'd had a buddy for a while named Gene and he was a good man to have as a friend, as long as he could stay sober. An older man in a vest and battered homburg had nursed me for a week outside of Biloxi. Then one morning I'd come wide awake knowing he was gone. Over the years, I'd tried to return the favor. Once in Texas and then again outside Leavenworth, Kansas. Only that fellow in Kansas had died on me. Bled to death inside himself after a couple of worthless cowboys beat the holy hell out of him purely for fun. Way I saw it everybody needs help sometime, and it only makes sense to pay it back.

Guess that's what I was trying to do there in that hospital room. The Ayers had hired me when I needed a job. She could be a pain, but she hadn't fired me, and the boss, well he'd always treated me square, like a man. Hurt me to see him there in that bed with all those tubes stuck in him and so pale and feeble looking. The man in bed almost looked like a stranger.

She was asleep now. I could hear the change in her breathing and all of a sudden I simply couldn't stand it in that room anymore. Not with her asleep and him looking like he was one step this side of death. Moving as quietly as I could, I slid my hand from under hers. She made a small sound, but I don't think she woke up. I took one final look at the boss, then tiptoed across the room.

Thirty-three

She found me in the cafeteria. I was on my third refill of bad coffee. It tasted the way the way water in a ditch alongside the tracks outside of Corinth, Mississippi had looked when the railroad bull kicked me out of the boxcar.

She came in real slow, hesitating just inside the door. Then she saw me, nodded, and crossed the floor. There was an empty chair across the table and she sat down heavy, like her legs were tired, and let out a long breath.

"You're a hard man to find. Didn't know if you were still here or not."

"I'm here. Thought about going home, but decided I needed a cup of coffee first. That was an hour ago."

She glanced down at her watch. Looked at it closely, then lifted her wrist and shook it. "Damn," she said, "it's stopped." A funny look crawled across her face. "No wonder I've totally lost track of time."

She turned and looked around the room. A white clock with black numbers hung on the wall. The little hand was on eleven. "Ugh, even later than I thought." She shook her head. Her hair swung loose and a strand fell across her face. She brushed it back with one hand and drug a bobby pin out of the pocket of her dress and pinned it in place. "I must look a mess." She rubbed at her face.

"You know, I can't remember the last time I took a bath. It's all getting away from me. My mother used to say there were times that she didn't know if she was coming or going. I used to wonder what she meant."

"And now you know."

"And now I know."

She shifted in her chair and let her eyes swing around the cafeteria. Except for an old man with his head down on a table and a young couple with long faces, we were alone. She closed her eyes and rolled her head on her neck. For the first time, I noticed the sagging skin under her jaw. "Oh, I'm tired, Judas. Tired to the bone." She opened her eyes. "That was Father's saying. He used to say that every day when he came in from the fields. 'Martha,' he'd say, Martha was my mother, 'I'm tired to the bone.' Funny how all those old sayings that seemed so silly turn out to be true."

"Life can be funny that way," I said.

"You got a cigarette, Judas? Think I'll take up smoking. Maybe nicotine would take my troubles off my mind."

"Nope," I said. "Fresh out." I grinned at her. "Do have a cigar at home. Been saving it for a special occasion. You're welcome to it."

"I'll give it some thought," she said. "Arthur smokes cigars, you know?"

I nodded.

"Big brown stinky things. Calls them bombs."

"I know, he's given me a couple."

She let her head settle to one side. "Now why he would do that?"

I rubbed at my eyes. The minute hand had moved to the bottom of the clock. Past my bedtime. "Could be that he's really a nice guy. Or maybe he was lonely and wanted some company. We talk, you know?"

She rubbed at her eyes. They were red-rimmed and blood shot. "Really?" She made a face. "We never talk anymore, not really."

Her eyes left me then. They wandered across the room, only I could tell they weren't really seeing anything in the sad little cafeteria either. I was only guessing, but I figured maybe she was looking back across the years. That can be a long look, not to mention a lonely one. I tried to read her eyes, but they were glassy. She came back slowly, in stages.

Her shoulders rose and fell and she turned to me. She was wearing a smile, but it didn't look real. "And what do you and my husband talk about, Mr. Cain?"

I gave her a smile of my own. It felt phony, like a magician had made it appear on my face. The woman was okay, but I was tired.

"Oh, nothing much. Fishing sometimes, and football. Once in a while he tells me something that went on at the bank. We used to talk about other things." All of a sudden I realized that I was taking a path I didn't want to go down. I flicked a glance at her eyes, then looked away and shrugged. "Well, you know—"

She gave me a hard look that chilled me some. "You mean things neither of us wants to talk about, or say?"

"Yeah."

"I see."

"There at the last we mostly talked about fishing. That, and when he was a kid. How things were back then."

She put her hands on the table, palms down, and stared at them. "Did he ever talk about me?"

I tried to think. If we'd ever talked about her, at least more than a passing comment about where she was, or what she'd cooked, or how hateful she'd been, I couldn't recall it. Part of me, the part whose feelings she'd hurt, wanted to tell her that. But if I told her the hard truth and the boss passed, she never get over my words, and I'd have one devil of a time trying to live with myself. It was too heavy a burden. "Sure," I said, "he talked about you right often."

She looked up through the shafts of hair that had fallen across her face. Right then, she looked like a child who has been left alone for a long time. Shy and a bit scared and anxious to please, all at the same time. "Really?" she murmured.

"Oh yes."

"And what did he say about me?"

I swallowed hard and wished someone would walk in. Lying was something I hated and wasn't good at. "Oh, lots of things."

"Like what?"

"Surely don't remember them all. But lots of stuff, like how nice you looked, or when you cooked him one of his favorite dishes. Like I said, I don't remember near all of it."

"He loves me, you know?"

"Sure," I said, "anybody could see that."

"Just because we argued sometimes doesn't mean anything. Not really."

"No, of course not. Couples argue all the time."

She opened her mouth like she was going to say something, but then her eyes changed and she closed her mouth. She lifted her head, then shook the hair out of her face.

"Do you have a girlfriend, Judas?"

"Like to think I do."

"What's her name?"

"Jessie."

"Is she pretty?"

"I think so."

Mrs. Ayers leaned back in her chair and let her eyes go almost closed. "I used to be pretty."

I felt awkward, unsure of what to say. Figured she wanted me to say something reassuring, but I couldn't think of any good words, so I held my talk.

"I used to be young. Young and slender and a good dancer. All the fellows told me I was a wonderful dancer." She cocked her head and peered at me. Her eyes were red rimmed and puffed up underneath, and her hair was tangled. "Are you a good dancer?"

"Not particularly."

"Oh, I bet you're being modest."

"Not really, just honest."

"Honesty is a good thing, too."

I nodded and wished I were somewhere else. It felt funny sitting here talking to her while upstairs the boss was hooked up to all those tubes and machines. Kept seeing his face and that hurt me inside.

She didn't say anymore and I thought maybe she was through talking. I wished she was. I wished she'd go back to his room or home or anywhere else, so long as she left me alone. I'd been alone for so long I could only take people in small does. Like castor oil. Besides, she rubbed on my nerves real quick.

Mrs. Ayers closed her eyes, then leaned back in her chair. Her head was turned in profile. With the loose skin under her chin and her protruding nose, it wasn't the most flattering pose. She made a groaning sound deep in her throat.

"I haven't danced in twenty years, and I doubt I'll ever dance again." She opened her eyes. "Still, I don't suppose that matters, not really. Not when you consider everything else."

"No," I said "don't guess dancing matters much one way or the other."

"It's only that it seems like once you begin to lose, you just keep on losing."

I knew she was thinking about her son, dead on some sand spit in the Pacific, and her husband, lying upstairs in a hospital bed in bad shape. He might die or he might live, but I figured he'd never be the same man again. She was eyeing me out of the corners of her eyes and I sensed she wanted me to say something, but I didn't have the faintest idea what.

I rubbed my face and wished I'd gone home. Footsteps squeaked in the hall and then a nurse stood in the doorway of the cafeteria. Reddish hair peeked out from under her nurse's cap and her face was full of bones. Her eyes worked across the room, lingering on my face for a second before moving on. In a moment they came back.

"Are you Judas?"

I nodded.

"Mr. Ayers wants to see you."

I felt my face growing warm. I nodded again and stood up. Mrs. Ayers was sitting right there, but I couldn't look at her. It felt like her eyes were burning into my spine as I walked to the door. I followed the nurse down the hall. Her back was straight and flat and she didn't say a word. It was a long walk.

Thirty-four

He looked like an old, worn-down scarecrow who'd been tossed in a bed and left there. His skin had a pasty look and his eyes were big in his face. But he smiled a little when I stuck my head in the door.

"Come in, Judas." His voice was scratchy.

I crossed the floor and sat in the chair by the bed.

"How you doing, Mr. Ayers?"

"Not so hot, I'm afraid." He looked around the room as if he were expecting someone else to be there.

"Once I came to, they called the doctor. He only left maybe ten minutes ago."

"What he'd say?"

His face worked all over and he shut one eye and squinted the other about half-shut, then turned his head so he was facing me. His half-open eye looked hot, like a fire was burning down under it.

"I'm going to give it to you straight, Judas. But don't tell Marilee. Okay?"

"Whatever you say."

"Well, Doc said that this last one was the real deal. Damaged the old pump bad. Told me straight out that the next one would be the end. Now, if I lay around and don't do much of anything and take my medicine and eat salad and Melba toast, I might squeeze out a year or two." Both eyes came open and his head settled deep in his pillow. "Not sure I call that living, do you?"

"Don't you think it's better than being dead?"

"Come on, Judas. You know how it is."

Sure, I knew how it was. Didn't make me want to say the words though. So I kept my mouth shut.

"That's why I wanted to talk to you, see. Before it's too late. Understand?"

I nodded.

"Good. Now you've got to promise me."

I didn't like the sound of that. Promises had a way of haunting a man. "Promise you what?"

"What we talked about before. That you'll take care of Marilee. She'll take it hard, especially after..." His voice trailed off and his eyes got that far away look eyes get when seeing something distant, or going back in time. I knew what he meant.

"Boss, you're asking more than I can deliver. Don't think Mrs. Ayers likes me much and I don't know the first thing about wills and settling estates."

"No, no, that's not what I meant. Don Trosper is a good attorney. He'll take care of all that. At least he better after what I've paid him. No, what I'm talking about is simply checking on her. Make sure she's eating and getting out some and not simply sitting around brooding. She's not a bad person. Only she's grown a hard shell over the years. Wasn't that way when we first met. Guess maybe I bear some of that responsibility, or it could be life itself shapes us over time." He gave me a lopsided grin. "Never have figured that one out."

A phone rang down the hall and I wondered who was calling and what the news was. I didn't want to answer the boss. Not right then, anyway. Probably because I didn't know how to.

His eyes stared at me. The fire in them had died down and they looked cool now, like glass, or polished stones. "You'll do that for me, Judas, won't you? Not much to ask as a last request, but it's what I want."

All the good things he'd done for me flooded my mind right then and I recalled how he'd treated me nice, like just another guy and not a yardman and I knew I couldn't say no. Maybe he wouldn't die, at least not for a long time. And when he did pass who was to say I had to keep such a promise. There would be nobody watching me and no one would know. Even Marilee would have no idea what I'd promised.

"You got it," I said. "I'll do my best."

He raised his right hand, grunting with the effort, and stuck it out at me. I put out my own right hand and his closed on mine. "Thank you, Judas. Eases my mind considerable knowing you'll be around to look after her." His fingers squeezed my hand. They felt cold, like death. I was glad when he let go.

"You'll never know what this means to me, Judas."

"It's nothing. You'd do the same for me."

"I'd try, for sure," the boss said and smiled. It was a tight-lipped smile. Even his lips were a bad color. They had a bluish tinge. Chilled me considerable to look at his face. Brought home the fact that we all came to this someday. Old Death might wait awhile, but he never lets anybody slide. I'd seen dead bodies, in hobo camps and such, and I'd watched two men die, besides the one I lost trying to doctor in Kansas. One old fellow had simply gone to sleep. The other, who been cut bad by a drunken Mex, had died with his guts in his hands, begging for his mother. For a bit I thought about how I might go. Then I pushed the chair back and stood up. Thinking of such things made me squeamish. The walls felt like they were closing in on me.

Thirty-five

Between one heartbeat and the next I came wide awake. I lay very still and listened. Something, or somebody, was walking across the clearing, headed for the shack. My first thought was of Jessie. Then I wondered if it was Brad Menifee and his boys. I slid out from under the sheet and padded over to the window.

The moon was down behind the ridge and only the first thin blue blush of daylight rimmed the eastern sky. A fine mist shimmered in the near dark. Trees rose out of the mist, misshapen and spectral. Grass and wildflowers seemed only a thicker element of the night and mist.

At first that was all I saw. Then I bent my head and looked off toward the west and a figure stepped out of the mist onto a rise of ground. For a moment it could have been a monkey or a man or old Scratch himself. Then the figure took another stride and I could tell by the movement that it was Moses.

I slipped on my pants and shirt and fumbled for a match. The lamp flickered just as he knocked on the door.

"Come in."

The door swung open and the old man stuck his head into the room. "You're sure an accommodating fellow. No telling who might be about this hour." He grinned. "Might have been Brad Menifee instead of an angel of mercy like me."

I laughed at that image. "You don't look much like an angel to me."

"Ever see an angel?"

"Well, that's a good question," I said. "Not sure if I have or not."

"So I might be one, huh?" He eased his cap back and scratched his head. "Don't the Good Book say something about entertaining angels unawares?"

"Yeah, something along those lines. Think it's in Hebrews."

"That's right, it is Hebrews." He tilted his head back, closed his eyes, and screwed up his face as though the effort to remember was a strain. "Let's see, best as I remembers it's in the second chapter of Hebrews, the second verse. 'Be not forgetful to entertain strangers; for thereby some have entertained angles unawares'."

"You've got a good memory."

"Been reading that old Bible for a long time. Eighty years and more, I expect. Started when I was a young'un."

I leaned against the table and studied the old man's face. In the flickering lamplight it had the cast and color of a statue carved by a primitive man. He hadn't said why he'd come and I wondered. Maybe he had something important to say and maybe he was only out wandering and decided to stop. Old men don't sleep well.

"Didn't think I had a good memory, did you? Probably thought I was too old."

"Try not to judge people."

"That's right out of the Holy Word, too. 'Judge not lest ye be judged.' You must be a Christian man at heart."

"Have been at times. Lately, I've not been practicing very hard."

"We all have our weak seasons."

I nodded. "You're out early this morning. Strolling for your health?"

He shook his head. "Nope. Like I said, I'm an angel on an errand of mercy."

"Meaning what?"

He bent his head and looked up at me from under his brow. I got the feeling he was studying my face. "Meaning afore daylight this very morning, Mrs. Arthur Ayers asked me to come and fetch you."

I had two questions to ask. The easy one, I asked first. "Where did you see her?"

"Down to the hospital. Don't recollect ever telling you, but I go there about every evening and haul off all their tore up cardboard and old newspapers and such and burn them out behind where the doctors park. I was gathering up trash on the third floor when she stepped out in the hall and called to me. Said she'd seen us talking together and asked if I knew where you lived. Told her I did and she asked if I would go and fetch you. She sure made it sound important."

The skin puckered up on the back of my arms and I made my face hard. "Fetch me for what, Moses?"

His mouth turned down. "She didn't say, Judas. Only said to fetch you to the hospital. Said you'd know sure enough what that meant."

I knew all right, and I turned my head away real quick and swiped at my eyes with my shirt sleeve. Then I went and put my boots on, washed my face, and combed my hair. Moses drank a dipperful of water while he waited for me. Daylight was coming hard when we stepped outside.

~ * ~

Shrouded in mist, the town lay quiet. The only sound was the echo of our footsteps. The streets were empty and the stores dark. Even the birds and squirrels still lingered in the nest. All that empty quiet gave a fellow an eerie feeling, like maybe he'd wandered into someplace he shouldn't have. If Moses had any misgivings, he kept them to himself.

Crossing Alexander, movement caught my eye and I turned my head in time to see a woman disappear around the corner. Maybe it was because she had been on my mind, but something in the set of the woman's back along with the way she walked going away made me think of Jessie. Longing ran through me like a dose of salts and I almost crossed the street to follow.

We cut across Veterans' Park, down the alley that ran between Roy Hoffman's Bakery and Levine's Dry Goods store. Then, out of the mist, the hospital loomed before us. Off to the east the sky was growing lighter and the mist was lifting as we crossed the street. We marched up the sidewalk to birds twittering in the maples.

I pushed open the door and started to step inside. Then I felt a hand on my arm.

"I'm leaving you now, brother."

I searched Moses' face. "How come?"

"Better for a colored man to go in the back door to a white man's hospital," he said.

"Aw, come on," I said. "I've got some dirty blood, too."

He shook his head. "Yours is Indian. Mine's black, which is altogether different. You know that, Judas. Besides, you work for the Ayers. That changes things, too."

"Come on," I said, "let's go. Nobody will say anything." I glanced down the hallway. It was empty. "Heck, nobody's up yet."

"Naw, man, that's where you're wrong. Nurses never sleep on duty. Nope, I'll slip around to the back door and get me a cup of coffee and a biscuit from the kitchen. Got a friend works there and she'll treat old Moses right. Catch you later."

He let go of my arm, turned and started around the building. I watched him until he disappeared. Then I went hunting for the stairs.

~ * ~

The door was closed. I eased it open in case she was sleeping. She was sitting in the chair, but her eyes were open. Open and vacant.

The room was quiet. Too damn quiet. I stood half in the room and half in the hall while I listened for the change. For a minute I couldn't figure it out. Then I knew. The machines had fallen silent. I made myself turn and look.

One eye was open, the other closed. It made it look like he was winking. The flesh had a waxen look and he was very still. His chest no longer rose or fell, even faintly. I looked back at her.

Her eyes changed slowly, in stages. When they were fully alive, they stared at me like I was a stranger. At that moment maybe I was. Maybe that was all I ever had been and ever would be.

She blinked. "He's gone."

My throat felt real tight. Heat surged through my body. Then all that heat turned to ice. A lump was forming in my throat. Felt like it was the size of young peach. I swallowed it down.

"I'm sorry," I said. That was all I could say right then. Meant it, too. Not that the words made one damn bit of difference. When did words ever make any difference?

"Arthur was a good man," she said, her head turned toward the bed. "Never gave me a minute's trouble, not really. Oh, I worried about his health and him eating right and drinking and smoking so much, but what wife doesn't worry about her husband?"

She pushed up out of the chair. Her legs were wobbly. She tottered over to the window and pushed her face close to the glass.

"You're not married are you, Mr. Cain?"

"No."

"Ever been married?"

"No."

"Then you've never had a woman to worry over you, have you? I mean really worry so that she can't sleep or eat or even think straight?"

"Guess the only woman that ever worried much about me was my mother."

"Is she still alive?"

That seemed like a strange question. In fact, the whole conversation seemed unreal. With the boss lying there dead it seemed really strange to be talking at all. Always heard you were supposed to show respect for the dead. Even when an old hobo had passed somewhere along the rails, the other men were silent for a spell. Still, maybe it was different with women like Mrs. Ayers. Maybe they needed to talk.

"No, she passed when I was nine."

"I'm sorry," she said, her back still to me. "Was it a long illness?"

"No, she was killed in an accident. She was walking along the side of the road one afternoon and a car came along and hit her. Driver said he was blinded by the sun. Dad always said the man was blinded all right, only it wasn't by any sunlight. Knocked her into a ditch. Police said she must of hit her head on a rock." I snapped my fingers. "Just like that she was gone."

I half turned toward the door then. It was like I could almost see them, my mom and dad, or their silhouettes or shadows or their ghosts. But that was foolishness. Nothing more than my mind playing a trick on me. I started to say something about Dad not lasting even a year after Mom passed. Instead, I shut my mouth. Already been blabbing too much.

A cart squeaked by in the hall followed by a car horn blew down in the street. Daylight was coming now. I wished it would hurry. The night seemed full of memories of the dead.

A new sound rose up in the room. Sort of a dry, hiccupping sound. Then it turned damp and I knew she was crying. Her back worked, twitching in spasms and jerks. For a long time, I stood and watched. Part of me felt like I ought to go over and give her a hug. But another part of me wouldn't let my legs move. It seemed like halfway to eternity before the men came with the gurney.

Thirty-six

Arthur Ayers was buried in a sweet, gentle rain at the cemetery north of town. The Ayers family had maintained a section there for over one hundred years, so at least he'd be lying with family. Didn't suppose I'd end that way. Mom and Dad were dead and gone and the rest of my folks scattered like dry leaves before November winds.

For him to have been a banker there wasn't much of a crowd at the gravesite. Then maybe bankers didn't have a lot of friends. Certainly they hadn't had many back in the hard times. On top of that, there had been so much death since Pearl Harbor that most people were worn down with funerals.

I was standing on a little knoll at the back end of the cemetery, in the shelter of a line of locust trees, watching the funeral with Moses. The Ayers section lay in the bowl below. Mourners stood around the gravesite. Beyond them was the hearse and four or five cars. A tall man in a black suit was standing next to Mrs. Ayers. Figured maybe he was her brother. The one from Clifton she talked about sometimes. Think he owned several filling stations. As I watched, Mrs. Ayers turned and appeared to say something to the tall man. He nodded and turned and started trudging up the slope.

Moses nudged me. "They've sent him to do one of two things."

"What do you mean?"

"Either they want you to come down and join the mourners or they want me to leave."

"Oh, you're crazy," I said, although I did wonder why the man had left the funeral.

He came up the hill slowly, moving carefully on the slick grass. Maybe I should have gone and met him halfway, but I stayed under the trees. Not that they gave much shelter, but they kept off the worst of the rain.

The man crested the rise and walked in under the trees. He was even taller than he had looked down below. I figured him for three or four inches over six feet and was pretty sure he must be Mrs. Ayers' brother. She was always talking about how she came from a big-boned family.

The man stopped a few feet away and readjusted his hat. "You Mr. Cain?"

I nodded.

"I'm Ralph Quinlin, Marilee's brother." He stuck out his hand and I shook it. As he let go, he glanced over at Moses and nodded.

"Mr. Cain, my sister would like you come down and stand with the family. She said you and Arthur always got along real good and that you'd been a big help over the last few weeks. Won't you come on down?"

I looked down at my clothes. They were my best ones, but that didn't signify much. "I'm not dressed for the occasion," I said.

"Oh, that's all right," Quinlin said. "Marilee won't mind." He smiled at me. "I think she'd feel better if you were there. Especially seeing how you were so close to Arthur. You should do it for him."

I didn't want to go. I'd look a fool down there and I knew it. Still, Marilee's brother was right about one thing. I did owe the boss. Figured I could do this one last thing for him. After all, I'd promised I'd keep an eye on Mrs. Ayers for him.

"Okay," I said and glanced at Moses. He was grinning like a possum. I made a face and started down the slope after Quinlin.

All the way down, I could sense the faces around the grave staring at me. Heat flashed up my cheeks. I kept my eyes on the ground.

I followed Quinlin around the circle of men and women. They were all dressed in black and wore somber expressions on their long faces. He stepped into the empty spot next to his sister and I eased up behind him. Close enough so that I wouldn't be asked to come closer, but not so close that I looked like one of the family. Mrs. Ayers turned her head and looked at me, but she was wearing a veil and I couldn't read her eyes.

The preacher stepped forward then. He was a balding man with glasses who reminded me of my Uncle Joe. Hadn't seen or thought of that man in years. Before I left home he'd run a grocery out to the crossroads. He'd been my dad's older brother and I wondered if he was still alive.

Even for a preacher, the man standing by the casket was windy. He talked on and on about birth and life and death. Actually, he droned. Like a wasp. For the first minute or so I listened close, hoping to hear even a handful of words that would ease the loss. But the longer the man droned, the more I sensed my mind drifting.

Death was something I'd always wondered about. Preachers and Sunday school teachers taught that if you lived a good life you went to heaven and if you didn't obey the commandments you went to hell. Which, I suppose, was the only way to say it from a religious point of view.

Still, nobody had even gone to either place and come back to tell about it. Least not anybody I'd ever run across. So who knew if either heaven or hell really existed? Who really knew?

Oh, it was nice to think about a heaven where there were streets of gold and always plenty to eat and drink and nobody got sick. God would be there, and Jesus. Even the old Holy Ghost. Not to mention all the people you'd lost over the years. Like my mom and dad. Only, I wondered how you would know them. Once, down in

Texas, along the tracks where they cut through the hill country, I'd gone into a pine thicket to answer a call of nature and stumbled across a skeleton.

Once I picked myself up, naturally I looked to see what had tripped me and saw right off that it was a human leg. Only the trousers had started to rot and I could see clear to the hide, which was all shriveled up, like it was starting to turn into a mummy, and I stepped around it and pushed some brush aside and there was the head. Something had been at the face and most of the skin and meat were gone and the bones were sticking up white. So that was it. Whether they put us in the ground, or if we fell unnoticed, we'd rot. Rotting flesh and gleaming bones. In the end, that's all we came down to.

The soul now, that's something I wasn't sure about at all. Course, I knew we were more than skin and bones and a heart and lungs and such. But that spirit stuff I wasn't sure about. Some folks, like from China or India, believed our spirits come back to earth in another form after we die. So we might come back as a dog or a horse or a gopher. None of that made sense to me. To come back knowing what you know as a man, but in the body of a coyote or a hawk, or even a piss ant. Come on, how could that be? But if not that, then what? It was all way too much for this hobo.

Mr. Ayers had been good to me, and whenever I thought about him being dead and lying in that casket it made my throat go all lumpy. Then to think about his skin swelling and cracking and going purple and green and black made my guts churn. So I stared up at the rain dripping off the tent that covered the grave and tried not to think about the boss, or that skeleton in Texas, or even the streets of gold.

Minutes seemed to move like cooling molasses. I didn't have a watch, so I didn't have any idea of how much time was passing, but it seemed like hours. Once, I glanced back up the hill and thought I could see Moses in the shelter of the trees. But that might have been my imagination.

I was powerful glad when the people began to sing. They sang "The Old Rugged Cross" and that one I knew some of the words to. So I sang along when I could and hummed the passages I'd forgotten. Then everybody took turns walking by the casket one last time and shaking hands with Quinlin and giving Mrs. Ayers a hug and, before I was ready, it was my turn. I made my face hard and stepped up and shook Quinlin's hand again and he nodded like we were old friends. Then, I stepped over to Mrs. Ayers and nodded at her and mumbled "Sorry for your loss," or something useless like that.

Hadn't planned to shake her hand and sure wasn't going to hug her, but she leaned in close and put out a gloved hand. Gloves made it seem not so bad, touching her that is, so I told myself I was only shaking a black glove with a hand in it and stuck out my right hand.

She took it all right, but instead of shaking it she pressed it between both hers and held on.

"Thank you for coming, Judas. I know it would have meant a lot to Arthur."

She spoke real soft and you could hear in her voice where she'd been crying and her throat was a little raw.

"Mr. Ayers was good to me," I said. "Figured I owed him."

"He thought a lot of you, too, Judas. He really enjoyed your fishing trips."

"They were fun. Didn't always catch a lot of fish, but we had some good talks."

"Oh, what did you talk about?"

I shrugged. "Lots of stuff," I said and eased my hand free.

"Talk about me?"

"Some."

"Haven't we talked about this before? I get so confused these days."

"You've been through a lot."

She bent her head and let go of my hand. All I could see was the top of her black hat. "Haven't I, though?" She made a catchy sound in her throat and then she squared her shoulders and lifted her face. A puff of wind caught the veil and tugged it open and I could see her eyes. They looked hot and damp and empty.

"I'll still need yardwork done. More than ever, I expect. I'm going to my brother's for a few days. Can you check on the yard while I'm gone?"

"Glad to, Mrs. Ayers."

"I'll be back in a week or so."

"Safe travels," I said and turned and stepped out into the rain.

Thirty-seven

Shadows moved like wild, alive things. The wind was up and the moon kept disappearing and reappearing as the clouds passed. They were headed for the coast and part of me wished I was going with them.

I was standing on the corner of Russell and Minter, leaning against an elm tree that had been old long before I was born. I was waiting for someone. I'd been waiting a long time.

Even for Saturday, the night was growing old. Noise from the bars downtown had died off to nothing more than an occasional "Good-night" or the toot of a car horn. All the restaurants had closed and the last show had let out down to the Alhambra. Lights were going out one by one, the way the stars came out at night, only in reverse. It had to be going on for two in the morning. My legs were tired from standing and my eyes ached with the need for sleep, but I'd made up my mind. I'd given up the last two nights. Tonight, I was going to wait. Even if I had to wait till dawn.

Guess I dozed off standing up. Remember letting my eyes shut for a minute, simply to give them a little rest. Next thing I heard was the clicking of high heels coming down the sidewalk.

She was tired, too. I could tell by the sound of her footsteps. I came awake instantly, but made my body stand real still. Not sure why. Maybe I wanted to surprise her, or at least not spook her too soon. They were almost the same thing.

The moon was shrouded and all the houses along the street were dark. The only light was the glow of her cigarette and a dim smear of light from the few streetlights along Main. Even in the near darkness, I was pretty sure it was her, but I held myself in check until I could be certain.

As she crossed Russell, the clouds parted and I got a glimpse of her face. It was open and unguarded and I knew right away. She never saw me. I was one with the shadows. I let her pass before I spoke.

"You sure can keep a fellow waiting," I said, acting like it was broad daylight and we were carrying on a conversation.

Her shoulders jerked and she made a small sound before she turned. "Judas, is that you?"

"In the flesh."

"Well what in the world are you doing standing all still in the shadows? Hell, you scared me out of six months of life sneaking up on me. What is wrong with you, acting like that?"

"Been missing you, Jessie. Haven't seen you in almost a week."

"Sorry, baby, but I have to work. A girl's got to eat, you know. And Brad Menifee don't give money away for nothing."

I reached out a hand and curled my fingers around her arm. Not holding her really, more touching than any sort of a grip. "I've got a few dollars saved back. You could have come to me."

She patted my hand with one of hers, then gently pulled her arm away. "Judas, you're one sweet man, but you're also a poor one. And I'm a woman with expensive tastes. I like you a lot, honey, but you can't afford me."

"That's where you're wrong. Soon as the boss's estate is settled I'm going to come into some money."

"You? How do you figure that?"

His attorney told me. Read it right out of the will. Most of it goes to the widow, of course, but I'm going to get a little something. For good and faithful service, something like that."

"Oh yeah, how much? Ten dollars?"

"Nope. Two hundred."

"You are going to get two hundred dollars?"

"That's right. Soon as the estate is settled."

She took a drag off her cigarette. The smell of smoke mingled with the other night aromas. "When will that be?"

"Couple of months, I suppose. Lawyer never really specified."

Jessie took a step closer. I could smell her perfume and cigarette and sweat. Against the darkness, her teeth were white. "Well, two hundred won't make you no rich man, but it sure beats a stick in the eye."

"We could leave town on it," I said. "Ride in style for a change. What do you say, Jessie? When I get the money let's go away and not tell a soul where we're going. On that kind of money we could go to Florida, or Chicago, California even."

I felt the palm of one of her hands against my cheek. It was warm and soft. "You're sweet, baby, but two hundred won't last long."

"It will if we don't blow it. Just get out of town and live close to the bone till I can find work. We can make it work, Jessie. I know we can."

For a moment she was quiet. Fireflies flickered across the night like tiny candles. Something made a rustling sound in the grass. I could feel my heart pounding and my hands were trembling. I put them in my pocket.

Jessie reached up and kissed me lightly on the cheek. Her lips felt like warm butterfly wings.

"I'll think about it. Now, come on," she said and slipped one of her arms through one of mine. "Walk me home, Judas. It's late and I'm tired and I keep getting a queasy feeling like something bad is going to happen. Walk me home, baby, and we can talk. But that's all, at least tonight. Only talk. I've been working and I'm hot, sweaty, and nasty."

I didn't say anything. Sometimes, a man has to play the hand he's dealt.

Jessie took a final drag off her cigarette and flicked it away. A tiny orange flame cartwheeled across the night. Then she took in a deep breath, let it out, and started walking. I walked with her. We went down the sidewalk arm in arm, like an old married couple. But I knew that was only wishful thinking.

Thirty-eight

She murmured in her sleep and I came sharp awake. The window was open and the curtains fluttered like they were alive. Beyond the window, the first pale light of day was covering the earth. The wind carried aromas and sounds: coffee brewing, bread baking, fresh cut grass, birds chirping, a man singing "The Star Spangled Banner" off key, the throb of a delivery truck motor. I turned back from the window and looked at Jessie.

She was asleep, her lips slightly parted. Strands of hair had fallen down across her forehead and her skin looked like dark silk in the pale, filtered light. Her face was unlined and her sleep untroubled, like a child's. Out in the street, a car horn blared and she moaned and turned away from me. I slid my arm out from under her shoulders and slipped out of bed.

As naked as the day I screamed my way into this world, I stood beside the window, feeling the cool morning breeze and catching glimpses of the world outside every time the curtains fluttered. I was feeling good, the way a man will feel when he's spent a sweet night with a beautiful woman. Going by the way I felt, I'd have sworn a dozen years of my life had fallen away overnight. If not invincible, I surely felt like I could whip the first three men I met on the street. In short, I was feeling dangerously good. Somewhere in the back of my mind, doubt started gnawing. Feeling that good couldn't last.

I heard the bed springs squeak. "Now there's what my mother would have called an eye opener. A naked man standing by the window in the cool sweetness of the morning. Oh, Judas, you are a lovely sight."

I turned and looked at her, blushing, quite aware of my nakedness. Usually that didn't bother me much with Jessie. Even though I had no evidence to back it up, I felt deep down that she was the one I'd been waiting for. Maybe that was crazy thinking, but I couldn't help it. A man can always help the way he acts. He can never help the way he thinks.

"You're a mighty sweet sight yourself."

She shook her head. "No, Judas, you're the sweet one." Her mouth rearranged itself into a funny little grin. "You don't know me. No you don't. Not really. When the chips are down I'm the most selfish person on the face of the earth, especially if there's money involved."

"Quit talking crazy," I said.

She let her head fall back onto the pillow. Her eyes stared up at me, dark pools that had no bottom. "You know, that's the funniest thing."

"What's the funniest thing?"

"That truth, the real truth, always sounds crazy when you first hear it. It's only when you look back that you can see the pureness."

"You sound like a professor, Jessie, or maybe a poet?"

She laughed and then she closed her eyes and snuggled down in the bed. "I'm no poet and for damn sure I'm not a professor. What I am is a lady, or, more precisely, a lady of the night. And right now, I'm a lady looking for a little love. Come away from that window, Judas Cain, and snuggle up with me."

She made a come-here motion with her fingers and I took one last glance at the morning and crossed the floor.

Her body was warm and soft and her nipples were hard and her lips were hungry. I kissed her bare shoulders and her neck and the curl of her throat. Then I closed my eyes and we seemed to meld together like something new being created sweet and natural.

~ * ~

"Come on, Jessie. This is the way it should be all the time. And it can be. All we got to do is get out of this town and start fresh. I've got a good strong back and I know I can find work on the docks in New Orleans or Mobile. What with the war on, they're always looking for good workers."

Her fingers traced patterns only she could see among the hair on my chest. She pressed against me and nibbled on my right nipple. "You're a sweet man, Judas, and a real fine lover, but I can't go. Not right now, anyway. I still owe Brad Menifee money. Besides, he likes me. Likes me a lot. More than once he's told me that he'll never let me go. Not with the money I bring in and the way he likes me. I wouldn't want you getting hurt."

"Hell, we can be gone before he ever knows. Like I told you, I've got enough money for train tickets anywhere you want to go. If you want to go west, why we can head to Chicago or Kansas City. Even go clear to California, if that's what you want. Lots of defense plants out there. We can probably both get work."

She sighed and rolled over. She went real still and I wondered what she was thinking. Before I could make up my mind to ask her, she sat up. Her back was shiny with sweat. I wanted to lick every single drop of that sweat off her. There were words I longed to say, but now didn't seem the time. I could tell she liked me, but I couldn't understand why she wanted to hang around this town and Menifee. Sure, he had more money than I'd ever make, but there was more to life than money. Ask Marilee Ayers. She had almost all of the boss's money now and where was she? Well, that was an easy one to answer. She was alone. And right then I felt all alone, too. Even with Jessie sitting on the side of the bed, I felt like I was the only man in the whole world.

She sighed again. "Not right now, baby. Maybe in a few weeks." She turned and gave me that smile that made my heart ache like a quirky tooth. "Give me a little time, sweet baby. Just a little time and a little understanding."

Reckon I should have said kind words right then, but my throat was all lumped up and the best I could do was to smile and nod. She stood up and I watched her fine, long legs carry her across the room.

"I've got to wash up and go out for a bit. Errands to run. May be a while before I get back."

I sat up in the bed and pulled the sheet up to my chest. "Want me to wait here?"

She shook her. "No, baby, you go on home. I'll come see you or send word by old Moses. Got a few things to take care of right now. You understand, don't you?"

I nodded. "Sure," I said, but that was a lie. Only things I was sure about was that my heart was aching something fierce and she was doing some kind of a shuffle on me. Lots of folks will tell you love is blind, but don't believe that. Love actually sees everything real clear, only the person believes just what he or she wants to. I was seeing things clear enough in the pale morning light that I couldn't even fool myself.

I lay there and watched her dip a washcloth in the basin on the dresser and wash her face and hands. Then I watched her get dressed. She was humming softly to herself. Her movements were smooth and unhurried. When she was dressed, she came over and brushed her lips across my mouth. That kiss made me want her all over again, but she was already walking for the door. Loneliness and longing merged inside me and ran through my veins like quicksilver. Seemed there was no one or no place for me. Nothing permanent. Nothing real. I felt a whole lot like crying, but I was a grown man, so I rolled out of the bed and strolled on over to the window, eased the curtains back and watched Jessie cross the street and head north, walking tall and proud and swinging her hips like they were hinged on ball bearings.

At the corner she looked both ways, then curled down Pink's Alley. I hustled over to the far side of the window so I could keep her in view a few more seconds. What I saw though was a cream colored Chrysler roll up from out of the shadows. The car looked familiar and something about the driver's face caught my eye. But sunlight was hitting the windshield and the glare was intense. Jessie opened the door and slid inside. The car started rolling. It turned left out of the alley. Jessie's face was a blur as it passed.

Thirty-nine

Another summer was dying. There was something in the air that made it feel different against your skin. Tree leaves were still green and the grass kept growing, but the difference was there. You couldn't touch it exactly, but it made you aware that you needed to be getting ready for winter. Cold, hard times were coming and piss ants and men had to prepare.

Earlier in the week, Mrs. Ayers had been talking about how chilly the house had been the winter before and I'd wandered around and taken a look at the windows. Most of them needed caulking. All morning, I'd been scraping away old brittle caulk and checking the panes to see if they were loose. Three needed to be replaced. But that required a trip downtown and I wasn't in the mood. Besides, I'd have had to ask Mrs. Ayers for the money and she had been moping around all day lost in sad thoughts, and disturbing her really didn't seem a nice thing to do. These days, I was trying to be nice. At least to her. Losing a son and a husband in the same year had to be an awful burden, and the passage of a few months didn't make it much easier.

I was around the back of the house looking at the windows and saw her pass in the hall. Before long she came back, then turned and strolled by again. I wondered if she was pacing because she was restless, or worried, or scared.

I was looking at the next to last window in what had been Mr. Ayers' library when she turned in at the door and crossed the room and sat down in a red leather club chair. The leather on one arm was cracked and the seat was stained where somebody had spilt something, but it looked comfortable. She let her head go back and closed her eyes.

Looking at her through the window made me feel like a peeping Tom. But I kept on looking, checking out the windows some, but studying her face, too. Her hair was brushed out today and hung down her on her shoulders in brown waves. The light in the library was kind and she looked younger than I knew she was. Since the funeral, she'd lost weight, but she was still a big woman.

Out in the yard there was a walnut tree that was starting to die and right then a redheaded woodpecker went to hammering on the trunk. Her eyes came open and before I could move they were looking into mine. My first thought was that she'd be angry, but instead of frowning, she smiled. It was a shy sort of smile, but a nice one, too. I smiled and waved back and moved on around the house.

I came out on the carport side and movement in the street caught my eye. I turned and looked. At first I didn't see anything but the street streaked with shadows. Then a Negro girl stepped out from behind the trunk of a cedar tree that grew just this side of the ditchline and made a come-here motion with one arm. Far as I knew I'd never seen the girl, but right off I thought of Moses' niece. I glanced around to make sure she wasn't motioning to someone else. Then I looked to make sure Mrs. Ayers wasn't watching. Strolling easy, like I was out to get the afternoon paper, I walked down the drive.

At the end of the drive was the girl, one foot in the street, shading her eyes with the flat of a hand. Ten feet away, I stopped and nodded.

"You Judas, ain't you?"

"That's my name. Who are you?'

"My name's not important. I'm only here to deliver a message."

"You're Moses' niece, aren't you?"

She cocked her head and peered at me like she was spooked.

"What if I am?"

I shrugged. "Nothing. Didn't mean anything by it. Simply had a feeling."

She took a step back and stared hard at me. She was short, even for a woman, and downhill from me, so it must have been like looking up at a giant. In a way, that made me feel funny.

"You want the message or not?"

"Give it to me."

"Jessie said to come see her this evening."

"How come she sent you to tell me?"

It was the girl's turn to shrug. "Guess she didn't have no other way to get you the message."

There were situations where that made sense. Maybe she had a headache, or Menifee was watching her. Could have been any number of reason. Yet, it didn't quite seem right to me. Still, I didn't aim to miss the chance.

"Okay," I said. "Where does she want me to meet her?"

"You know that old church down to the crossroads? One where the chimney has done fallen down."

"Out on the McCone Road?"

"That's the one, about twenty yards beyond Draper's Grocery."

"I know it."

"Well she said come just afore dark. Said she'd be waiting for you around back."

"What about Menifee?"

"Oh, yeah. I remember now. I was to tell you he's gone out of town on business. Won't be back till tomorrow night at the earliest."

I didn't believe her. I didn't disbelieve her. Probably there was some truth in everything she said, and then, too, she probably never told the whole truth about anything. "Okay," I said. "Tell her I'll see her then."

The girl smiled and nodded and I could see a gold-capped tooth shining up near the roof of her mouth. When she smiled she looked a lot younger. Seeing her smile like that I'd have guessed sixteen, but surely she was eighteen or nineteen.

"Well," she said, "I'd better go then. Got things to do, you know."

"Yeah," I said. "Better be getting back to work myself." I should have asked her more questions. Something about the message bothered me. Bothered me the way a blackberry seed will get between your back teeth and aggravate. But part of my mind was worrying about Mrs. Ayers, her sitting so quietly and all, and anyway most of the story sounded good. Plus, to tell the truth, I wanted to believe it.

The girl nodded again and turned and started down the street. She walked steady, only slow, like she was going somewhere on purpose but her feet hurt. I watched her till she reached the end of the block.

Forty

She was standing at the kitchen counter and turned with a knife in her hand. With her free hand, she brushed a strand of hair out of her face. She worked up a smile.

"I'm making myself a ham sandwich. Would you like one?"

Pickings had been slim around my shack the last few days and my mouth watered at the thought of food. "Wouldn't mind," I said.

"Good. Now go wash up and sit down at the table and I'll bring you one."

"Okay," I said, feeling a touch uneasy. I'd never eaten with Mrs. Ayers at her table before. The boss and I had a eaten a sandwich together a few times, or a cookie, or a piece of pie. And, of course, we'd drunk plenty of beer and a little wine. But we done that in the yard or on fishing trips. Thinking about eating in the kitchen without the boss there made me feel all squiggly inside.

I walked down the hall to the bathroom and washed my hands and face, then wet down my hair and combed it with my fingers. I stared at my face in the mirror. It looked right ordinary to me. I wondered what Jessie saw in it. Then I wondered what she didn't see. That sort of thinking wasn't getting me anywhere, so I dried my hands and headed for the kitchen.

Mrs. Ayers was seated in her usual chair at the end of the table closest to the stove. I hadn't thought about where I was going to sit. There were four chairs and the one at the opposite end of the table was where the boss had sat. I'd sure didn't want to sit there. Merely thinking about it made me feel nervous.

On the other hand, the other two chairs were closer to Mrs. Ayers. That wasn't any good either. My thought was to tell her I'd eat my sandwich outside while I worked. She nixed that right away by pointing to a plate at the boss's old spot. There was a sandwich on it and a scoop of potato salad. There was glass of tea beside the plate and a cloth napkin. I'd already lost my appetite.

"I'm not really so hungry"

"Oh, go ahead and sit down, Judas. A working man needs to eat to keep up his strength."

I started to say something about not liking to sit in the boss's chair, but then I thought that maybe that would only make her think about him again. I surely didn't want to spoil her better mood. I eased on around the table and sat down.

Sure felt funny sitting there at the head of the table, right where the boss had sat. Although I knew he was in his grave, it seemed like he was watching me from somewhere in the room. I glanced over my shoulder at the corner. It was all way too spooky for me. I swallowed hard and looked down the table. Mrs. Ayers was smiling at me.

"Would you like to say grace, Judas?"

Praying wasn't something I'd ever gotten good at. Other than the prayer I said at night right before I went to sleep, I didn't do much of it. As far as public praying went, I was pure rusty. "Why don't you go ahead," I said.

She looked at me funny for a second. Then she nodded and smiled. "All right. Shall we bow our heads?"

I closed my eyes and lowered my chin. Not having to look at her made things easier. "Dear Lord," she said, "bless this food we are about to eat that it might be used to the nourishment of our bodies. Be with our friends and family, and help us to be better Christians in days to come. Amen."

"Amen," I said and opened my eyes. She was looking at me again. I stared down at my plate.

"Go on and eat, Judas. That sandwich will get stale lying there."

I nodded and picked up my ham sandwich. The bread tasted like sawdust and the meat had a slimy texture. I kept my eyes on my plate and chewed with vigor.

"Afraid I'm not much of a cook these days. After Arthur, well, you know."

My mouth was full of bread and ham, so I only nodded.

"Do you have family somewhere?"

"Not that I know of, Mrs. Ayers. Least not for sure. My folks passed a long time ago and I've lost track of the rest of my kin. We never were much for the family thing."

Mrs. Ayers put her hands in her lap. "We were always a close family. Real close. Only now you and I are just about paddling the same canoe, aren't we?"

I thought about what she had said until I figured out what she was driving at. "Reckon in some ways we are."

"On the radio, they say the war will be over soon."

I washed my mouth out with tea. "That's good news."

"Yes, only I wish President Roosevelt had lived to see the end of this awful conflict."

I nodded. "Hated to hear about him passing. Been president a long time, hadn't he?'

"Elected to four terms, but didn't live to serve out his final one."

"Truman seems like a stand up guy."

"Harry Truman is not Franklin D. Roosevelt."

"No, but he seems like a pretty down-to-earth fellow."

"He's a bit earthy for my tastes. Gambles and drinks. Hardly fitting for the office."

"Oh," I said, "don't reckon a drink and a hand or two of cards ever hurt anybody."

"Poker is not Rook."

"No," I said, "don't suppose it is." I couldn't see where it hurt if President Truman played a few hands of poker with his cronies, but it was clear Mrs. Ayers was down on gambling. That made me wonder if the boss might have lost money playing poker on those Friday night get-togethers with the boys he'd told me about.

She went quiet then and sipped at her tea. I concentrated on eating, hurrying now, anxious to get away from the woman. She bothered me in ways I couldn't explain, even to myself.

Her head went up and she looked out the window. She stared like she was seeing something real interesting. Everything looked ordinary to me.

"There were a lot of flowers at the funeral."

"Sure were."

"Such pretty arrangements."

"Shows people cared, spending money like that."

"Arthur was well liked."

"He was a good man."

"And what good did that do him?"

"Huh?"

"He's dead, isn't he?"

"Yes."

"So, being well-liked didn't amount to anything, now did it? Didn't stop him from dying. Didn't stop our son from being killed by a damn Japanese on some God-forsaken island in the middle of the Pacific." She turned away from the window and her eyes settled on my face.

She didn't say anymore. Maybe she had run out of words, or maybe she was waiting on me to answer. If she was, she was fresh out of luck. She was only asking questions I'd already asked. Best I could tell, there weren't any answers. Not to questions like hers.

Somewhere in the crepe myrtle, a bird took up singing. I sat and listened and tried not to think about anybody dying, or the woman with the sad eyes. After a while, I got to thinking about when my folks died and when some guys died lonely along the tracks where nobody knew their name.

Rich guys died in their beds or hospitals. Poor folks simply died where their affliction took them. Finally, I got to wondering how I was going to die. For a second it was like I could almost see it coming. Foretell my own death, you might say. Thought I saw visions of a knife shining in moonlight and then I saw blood. I thought of the conjure woman Moses had mentioned. Then I went hot and then cold before sweat broke out on my face liked I'd been caught in a rain shower.

"Are you all right, Mr. Cain?"

Her voice jerked me back in the room and I nodded and slugged down the last of the tea. "Yeah, I'm fine." I pushed my chair back. Her eyes were on me again, only with a different look this time, like she could see right through my clothes and skin, right straight into my mind. That threw a chill on my bones.

I quit looking at her and stood up. "Thanks for the sandwich, Mrs. Ayers. 'Spect I'd better be getting to work."

She didn't say anything. Only kept looking. After a moment, she nodded. I nodded back, turned and stared for the door. Her voice called me back into the room.

"It gets lonely at times, Judas. I'm sure you can imagine." Her eyes were still on me, but they looked brimming with tears. Daylight slid in through the window and landed softly her face. Hitting her that way, it made her look younger and more vulnerable. Even somewhat pretty, in a faded sort of way.

I looked away real quick. That wasn't the way I should be thinking. Not the way I wanted to think. Being good was harder than anybody ever let on. Sometimes a man's thoughts were like wild horses.

"Yes, indeed," I said. "Lonely is something I sure enough know." I nodded again and hurried out the door before she could speak again.

Forty-one

Moonlight streaked the McCone Road. In the pale light, it looked like a page right out of a picture book. I was coming up from the south. I'd crossed over the tracks at the edge of town, down the gully behind the ball field, then worked my way across the open ground before picking up the McCone Road below the old stone bridge. It wasn't the quickest way, but no one could have followed me across those open fields in the moonlight without me seeing them.

Draper's Grocery sat by the side of the road maybe forty yards ahead, right past where the road bent to the north. In the moonlight, it looked like a ship leaning to port. Locust trees lined one side of the road and I stopped under them and peered into the darkness. Why Jessie wanted me to meet her out here was more than I could figure. But Jessie was that kind of woman. Once, we'd made love once in a parked car. What was strange about that was that neither of us had the faintest idea who the owner of the car was. That was Jessie. She had a wild streak in her that made me nervous and excited at the same time.

All I could see was the old store and shadows slow dancing in a light breeze. All seemed quiet. Too quiet. A spookiness ran through the silence that was broken only by the rustling of the locust leaves. Usually at night you could hear a cow low out in a field or a dog bark outside some lonesome farmhouse. Tonight, though, was as quiet as an empty funeral parlor. I stepped out from under the trees and started down the road.

~ * ~

It was a small sound. Nothing more than a board creaking. So small it almost didn't register. Draper's Grocery store was on the far side of the road and the night was as dark as the bottom of any well and there hadn't been any sign of anyone or anything. A dog could have wandered up on the sway-backed porch, but…I started easing off the road.

The county had cleaned out the ditchline within memory and I crouched down and duck-walked down it toward the store, moving slowly, placing my feet as carefully as I could. It was my good luck that the porch jutted at an angle away from the ditch.

Fifteen yards from the store the ditch petered out and, after a long look, I came out, going slow and low, searching for cover.

Old crates and pallets were strewn around the yard, but they were too low. Fortunately, there was an old farm wagon standing in the middle of the side yard. One of the wheels was off and the axle was propped on the stump of what had once been a huge tree. I slipped into the wagon's shadow.

The night had gone all quiet again. I could hear the faint sound of my own breathing and the whisper of the wind high up in cedar that grew at the edge of the cleared ground. Then I heard the creak again. I held my breath and heard a whisper. It was only a word. Merely a name. But it was enough.

"Tom, Tom?"

"What?"

"You see that?'

"See what?"

"Something moved over there by that old wagon."

"You sure?'

"Shut up, you two. Just keep your mouths shut. He'll be along any minute. The girl said he fell for it all the way."

Maybe he whispered a few more words, but I was already moving. I curled around the end of the wagon farthest from the porch and eased around the back of the grocery. It was dark there, which was good and bad. Good because nobody could see me; bad because I couldn't see what was under my feet and the place was littered with broken bottles and empty tins and scraps of paper and beat-in cardboard boxes. A shaft of moonlight sliced through a gap in the trees and I could see the mess before me. A likely looking stick lay in the dirt and I picked it up.

It was all clear now, clear as polished glass. My gut had been right. The story Moses' niece had told had been a lie from start to finish. I wondered what the three men had in mind. Another beating? Or something worse? My brain was churning trying to figure out all the angles. I could sort of see a picture of the way things were coming down, but it wasn't clear. More like looking at a car off in the distance through a shimmering mist. Sure, you could tell it was a car, but you couldn't make out whether it was a Ford or a Chevy or even a Lincoln.

In the end, I figured they weren't planning on taking any half-measures tonight. If the deal had been for another beating, Menifee would have been there in person to dish some of it out. Murder, though, was another story altogether. He'd want no part of that and would be miles away, maybe even out of state, equipping himself with an iron clad alibi. I could feel my stomach churning.

I thought about Jessie and what a damn shame it was that we never got a chance to really be together the way we wanted to. Well, at least the way I wanted to. I wondered if she'd miss me. Then Mrs. Ayers' round white face flickered across my mind like a moon gone wandering. Then it was gone and I was moving again. A cold sweat had broken out all over my body.

My plan was to ease around the store and curl back through the second growth timber that lined the old limestone quarry. I'd have to keep an eye out, but with the moonlight breaking through the clouds I figured to be okay. What I hadn't figured on was the man coming around the far side of the building.

Guess it was a tossup as to which of us was more surprised. His eyes went wide, and quicker than I could move he reached for something jammed between his belt and his gut. I caught the glint of moonlight on metal as he was drawing it free. I was already swinging the stick like a baseball bat.

It thumped his head like it was smacking a ripe melon and he groaned real soft like and slumped to the ground. The knife spun free and I picked it up and started running, remembering the conjure woman's warning. Ten yards from the timber, I heard a man shout. A shot rang out, then another. Something smashed into my left arm and I spun like a top and went stumbling into the dark under the trees.

My arm was burning like fire and blood was running hot down my skin. My brain was woozy and I was seeing spots. More than most anything, I wanted to lie down and let the world stop spinning. But I knew that would be the pure end of me. I pushed on through the thick underbrush, brambles catching my clothes, ripping at my skin. Behind me, men were shouting and I could hear footsteps.

I didn't turn around to look; just kept running as fast as I could. Roots tripped me once and I fell heavy, but the ground was forgiving and I rolled smooth and came up with the knife still in my hand. In that second, I caught a flash of the vision I'd had at the lunch table.

I looked ahead for a second, then caught a glimpse of large, pale stone and hurried on. My right foot slipped and I stumbled into a big sycamore, bounced off and kept moving. Between one step and the next I felt the ground fall away beneath me and then I was flailing through the dark air.

Forty-two

My eyes flickered open and I was looking straight up at the moon. My left arm throbbed and my head felt like it had been cracked open by a ball-peen hammer. I was lying flat on my back and the sharp edge of a rock was gouging me in the ribs. I decided to sit up.

Although that was a fine idea, my body didn't want to cooperate. So I made another decision. This time I decided to lie still and listen.

First thing I heard was my own breathing. It sounded like I was having trouble catching my breath. About the time I got that under control, I could hear the wind worrying the top leaves of the trees that grew on all sides. I studied the ground and finally figured out I was in the old quarry.

Not much moonlight made it down to the bottom of the quarry, but from what I could see the timber was second growth stuff that didn't amount to much. Probably whatever had grown up volunteer after the quarry shut down. It wasn't worth cutting, but it did make for reasonably good cover.

Best I could tell, I'd fallen into the shallow end of the quarry. I made up my mind to try and sit up and get a better handle on my situation. On the third try, I made it. When my head quit spinning I had a look around.

It was about like I'd figured. Looked like I'd ended up in the last section they worked before the rock ran out, or the money did. Seemed I'd more tumbled down the bank than fallen all the way straight to the bottom and that had probably kept me from being hurt a lot worse.

Blood was still oozing down my left arm from where one of the men had winged me before my fall. I worked my handkerchief out of my hip pocket and tied it around the wound in a sort of a tourniquet.

Where the bullet had burned my hide it stung like fire, but, best I could tell, it was more a flesh wound than anything serious. Long as I didn't bleed too much or get the wound infected it shouldn't be too bad. Thing to do was to get out of the quarry without running into those three thugs up above. I got my right hand on a nearby sapling and started pulling myself up to standing.

What light made it to the bottom of the quarry was thin as watered milk. Trees rose out of the darkness without warning and bushes, brambles and snaky vines clawed at my legs. Rocks slid under my feet and I stumbled forward like a drunkard, holding my bleeding arm one minute, grasping for a hold on a tree trunk the next.

Time didn't have a lot of meaning. Funny about time; given the fact that I might be a goner before the hour played out, I figured I'd have been counting every second silently in my head and praying under my breath for another one. But that wasn't the way it was. No, it was more like I was in a fog where nothing looked normal and nothing much mattered.

When a man gets in a bad way he thinks of one of two things—heading for home, or finding his woman—and I thought of both. At first, I planned to work my way out of the quarry and curl around the edge of the swale and head for home. Five minutes later, I got to figuring that at least one of the desperados might think of that very thing and be waiting in ambush. Naturally, my next thought was of Jessie.

She came into my mind full blown, like a vision from God, and she looked so real and close that I could almost touch her face. I spoke her name aloud, but only the wind answered. I said her name again and lurched forward.

The going was harder now. I'd lost whatever path I'd been following and now was clawing and rooting my way along like some wild animal. Grunting sounds rose up in the night and I paused to listen. All I could hear was the whisper of the wind interspersed with the call of a night bird. When I started climbing again the sounds returned. Worried more than ever, I pushed on. Then it came clear in my mind that the sounds were my own. Not only was I crawling over the rocks like a wild beast, I was grunting like one, too.

Time floated like a cloud and my mind began drifting, thinking first of hobo days and then back to when I was kid. Even thought about the last time I'd seen my mom and dad. Maybe it was the loss of blood, or maybe I had the shell shock some men coming back out of the service had. Anyway, I quit caring about much of anything except moving. Vaguely, I noticed that the incline had eased, then I could see the tops of trees and off in the distance reflected lights. I slipped around a boulder as big as a steer and there was the rim of the quarry. I climbed up on a shelf of jagged rock and stepped up and out into a halo of moonlight.

~ * ~

Guess I was like a bird or animal with a homing instinct. Without realizing exactly what I was doing, I began to curl off to the south, staying in the shadows where I could, moving as quickly and quietly as my wobbly legs and the knee high grasses would let me.

The wind was starting to come up and there was good and bad in that. Good was that it covered some of the sound of my stumbling. Bad was that when it was blowing I couldn't hear the men who wanted to kill me. Once it fell away all of a sudden into a hush, reminding me of the silence you encounter when you enter an empty church. There was something mysterious in it, and something holy. I stopped and listened. I heard the murmur of voices, but then I decided it was only the surge and ebbing of the pulse pounding in my temple. Weakness washed over me like the wake from a big boat passing and I stumbled on. Blood was seeping down my arm, but there was nothing I could do about that.

That journey was more like a dream than anything real. Half a dozen times I felt the night slipping away from me, the sky going black, swirling away like water going down a sinkhole. Then it would come back and I'd feel as cool-headed and calm as if I'd woken from a restful sleep.

My legs moved all right for the most part, although I stumbled a few times. Once, I tripped over a root or rock and fell face first into a patch of clover. Dew was starting to fall and the temptation to lie there on that cool damp softness was strong. But that was only another way to spell death, so I rolled over, got my back up against the trunk of a big tree and carefully worked my way to standing.

Somewhere in the night I started talking to myself. Nonsense undoubtedly. I could hear my voice and some of the words made sense, but not all of them, then I had another sinking spell and then I was singing. Singing some silly song I vaguely remembered from childhood, then suddenly I was singing one of those old church hymns the Baptists used to sing. Then I could hear myself crying, only it was like I was far away and I was growing cold. After a spell, I could hear the faint murmuring of the river and smell the thick scent of cedars growing tight together. Their branches scratched at my face while birds fluttered up in the night. Then I was stumbling out from under the thicket and the shanty I'd been journeying to loomed before me in the night like an abandoned castle in some dusty school book.

Forty-three

Voices murmured out in the sweet darkness and I felt drawn to them and let myself go, flying silently like some giant bird.

A gravelly voice said, "He's coming round."

Then a softer voice said, "Bring me some fresh water. I want to wash his face."

The voices seemed familiar, but my brain was sluggish, full of used motor oil and cracked in important places. I forced my eyes open.

Daylight had come and the little shack was filled with sunlight. For a moment, I simply lay there on some sort of cot, blinking and coming awake. Then I started to roll over.

"Damn, that hurts." I gently pressed my right hand over the bandages on my left arm. How a man could forget about getting shot was beyond me.

"Good to have you back with us, brother." Old Moses bent his head low and smiled in my face. If he had more than five teeth in his head they were off hiding somewhere.

A soft hand brushed fallen hair off my forehead. "Yes, you had us worried there for a bit, Mr. Cain."

Of all the people I'd expected to see, Marilee Ayers wasn't even on the list. Trying not to move my hurt arm, I eased my head around until I could get a good look at her. She was soaking a rag in a basin of water. As I watched, she pulled the rag up and twisted water out of it. "Hold still, Mr. Cain, I need to scrub on your face. It's a bit dirty."

"Yass," Moses said, "looks like you been lying with swine, friend."

"Swine about covers it," I said. My tongue felt thick and rough and the words came out slurry. "How about a sip of water?"

Moses rooted around, found a cracked coffee cup that looked reasonably clean and filled it with water out of his bucket. The water was still some cool from the river. After one sip, I drank the rest of it straight off.

"That's better. Ouch."

"Sorry, but you've got nicks and abrasions all over your face. What happened?"

"It's a long and sad story. Let's just say I fell among evil companions."

Moses snorted like he'd been stung by a bumble bee. Mrs. Ayers squinched her mouth tighter and scrubbed with more vigor. Probably figured I'd been out drinking and got clipped in some honky-tonk brawl. Well, that was all right. She didn't need to know too much of my business.

Mrs. Ayers probed at one of the cuts with the tip of a finger. For a big woman she had gentle hands. She was wearing perfume, too. Faded lilacs. It was a nice scent. Made me think of summer evenings.

"And one of these, er, companions shot you?" Her breath was warm against my cheek.

"Something like that."

"Why would they do that?"

I shrugged. "People do crazy things all the time."

"Yes," she said, "I suppose that's true."

She went back to working on my cuts. Made me feel funny inside, her standing so close and all, but I was feeling weak and washed out and I didn't have any real strength. Losing all that blood last night had taken the starch out of me.

Anyway, her hands were soft and she smelled nice. Even her breath smelled faintly of peppermint and, more faintly, of coffee. It felt pleasant to have a woman fussing over me, even if she was a little overbroad in the hips and extra full around the middle. That, I didn't really mind. Was a bit puzzled though about how in the world she had ended up at my shack.

I closed my eyes and let her wash my face. As she worked, I got to wondering if since the boss and the kid had both died it made her feel good to be doing something for a man again. She was a private person and had never talked to me much about anything personal, but I'd got the feeling that she was the kind of woman who liked to do for others.

When a car horn blew, I was half asleep and half wanting a cup of coffee. I jerked awake and looked around right sharp. Getting shot tenses up a man's nerves considerable.

Mrs. Ayers dabbed once more at my forehead. "There's the cab. Hurry up the path, Moses, and tell him I'll be along in a minute, will you?"

"Sure thing, Mrs. Ayers. I'm on my way." Moses waved a hand and ambled out the door. I watched him hump it across the yard, moving spry for a man his age.

Mrs. Ayers put one hand on my shoulder. It felt heavy and strange, yet there was comfort in her touch. "There you go, Judas. I've bandaged you up as best I could. Your need to see a doctor about your arm. You were very lucky. The bullet bit a chunk out of the flesh, but I don't think it damaged any nerves or muscles." She patted me on the shoulder and stood up straight. "I cleaned it out pretty well, I think, but a doctor needs to work on it. I'm sure you'll need stitches."

I nodded. We both knew I didn't have the money to see a doctor. Best bet was old Doc Haney, who was mostly retired, but would take a patient if he knew he was their last hope. People paid him mostly in fish or chickens or vegetables, even yard work. Once I got back on my feet I could manage something.

"Thanks for the nursing."

"You're most welcome, Judas." Mrs. Ayers smiled. She had full lips and a pleasant smile. Probably down deep she was a nice person. It was only that outer crust was hard and sharp and sour. "But you know you really need to quit messing around with undesirables. Keep it up and you may well need more nursing than I can give you."

"I'll try."

"You must do more than try, Judas. The Lord will help you if you really want him to." She rambled on like that for a minute or two. Then I guess she saw that I wasn't paying a lot of attention, cause she sighed and shook her head. "Have it your way. You're a stubborn man, Mr. Judas Cain."

"Guess, I am, Mrs. Ayers, but I do appreciate your help. And I'm working on my life. Seems like things keep happening, though."

Her mouth came open and I reckon she aimed to say something. Instead, she shook her head and closed her mouth. Then she touched the tips of her fingers to one side of my face, turned, and walked straight-backed out the door. Probably I should have said something more. Part of me wanted to. But I just sat there and watched her walk down the path until she rounded the bend. After a couple of minutes, Moses came strolling along. He walked on inside and gave me a hard look.

"Judas, you sure living on the edge. The Lord Himself must have been watching out for you, sending me over to your place last night. Something inside me told me to come. Yes, brother, you surely are living on the edge of destruction."

"Didn't aim to. Three men jumped me last night on my way to see Jessie. Figure they were Menifee's men."

"Probably so, but what you mean about going to see Jessie? Surely they didn't jump you in town."

"No, she sent word that she was out the McCone Road, on past Draper's. We were supposed to meet around back of that old church at the crossroads, the one with the chimney fallen down."

Moses shook his head. "Man, you dumber than I allowed. Jessie ain't never going to meet nobody back of no church, certainly not one way out in the country. She ain't religious like that."

"That was the message I got."

"Who gave you such a message?'

I started into his eyes. They looked watery and sort of cloudy. I wondered how well the old fellow could see. "Your niece brought me the message."

"Which niece?"

"One you told me about."

Guess he read the rest in my face. "Oh," he said, "that sure ain't good. Two bits says Menifee is mixed up in all this. That niece of mine is a sweet girl, but plumb crazy about that man. Does whatever he tell her." He looked off, out the door, seeing something in the distance I could only guess at. "She's a burden to me, Judas. A burden and a shame."

I didn't say anything. In my day, I'd been both. For a spell we didn't say anything. Simply sat there seeing what we were seeing, thinking our own thoughts. After a bit my arm started hurting, so I got up and walked outside and sat on a stump in the sunlight, hoping the heat would help. Plus, I had some half-crazy thoughts rolling through my mind and I didn't want Moses reading my face. In a bit I heard him banging pots and pans. Shortly thereafter, he called me in for breakfast.

Forty-four

Intermittent rain pecked against the window glass. Drops struck with a rhythm that sounded like code. Drop, drop-drop, drop, drop-drop-drop. I stood back a little from the window, watching what little traffic there was, trying to decipher what the rain was trying to tell me. Behind me, Jessie stood in front of the mirror, doing what she called making up her face. I turned away from the window.

Jessie eyed me in the mirror. She'd done something with her eyes. She didn't look like Jessie.

"You're crazy," she said, "Brad will never fall for anything like that."

"I tell you it will work, Jessie. At least if you keep your mouth closed."

"Like I'd have anything to do with your foolishness. The less I know, the better it is for me. So please don't tell me anymore."

Out on the street somebody tooted their horn. "You're always doubting me, Jessie. I wouldn't take this chance if I didn't think it would work. I'm only doing it for us, you know. We can't go on the way we have. Getting the hell beat out of you gets real old in a hurry."

She patted her hair with her hands. "You're a silly man, Judas. Even if your plan was to work, I tell you I'm not ready to settle down."

"Oh, you're only mouthing," I said.

"There are none so blind as those who will not see."

"And what is that supposed to mean?"

She threw her head back and laughed. Her throat was very lovely. I wanted to kiss it. "You're one of those men who has to learn the hard way, Judas. My conscience is clear. I've tried to tell you I'm not one of your model little stay-at-home and mind-the-kids women."

"You're only saying that to spare my feelings."

She twisted her face into a grimace. Then she blinked and looked down. Her hair swirled across her face until I couldn't see it at all. "Have it your way," she said.

"I tell you it will be all right. I'll work everything out and then we'll be together. A man like Menifee is always ready to do a deal. Doesn't that sound good?"

Jessie turned then and stared at me. Her face was without expression. I couldn't tell what she was thinking. She was a hard woman to figure out. But then, I think all women are that way.

I didn't know what else to say and she wasn't talking. The room grew so quiet that it felt like we were the only two people in the world.

Finally, she smiled. It was a quiet smile, but a smile nonetheless. "Yes, that would be nice," she said. Then she turned around and went to brushing her hair. There were lots of words I wanted to say, but somehow I didn't think that now was the time to say them. Maybe for some words there was never a good time. My plan sounded good to me, and I wanted it to work. Wanted that more than anything in the world.

The hotel room had gone quiet again. Voices drifted in from down the hall. That was all – only voices. Merely people talking. I wondered what they were saying. The rest of the world might be talking, but in Room 36 Jessie was brushing her hair and I was standing in front of the window watching her. Raindrops peppered harder against the glass, as if there was a new urgency to their secret message.

Forty-five

The scent of pines was sharp. Unseen birds fluttered restlessly above me. Through an opening in the branches, I could see a smear of moon and a single star. The moon was up high enough for me to guess it was near midnight. Since dusk, I'd been lying on pine needles that carpeted a ledge at a bend in a narrow trail that wound through a stand of second-growth timber.

It had taken the better part of two weeks to set things up. Moses and I must have planned it out two dozen times, going over it till it sounded perfect. Now, lying on my stomach peering into the darkness, my nerves were whining and the whole thing seemed as lousy as Confederate money.

The setup was actually pretty simple. Moses had told him I'd be down at the end of the trail all alone, just this side of an old sinkhole, waiting for Jessie. Only Jessie wasn't going to come. Instead, Menifee would show up, believing I was alone and unarmed, and finish the job his hired hands hadn't been able to.

Only I'd have a long heart to heart with him, work something out. If it was money he was after, I'd make sure to cover what Jessie was bringing in. I'd also tell him the sheriff was on to him and he needed to get out of town. Listening to the boss, I'd picked up enough names of the men who ran the county to make the storyline sound real convincing. And I'd practiced my story a dozen times. Had it down smoother than rabbit fur. To make sure he'd listen, I'd helped myself to one of the pistols the boss had collected when I was painting for Mrs. Ayers earlier in the week. My arm wasn't back to one hundred percent, but it was good enough. The plan was sure to work.

At least it had seemed that way this morning. Now my plan seemed hollow, my throat had gone tight and I could feel my heart pounding against the pine needles. Some animal scurried through the underbrush and my body jerked in response. My mouth had gone so dry I'd have given a lot for one good shot of something strong. Moonlight grew dim. Clouds had drifted across what there was of the moon.

Voices came then, indistinct, but loud enough so that I could tell there were at least two. That was all right. Moses was supposed to show him the way.

At first, having Moses there bothered me. I'd worried that if something did go wrong, once Menifee had taken care of me he would take care of Moses. Moses had said that wouldn't be a problem. Menifee considered all Negroes too dumb to come in out of the rain and was convinced that no one would believe an old, wooly-headed uncle. Besides, as Moses pointed out, Menifee would be figuring he could always keep Moses in line by threatening his niece. Like I said, the plan had sounded good over fried fish and cornbread. Now it tasted like ashes.

The night grew quiet and the voices came again, more distinct this time, but I still couldn't make out the words. The light faded a few more degrees and I scooted closer to the edge.

Twigs cracked under their feet as they drew closer. One of them sneezed. I stretched out an arm. After only a few inches, all I could feel was air. A nerve twitched in my cheek. I craned my neck and there they were, two blurry figures stepping round the bend.

Two men was all right, as long as one of them was Moses. The figure on the left favored him considerable, but in the near darkness I'd have to wait until they got closer, or spoke, to be sure. Way off in the distance an owl hooted and then another answered, closer, less than twenty yards away and deep in the timber.

"You sure he's down here?" Menifee said. His voice I knew. Chilled me off some, like ice water.

"Oh, yes sir," Moses said, sounding like they were two old friends chatting after Sunday services. "He sure enough thinks that Jessie's going to meet him down here. Crazy about that woman, old Judas is."

"Must be half crazy himself to think she'd come all the way down here by her lonesome."

"Oh, I don't know about that, boss. That Jessie, she's got a wild streak in her. Leastways that's what I hear. Word is she ain't afraid of hardly nothing."

"Well, she better be afraid of me if she keeps on messing with Cain. That's one man I purely do dislike. Acts likes he's some kind of a good man, only I know for a fact that he ain't nothing more than a lousy hobo. And no woman of mine is going to mess around with a damn bum. If Jessie don't know that, she damn well better be learning it, and pretty damn quick, too."

They'd been walking as they talked and were dead in front of me now. Menifee's face was a pale shaft. They kept moving, curling into the darkness. I took a long look back up the trail and came up empty. Then I eased back off the ledge and went down the slope. I'd walked the route a dozen times and could have done it blindfolded.

~ * ~

The path curled around an outcropping of shale and then skirted a bramble patch before opening up into a shallow clearing inside a stand of oaks that had to be forty years old. I had the shortcut and if I hustled I'd be in the timber before they came out of the overhanging pines.

Last year's acorns crunched beneath my feet and my breath caught in my throat, but I'd been quick enough. They were still twenty yards away and I got my back up against the biggest oak I could find and tried to breathe real shallow. The gun in my hand felt like a bar of iron. I took the time to make sure the safety was off. Then I heard the owl in the timber hoot again and they stepped out into the clearing. I made myself wait until they were ten yards past.

"That'll be far enough, Menifee. I've got a gun and it's loaded. Now turn around real slow and keep your hands out where I can see them."

"What about me?" Moses said. He managed to get a goodly amount of fear in his voice.

"I don't care what you do, so long as you get. This is going to be a private conversation."

Moses mumbled something and started shuffling back up the trail. I didn't dare more than a quick glance, but he looked all right. I counted to twenty then stepped clear from the oak.

"Well, look at the snake what crawled out."

"I don't want trouble, Menifee. Only talk. Oh, and keep your hands out where I can see them."

"We can talk all right. But you just bought yourself more trouble than you can handle."

There was a whine in his voice, and a growl. Just hearing him speak brought my nerves up. A trembling ran though me. The gun felt terribly heavy. My hand was shaking.

"Jessie and I don't want trouble with you, but you need to let her go."

He shook his head. In that movement, he also eased a step to his right. "Hate to spoil your party, Cain, but Jessie belongs to me. I've tried to be a nice guy about all this. Sent you messages and all, but you don't seem to listen."

"You're the one what hasn't been listening, Menifee. Slave days are over. President Lincoln freed them years ago."

He laughed then. "You're dumber than you look, Cain. Slavery still exists. One way or another we're all slaves. You ought to know that. You ain't nothing special, just a lousy hill-jack wage slave."

"My personal life doesn't matter. What matters is the way Jessie and I feel about each other. We want to be together and you can't stop us. Thousands of men have been dying to make sure we're all free to live the way we want to."

"Don't talk to me about war. I fight my own battles. And I don't need your help or Uncle Sam's or any damn body else's."

All the time he was talking his feet were easing ever so slowly to the right. I eased half a step to the left myself. My heart was hammering and there was a whine in my ears. I'd never held a gun on anybody before and the palm of my right hand was slick with cold sweat. I wanted to dry it off, but I was afraid to switch hands. I didn't trust him. Right then it occurred to me that I ought to have searched him. Being Menifee, he probably had brought a gun. Day late and a dollar short. Story of my life.

He was talking again and I made myself focus. Letting my mind wander wasn't good business.

"Besides, you don't know Jessie. She's one mixed up woman. Never knows quite what she wants. Oh, one minute she'll want one thing, let's say a good wholesome man like you, and the next, something else. Probably getting liquored up or dancing till dawn with strangers. I'm the only man who really knows her. Knows how to deal with her. See, Jessie's a beautiful woman, but she's also a woman with lots of needs. And I'm the only one who can take care of her the special way she needs to be taken care of."

He paused then and tilted his head on one side, and in that moment, with his face coated in moonlight, he put me in mind of a painting of an ancient Greek philosopher I'd seen in a book in an abandoned library in Kilkenny, Texas.

"Guess in certain ways me and Jessie are a lot alike. Only she's weak and I'm strong." He grinned and his teeth were white against his tanned face. "Strong enough to take care of you anyway, Cain. My only mistake was not doing it myself. Good help is real hard to find these days."

He laughed then and it wasn't a pleasant sound. "Look at you, having to use that old nigger to get me down here, instead of being man enough to come see me face-to-face." He shrugged and I noticed his body didn't quite come back to plumb. "Oh well, I'll tend to him, too. Guess a man has to do certain things himself. I've learned that lesson now."

He lifted his chin and stared at me real cool like, as though we were old friends, or maybe debating contestants. "That's what sets me apart from the riff-raff, Cain. I'm smart enough to learn a lesson." He leaned a little toward his right. "Are you a smart man, old Judas buddy?"

"Maybe," I said. "But that's not what I came here to talk about." I didn't like all this mouthing. Made me nervous down in my gut.

He shook his head. I could hear the owl off in the distance mingled with the rustle of something small and alive in the brush. Pine scent drifted on the breeze.

"You might be a man that could learn out of books. But you ain't natural smart. Not like a fox or a crow. Not like me. You're like most men, Cain. You let your feelings get in the way of your thinking. Specially when it comes to women."

I recognized my cue and jumped in. "Speaking of women," I said, "that's what I want to talk about. Let's talk about Jessie. She doesn't belong to you or any other man and if you don't leave her alone, well, all anybody has to do is drop a word in the sheriff's ear and you'll be going away for a long time. Word on the street is that he's on to you anyway. Just waiting for you to make one more jump and then you're doing hard time."

Menifee snorted. He sounded like a mad bull. "So that's your little game, Cain. Well, there's hard time and then there's real hard time, which is dead time. And, old buddy, that's the only time you're going to be doing."

It was like catching a glimpse out of the corner of your eye of a rattlesnake striking. I'd seen one kill a dog that way down near Laredo. One second Menifee and I were talking and the next second he was whipping a pistol out from behind his back.

One of us screamed. Might have been me.

Don't even remember squeezing the trigger.

All in a roar the night came alive. I saw the flash of his gun and felt mine buck like something gone wild.

Remember thinking, I hadn't even taken good aim.

I closed my eyes and sank to my knees waiting for pain and death. They didn't show. I opened my eyes. I look around, and I was so scared that maybe I wasn't seeing real good right then, but all I saw was darkness and silhouettes of trees. Then I heard Menifee groan. I got to my feet and stumbled toward the sound.

Menifee was on his back in a swale. Moonlight covered him. His hands were digging at his guts. His eyes were open and he was looking at me. I'm not sure he was seeing anything. He made a small sound down in his throat, then his body jerked and went still. To me, he looked like a pile of wet gunny sacks. My stomach turned over and I bent over and vomited. I was sweating and chilled to the bone all at the same time. Far off in the timber the owl hooted at the moon.

Forty-six

Clouds had covered the moon and the night had gone hard dark. I stood in the deep shadows of the big oaks at the bottom of the drive and peered up toward the house. It was as dark as the night.

It had taken me some time to figure out to come here. After I drug Menifee's body deep in the woods, I'd come on the sinkhole. It wasn't a big one, like I'd seen down in Florida, but when I'd pushed his body over the edge it fell what sounded like at least thirty feet. I'd shoved in fallen branches along with last year's leaves, hoping they were covering his carcass. For some time, I'd stood there thinking about the enormity of what had happened and trying to figure out what needed to happen next.

No way of knowing whether or not Menifee had told some of his men where he was going, but I'd had to assume that when he didn't show up for breakfast somebody would go check on him. If he'd mentioned my name, and it had struck me that he was the type who would, they'd come looking for me. That meant I couldn't go home. Moses had been seen with me too many times to take a chance of putting him in danger. Menifee's men would check on Jessie right away, so I couldn't go to her place. That pretty well used up most of my options.

Guess I could have cut and hightailed it for Louisiana or Arkansas. But I figured that Menifee's boys wouldn't bother with extradition papers. After what seemed like a long time to be thinking about anything, the only plan that made sense was to come to the Ayers place.

Surely there were better options. But I couldn't think of them. Now, looking up the dark drive, this option didn't seem so smart. I wondered, what with the boss gone, if Mrs. Ayers kept a loaded gun in the house. Headlights pierced the darkness and I stepped deeper into the shadows and watched a car roll by. Stumbling around in the dark seemed like a real poor plan. Either Menifee's men or the police were likely to spot me if I stayed where I was. I started walking.

Most likely it was simply habit, but I slipped around to the side so that I came in under the carport. Seeing the boss's car gave me a start. Funny, but I'd not thought of it since he passed. For a moment, I stood with my hand on the hood wondering what happened to a man's possessions when he passed. All men have some possessions: clothes, a few tools, maybe some books or old photographs that once meant a lot to them. Some, like the boss, had cars and houses and bank accounts. Menifee had surely had all those, too. I wondered who was going to get his stuff.

Then I wondered what would have happened to my few things if Menifee had shot straighter. Nothing I had was worth much. Only a few shirts a few underclothes, some slacks and a well-worn jacket. I had a few books I'd picked up along the way, usually when somebody had set them out to the curb. There was an iron skillet along with a couple of pans. Except for one grainy picture of my mom and dad on their wedding day, that was it. How that photo had survived my journeys was amazing.

Nobody would want that picture. Wouldn't mean a thing to them. They wouldn't want the clothes or the pans. Even the shack had been abandoned when I'd moved in. Nobody would be interested, and if I'd bought the farm instead of Menifee, it would have been like I'd vanished. Or maybe it would have been more like

I'd never existed. Sad, when you thought about it. But what was a man to do? He lived; he died. And that was it. Once he was gone he started to fade, the way chalk fades on a sidewalk when it rains.

Menifee would be missed by some for sure, but soon he too would start to fade. Already the picture in my mind of the boss was starting to dim around the edges. I could hardly remember what the kid had looked like before he went into the service. Someday, I'd be nothing more than a blurry memory to a precious few. And when they were gone, well I'd been gone, too. Dust in the wind, as they say in Kansas. Dust in the wind.

I pushed off the hood and went up the back steps and knocked on the door, moving quickly before I changed my mind. I waited a minute, but couldn't hear sounds of anyone stirring within. Part of me sure hoped she was home. Another part wished she had gone to her brother's. I knuckled up and rapped on the door again.

I stepped down to the bottom step and waited. I'd made up my mind I wouldn't knock again. Don't know why. Reckon that's simply the way my mind works.

All that knocking had sounded loud to me so I turned and peered out into the night. Half expected lights to be coming on in every house. All I could see were the outlines of trees and shadows slow dancing in the wind. Then a small band of light fell across the lilac bush at the far corner of the house and I knew somebody was home. I turned back around and ran my fingers through my hair. Seconds later I heard footsteps.

The porch light snapped on and I blinked at the brightness. Then the curtains parted at the door glass enough so I could see the image of her face, blurry with the dusty glass between us. She mashed her face up against that glass and called out, "Who's there?"

For reasons I don't pretend to understand I didn't answer right off. She called again, her voice croaking at the end, "Is anybody out there?"

Easy to hear that she was scared. Well, that was all right. I was still shaking a bit myself, which I suppose was understandable. Not every night one man shoots another, especially if he happens to kill him.

"I'm going to call the police if you don't answer. You hear me?"

She sounded like she meant what she had said. I swallowed whatever had been holding me back and called out, "Mrs. Ayers, it's me, Judas."

"Well, what in the world are you doing out there at this time of night?"

"Can I come in? It's important."

The curtains fell back and then the regular door came open, at least as far as the chain would allow. I could see a slice of her face. One eye glistened.

"Is that really you, Judas?"

"Yes, ma'am, it's me."

"Well why are you out there at this time of night? I mean do you really know what time it is?"

I stepped back onto the carport and looked up at the moon. "Figure it's gone after midnight," I said.

"Well, I should think so," she said.

As if it were a mind reader, the old Seth-Thomas on the mantle chimed twice. Ever since I was a kid I'd wanted a mantle clock. Always found comfort in their chiming.

"Hear that?" Mrs. Ayers said. "It's two o'clock. No time to be out gallivanting around, if you ask me." She paused and I could see the eye twitching.

"No decent person lays out till such hours. Have you been drinking, Judas?"

"No, ma'am, not one drop. Could use a shot, though, now that you mention it."

"Well, don't expect a drop from me. Not when you come knocking on my door at two in the morning." The eye was fixed hard on me. "What are you doing here anyway?"

"Aim to tell you if you'll let me in."

"Well—"

"Oh come on, Mrs. Ayers. If I meant to harm you, I wouldn't knock on your door, now would I?"

"Well, I don't know—"

"You'd better let me in before the neighbors get curious."

Figured maybe she'd argue some more, but the threat of the neighbors knowing her business was more than she could handle. The chain rattled and then the door swung open. I went up the steps and slipped inside before she could change her mind.

She made a funny little sound, halfway between a gasp of surprise and a snort of irritation. Her body leaned away from me and her eyes were half-hooded with sleep. Or maybe that was fear. No doubt I looked a sight. At my best I wasn't a thing of beauty and a joy forever, and I sure as hell wasn't at my best.

"Don't worry, Mrs. Ayers, I'm not here to do you harm."

She leaned against the doorframe and gave me a long, hard look out from under the swatch of hair that had fallen down across her face. That wave of hair gave her a sort of wild look, and, in some way I couldn't explain, it made her look younger. I could see that she might well have been a pretty girl.

"Then what are you here for?"

Now that I was here, I didn't know what to say. Or maybe it wasn't that I didn't know what to say, but that the words didn't want to come. I took a deep breath and wished the boss was sitting at the table. If he'd been there, I'd have asked straight up. He'd have understood and helped for sure. Her, I wasn't sure of. I waited for a moment, just to see if any bright ideas popped up.

"I need a place to stay. Just for a little while," I said, only looking up at her after I'd said it. The night rose up and sucker punched me. My legs went wobbly and I leaned against the sink.

She brushed the hair off her face. Without her makeup she looked different. Softer, and more vulnerable. "You look like something the cat drug in, Judas. Are you sure you haven't been drinking?"

"Yes, ma'am, I'm sure. Haven't had a drop tonight."

"Well, what is wrong with you then? Why do you need a place to stay? Are you sick? Did your place burn down?"

I couldn't tell from her voice if she was worried or angry. "No, I'm not really sick and my place is all right. I'm just in a bit of a jam."

"How bad a jam?"

"Pretty bad."

She looked at me funny. Out of the corners of her eyes, like she was afraid to face me. "Your voice sounds funny, Judas. Has something happened?"

"Yes."

"Something I need to know about?"

I thought about that one for a second. Couldn't see any way, but to say it. "Yes," I said, keeping my voice low. "I had to shoot a man tonight."

"What did you say? You're mumbling, Judas. I believe you are drunk," she said and drew herself up tighter against the table.

"No, I'm not drunk, Mizz Ayers, and I expect you did hear me clear enough. It wasn't anything I wanted to do, but I had to shoot a man. It was his play all the way, but that doesn't change the fact that I had to shoot him."

The skin on her face seemed to tighten and her eyes went wide, then narrowed. A lock of hair had fallen down again and she lifted a hand to sweep it back. Her hand was trembling. "Well, if you had to defend yourself, why don't you call the police and report it? This is America, the police won't mistreat an innocent man."

"It's not the police I'm worried about. It's the friends of the man I had to shoot."

"Surely the police would protect you."

There was nothing for it, but to say a name. Say a name and hope she understood.

"I shot Brad Menifee."

For a second, it was like the name meant nothing. Or that it was a name she'd heard before, but couldn't quite place. Say a name like Wiley Post or Urban Shocker. Then I saw her eyes change and she drew her breath in sharp.

"Oh my," she said, "all of a sudden my legs feel weak. I'd better sit down." Her hands fumbled for a chair and then she flopped down.

"You know Menifee?"

"I've heard of him. Arthur mentioned him a few times. I gather Mr. Menifee is rather a villain."

"Yes," I said, "he was."

She had a delayed reaction, but she got it. Say what you will about Mrs. Ayers; she wasn't stupid.

"Oh," she said. "That does make a difference."

"Considerable," I said.

She sat there quietly. I wondered what she was thinking; I wondered what she'd say. She lowered her eyes, then lifted them and looked around the kitchen as if she'd never seen it before. After a bit, she let her eyes drift back to my face.

"I'm frightened, Judas."

I nodded. "I understand, Mrs. Ayers. I'm scared enough, myself."

"Mr. Menifee has a sort of a gang, doesn't he? People who carry out his orders, I mean." She nibbled at her lower lip. "Bad men."

I felt sorry for her. In the space of a few months, she had lost her husband and her son, and now this crazy yard man, who was supposed to be helping her, was knocking on her door in the middle of the night, pleading for sanctuary. No wonder she looked scared. Anybody with sense would be. No use sugar coating anything. I could only tell her the truth then hope for the best.

"Yes, ma'am, real bad men. I hid the body best I could, but—"

She opened her mouth, but nothing came out. After a moment, she must have realized that the pose wasn't good for her, and she pressed her lips together. Figured she had something she wanted to ask, but for some reason was reluctant to. I tried to read her mind.

"I won't stay long. As soon as I figure out where to go, I'll leave."

She shut her eyes. I looked down at my hands. Hands that had killed a man. They weren't trembling any longer, but I still felt fluttery inside. It was like a cloud of butterflies were flying around in my stomach.

Mrs. Ayers opened her eyes. For a second, she almost smiled. "I guess one night will be all right. Nights are not my best time. I'm too tired to think straight and I imagine you aren't doing much better. Maybe we'll both see things more clearly in the morning."

She pushed up out of her chair and tugged the belt of her robe tighter. "Obviously, you'll need a bed. Would it bother you too much to sleep in Lenny's room?"

"The couch would be fine."

"You'll have more privacy in his room."

I didn't want to sleep in a dead kid's room. But, like the old saying went, beggars can't be choosers. Besides, the room was on the back and there were a couple of windows that offered possible escape in case Menifee's boys tracked me down.

"Okay," I said.

She smiled and nodded toward the hall. "Come on, Judas, let's get you tucked away for the night."

I followed her down the hall. My mind was whirling with crazy thoughts. I told myself to get a grip.

~ * ~

I lay on the bed. I lay very still and thought. I thought about dead men. I thought about the man I'd killed. Then I thought about being in the boss's house and him being dead. For sure, I thought about the kid, about Lenny, about him being killed by some Jap on some lousy island that I didn't even know the name of a thousand miles or more away. I lay on that bed with my eyes closed, seeing their faces, thinking about all that death, and it made me half sick to my stomach. Knew I'd never sleep. Told myself to get up off the bed and put my pants and shirt and shoes and socks back on and slip out into the darkness. Yeah, that sounded good, but what then? There was always the kicker. In my life there was always a kicker. This time the kicker was where would I go? Once I got out in the darkness, where would I go? Yeah, where would I go? When a man is really hurt or scared or lonely, he needs to go home. So where was I supposed to go? Where?

Forty-seven

I blinked and instantly came wide awake, feeling refreshed the way a man does after a nap when he's really tired. It took me a minute to realize where I was. Then I knew I was at the Ayers place and I lifted my head and looked out the window. It was just going daylight and I wondered what the morning would bring. I told myself to roll over and go back to sleep, but my heart was pecking away inside my chest and I knew I wouldn't. I rubbed at my eyes and sat up in the bed.

"You're awake, Mr. Cain?"

I jumped like a gut-shot rabbit. Then I turned to her voice. She was sitting in a big soft chair with her big soft body all sprawled out and suddenly I was very conscious of my bare chest. I looked around for my shirt.

"You cried out in your sleep, Mr. Cain. I was worried. You must have had a terrible dream."

"It's Judas," I said. "Guess I must have. But I'm all right. You needn't sit up with me like some sort of nurse."

Mrs. Ayers smiled a little. She looked almost pretty when she smiled. "It's funny you saying that. Before I met Arthur, I was going to be a nurse. They trained us to listen. Nurses learn a lot by listening."

She shook her head. "Then I was going to be a school teacher. That was a position which fit in more with Arthur's notion of how our lives should be. Only I never became a teacher or a nurse. Just a wife and mother. Now Arthur is gone and—"

She turned her head and looked out the window. Daylight was licking at the grass. "What am I supposed to do now, Mr. Cain? Judas. One must get with the times. I recognize that." She twisted up one corner of her mouth, which made her look like she was laughing at herself.

"My husband is dead. My son is dead. My mother and father are dead. I have no one in this town, Mr. Cain. What do you think I should do?"

She seemed very serious, as though the next ten minutes might make or break her. I wished I had something helpful to say to her. I didn't know what to do. After a minute, I decided to try and be funny.

"Maybe you should hop the midnight freight when it leaves the station," I said.

Hers eyes widened, then narrowed. "Are you trying to be funny, Mr. Cain?"

"Yeah," I said.

"Well, you're not."

The expression on her face made me feel bad. "I'm sorry," I said.

"You should be." She buried her face in her hands. Her shoulders started going up and down.

Well, I was sure enough was sorry for what I'd said. The woman had been through plenty. But what was I supposed to do about anything? Sticking my foot in my mouth was one of the few things I was good at. I took a deep breath and reached for my pants. I slipped them on under the sheet and then swung my legs out.

Standing there in the middle of the bedroom with no shirt on, I felt like a fool. I sure wished the boss was there. He'd have got things straightened out quick. But like Fast Eddie Brown always said, "If wishes and buts were candy and nuts, what a merry damn Christmas we all would have."

I needed to do something to make up for my mouth, but I didn't have a clue. I stood there like one of those Greek statutes, trying to think of the right thing to do. If there was a right action to take, I never did come up with it. After a bit, I walked over and put a hand on one of her shoulders. Her robe was soft and white. Standing there, I had an unbidden thought about that big, soft body under the robe.

After a bit, her shoulders stopped heaving. She reached up and put one of her hands on top of mine. Her hand was warm and soft and damp. I let my hand lie there. Figured it was the least I could do.

She sniffed and lifted my hand and pressed the palm against her cheek. Her skin was softer than I expected. Touching her like that made me feel real strange. Down the block a dog barked. A car rolled by, headed toward town   . She turned her face and pressed her lips against my palm. I could feel my cheeks blushing, but I didn't say anything,

For what seemed like a long time, she held my hand very tight. Then she kissed it again and stood up. Somehow her arms got around my neck and I pulled her to me. Her body was soft and she smelled of lilacs. Outside the window a bird twittered. Our lips found each other. I reached down and untied her robe. I took her hand and we walked together to the bed. The springs squeaked. Voices from the street drifted in through the open window, but I wasn't listening to the words.

Forty-eight

Her back was long and smooth and seemed to be inviting me to stroke it with my hands, or maybe even lick it with my tongue. I'd have been glad to do either. I tried not to think about Marilee.

Men made mistakes, I told myself. You made a mistake. You simply made a mistake. Or maybe it was two lonely, scared people who need each other for an hour. One sweet hour. That was all it had been. One sweet hour three days ago. One sweet hour. That's all. That's what I told myself.

Jessie was standing by the window, a step back so the curtains concealed her from the street. Late afternoon sunlight reflected on her skin like Hollywood lighting. Longing rose in me and nearly choked me down. I wanted her more than words could say. We had made love earlier and then we had stayed in bed, talking about odds and ends, smoking cigarettes, and watching the afternoon start to die.

I tried to curl the talk around so that it was about us. Specifically about us going away together. Even with Menifee gone, this town was full of problems, for both of us.

Since the boss passed, nobody in this town gave a damn for me. Except for Moses, and he was an old man who was struggling to get by. Well, there was Mrs. Ayers, but I wasn't sure what was on her mind. Like I freely admit, women confuse me.

And as for Jessie, well lots of men liked her, but not the right way, and lots of women hated her, for all the obvious reasons. On top of that there were Menifee's buddies and employees. When he didn't show up after a few days, they would start looking. Probably already were. I wished I'd taken time to toss more branches over his body. His boys played rough.

The biggest problem, though, was Jessie. If she would cooperate, we could run away from all our troubles. A few hours on a fast train and we were long gone. She simply wouldn't go. Why I hadn't figured out. I closed my eyes and tried to think.

"Baby, Menifee's out of the picture. We can focus on just us. You can trust me on that."

She gave me a long hard look. "What makes you think he's out of the picture? Brad's a hard man to get a handle on. I should know. Been trying to do it for years. Just when you think he's acting one way, he turns around and does something you don't expect."

I sat up and propped my back against the headboard. "I got it straight from a totally reliable source, Brad Menifee is going to be out of town for a very long time."

"Huh." She flipped her hair and bent and picked up her dress and underwear. She slipped on her underwear. They were white. "And who is this source?"

"Promised to keep it a secret," I said, and winked. "But you can trust me, Jessie, this info is the real deal."

She slipped her dress on over her head. Behind the material she said, "I gave up trusting men a long time ago." Her head popped out. "Trusting a man always gets me hurt. Any man."

"I'm not any man."

An expression I couldn't quite place worked its way across her face. She turned, sat down on the only chair in the room and without replying started putting on her shoes. I swung my legs out and reached for my clothes.

"You getting hungry?"

I hadn't been thinking of food, but maybe eating was better than the tension I could feel simmering. I couldn't understand what she was so nervous about. Sure, Menifee had been a real bad man, but I'd told her he wasn't a factor any longer. Maybe she didn't believe me. Maybe she was scared so bad so deep down inside that nothing could erase the fear. I didn't know. Could be that she might not know herself.

"Let's go eat, we can talk things over while we drink our coffee," I said, giving her a smile I didn't feel. I loved her in a way I'd never loved any other woman and I wanted her and I needed her the way a man dying of thirst needs water, but I didn't understand her. Couldn't get a handle on how she really felt about me. That made my stomach hurt.

She stared at her reflection in the mirror and painted her lips. Her eyes glittered like hot metal. She turned and smiled that certain smile that made my heart thump extra hard. Then she crossed the room and slipped her hand through my arm and we walked out of the room and down the hallway like a freshly married couple. I couldn't ever recall feeling more proud.

Forty-nine

"You surely have been working."

I'd been so lost in thought that I had no idea anyone was within a hundred yards and her voice made me jump. I whirled around, the axe in my hand, and she stepped back like she was afraid. Well, maybe I would have been, too.

"Sorry, Judas, didn't mean to startle you. You've been working for almost two hours without stopping and I thought you might like something to drink. I made some lemonade." She shook a glass at me.

"Didn't mean to turn on you with an axe in my hand," I said. "Seems like I'm jumpy these days." I didn't really want the lemonade, but she had gone to the trouble of making it and bringing it out to me. Not many people had done that much for me. I'd be ungrateful if I refused. "Lemonade sounds fine," I said.

Her smile was a nice one. I wondered why she had come all the way down to the bottom of the yard. She could have just yelled from the steps. I sipped at the lemonade and eyed Mrs. Ayers over the top of my glass. Dark circles had formed under her eyes. She was still a big woman, but her dress hung loosely. Looked to me like she had lost about twenty pounds since the boss had passed. I tried to recall exactly how long ago that had been. Remembered him passing, every detail, but the actual date he breathed his last wasn't etched on my brain. Had it been a year? Time seemed elastic to me these days, elastic and out of focus.

Fall had come with a hard freeze a couple of weeks ago and the yard was awash in yellow and red leaves. I could smell wood smoke and a jacket felt good in the morning.

The lemonade had a twang to it and I figured she must have shorted the sugar. Well, that was okay. Even with the insurance money, the loss of his big salary had to hurt. On top of that, funerals weren't cheap. Dang morticians ought to all be millionaires the way folks were dying. The long hot summer had been hard on the old folks and some of the young ones had come home from the war to die. Then there were plenty of fools who shot each other or smashed their car into a tree. Course not everyone who died got buried. At least not official like. I thought of Brad Menifee and smiled into my lemonade.

For a couple of weeks after he disappeared the town had been thick with talk and rumors. Some said he'd gone to California, where he'd talked of going. Others thought he had been killed by the Williams brothers who ran shine, women, and stolen cigarettes over near Moreland. The guy who ran the barber shop knew for sure that Menifee had run off with the Baptist preacher's wife who had also gone missing. A few of the old Negroes laid his disappearance onto the Mulberry Black Thing, which, as I understood it, was some sort of creature that lived down in the low swampy ground east of town.

Only two people in the world knew for sure where Menifee was, and one of them was dead and the other had no intention of talking. Old Moses had to suspect plenty, but he didn't know, not for certain.

"You're gathering wool, Judas."

That woman kept sneaking up on me. I'd been thinking so hard that I'd forgotten she was there. My shoulders jerked again and I swallowed my aggravation. I still liked to eat.

"Just thinking."

A hard windstorm had blown through the week before and three of the old rotten trees down in the swale had fallen. Today, I'd chopped up two of them. She was sitting on the third, staring at me. Having a woman look at me like that gave me the willies.

"Must have been thinking pretty hard. What were you thinking about? That is, if you don't mind my asking."

"Oh, about all the work I have to do," I said, sweeping an arm in the direction of the bottom. To tell the truth, a good-sized gang of men could have gone in there, worked steady for a week and there still would have been work to do. So as lies goes, it wasn't totally black.

She cocked her head and smiled. I noticed she had a nice mouth. "Sure it wasn't a woman? Word around town is you've been seen squiring a girl around. Understand she is right pretty."

In spite of the chill, I'd been sweating and I rubbed a shirtsleeve across my face to keep it out of my eyes. "You can hear about anything," I said.

"Suppose that's true enough, but you have all the symptoms."

"Such as?"

"Being real quiet and moody and staring off into space a lot. And not eating near as much as you used to." She shook back her hair. "I know them all. After all, I used to be a girl, believe it or not."

I nodded.

"When I was young, lots of men thought I was pretty." She shook her head and I watched her hair swing like moving water. There was more silver among the brown than there had been when the boss had been around.

I wasn't sure what to say. I wondered if she was fishing for a compliment. Didn't see where it could hurt to say a kind word.

"You still look nice," I said. Once they were out I could hear that the words sounded vague and phony, which about covered it.

"Why thank you, Judas. A woman always likes to hear sweet words."

I couldn't see where they were so darn sweet, but if she liked them, so be it.

The train sounded down by the depot and we paused and listened. The wind was pushing out of the west and you could hear it in the white pines and see the leaves falling from the oaks and beeches and water maples. It looked like it was snowing leaves.

"What's your girl's name, Judas?"

That really wasn't any of her business, but I didn't see where it could hurt to say it. Lately, we hadn't been keeping it a big secret and people around town had seen us. And, of course, some people have to tell everything they know and maybe a little more besides. I favor folks who keep their business to themselves. Anyway, I owed her something after that night.

"Her name is Jessie," I said, not looking at Marilee Ayers.

"Is she pretty?"

"I think so."

Marilee wiped a leaf off her sweater. "Why do you want to be with her?"

I shrugged and bent over and lifted a cut limb and tossed it on the pile. Figured she was remembering when we had made love.

"Yes, you're right, it's really none of my business. I apologize."

"Don't worry about it. No big deal."

"Arthur often said I had a real talent for sticking my big nose where it didn't belong."

I swung the axe back and forth, like a pendulum, hoping she'd take the hint. "Guess we all do that from time to time."

"Perhaps, but I need to stop it." She stood and looked straight at me. "A woman of certain age with time on her hands does a lot of wondering, Mr. Cain. I hope you can understand."

"Sure," I said.

I think she planned to say something more, but she didn't. I wondered if she wanted to talk about that night. I hoped she didn't because I wasn't sure what I would say. But she simply stood there staring at me, until I began to feel funny, like I had a smudge on my nose.

I moved my head in a way that she could take as a shrug or not and glanced up at the sky. Dark clouds were whirling in from the west, driven by the wind. A chill ran through that air, and she pulled her sweater tighter around her. Her breasts pushed out against the sweater and, before I could stop myself, I remembered how they looked. That sort of remembering was best left undone. Cold air was working in under my shirt and I hunched up and wondered if we were going to have a hard winter.

"Reckon I'd better get back to work," I said, trying, in a nice way, to let her know it was time for her to drift on back to the house.

Only she didn't go. She just stood there looking at me. Finally, she took a deep breath and let it out. "I hope your lady friend appreciates you." she said. A smile rippled across her lips, then faded.

I didn't know how to take that, so I just nodded. In the silence between us, you could hear the wind working through the trees. A church bell started to toll. It sounded like it was tolling somebody's passing. It tolled five times. A dark bird swirled up out of the woods and winged hard across the open ground.

Mrs. Ayers half turned to go. "You're a good man, Judas Cain," she said, reaching out a hand and letting the tips of her fingers slide across one side of my face. Then she finished the turn and began walking up the hill. For a big woman, she had nice legs. Her words had confused me so that I didn't answer. Instead I stared at her back until she reached the top of the slope. There she turned and looked back and lifted a hand. I lifted one in return and then turned to the remaining fallen tree. The axe felt good in my hands and I smiled as I swung it.

Fifty

Thunder rumbled off to the west. It was still distant, but coming closer. Lightning flickered, and then was gone. The scent of rain was faint, but distinct. I lay as still as stone in the bed, staring out into the night, listening to her breathe.

Her breathing changed as she rolled over. Her breath was warm and moist against the side of my neck. Her fingers traced patterns down my arms.

"Is it going to storm, baby?"

"It's coming," I said, "weather's really been changeable of late."

"Storms excite me, you know."

"Is that right?" I said, rolling over onto my side, facing her. Only a faint glimmer of light from a room across the street slanted in through the window. Her face was a dark moon rising. I snuggled closer. Her scent drifted through the darkness.

"I want you, baby," she murmured.

I snaked an arm around her body and pulled her to me. Her breasts were soft and warm against my bare chest. Her nipples pressed against me. I buried my face in her hair. "I want you, too, Jessie. More than anything."

"Love on me, honey." She pressed her lips against mine. They were soft and warm and thick and her breath was sweet with whiskey and promises. I pulled her so tight that she gasped a little.

"Don't break me, sweetie."

"Don't worry," I said, "I don't aim to."

Thunder rolled again, closer still.

"Let me have you, Judas."

I shifted my hips and pushed against her. She was open and wet. I said her name like I was praying. She moaned softly and mouthed words against the side of my neck. Her breath was like a warm wind in May. She arched her back and wrapped both arms around me.

Thunder rolled so close it sounded like it was coming down Main Street. Lightning fired in the sky and you could almost see God in the after-reflection. I said her name and thunder rolled like the end of time.

Fifty-one

I came awake slowly, swirling up out of a dream as dark as a river. The dream had scared me and the fear lingered, even as the dream began to fade. I reached out for Jessie. All my fingers touched was the cool slickness of the sheets. I opened my eyes.

Sunlight filled the room. A stiff breeze was blowing out of the south and the curtains fluttered at the window like flags. I looked around for Jessie, but all that remained was a hint of her perfume, mingled with her more personal scent. To me, that smelled warm and slightly wild and I wondered where she had gone, and why she had gone without waking me. I sighed and rolled out of the bed.

Out of some kindness, I suppose, Jessie had left two dollar bills lying on the dresser. I got dressed and stuffed the bills down in the front pocket of my trousers. Then I headed for the hotel dining room. Halfway down the stairs I wondered if Jessie had simply forgotten the money.

I ate ham and eggs and toast and washed it all down with hot black coffee. I lingered over the second cup of coffee and read a newspaper somebody had left behind. Two brothers were missing on a canoe trip in Montana. A bank in Joplin, Missouri had been robbed for the third time in two weeks. Unemployment was up and so was the price of steak. Truman's popularity was falling and out in Kansas a preacher had run off with the choir director. Seemed like times were tough all over. That I could understand.

What I couldn't understand was where Jessie had gone. There were chores to be done at Mrs. Ayers' place, but I didn't feel like working. I felt like seeing Jessie and talking to her. I wanted to make sense of the situation. But I didn't know where she was. An image of Marilee pushed to the surface of my mind. Coming like it did, right in the middle of thinking about Jessie, made me feel guilty. She never mentioned that special time, but I could tell it was on her mind. Mine, too, if I wanted to be honest. Women, I thought, are impossible to get a handle on. I paid my bill and left a small tip. Then I walked outside.

The day was going to be a fine one. The sky was a polished blue. A few streaky white clouds highlighted the western horizon. The sunlight was bright, but without heat. For the better part of an hour I wandered up and down the main street. I glanced in a few windows, but didn't speak to any of the people passing by. I didn't know them and they didn't know me and not one of us cared enough to make an effort.

If my mind had been straight I'd have gone on and done the couple of jobs Marilee wanted me to take care of. What with her being a widow and all, I should have done that. Especially since she'd been so nice to me of late. But my mind was full of Jessie and in the end I didn't go. Funny thing was, in a way I did want to go. Even if it was nothing more than seeing Marilee and making sure she was all right. Felt like I owed the boss, plus that hour she and I had shared had to signify something. Still, I couldn't make myself go there. And I didn't want to go to my place and sit alone. Suppose I could have gone back to Jessie's hotel room, but that morning that little box of a hotel room seemed stifling. Finally, somewhere along the prime of the morning, I stared meandering off toward old Moses' place.

~ * ~

He was sitting on a stump in the sunlight wearing a red jacket and a greasy ball cap. He smiled as I came up the path.

"Brother Judas, long time no see."

"Yeah, thought I'd pay you a visit."

He nodded and cocked his head so that the sunlight wasn't directly in his eyes. "Mighty nice of you. Not many will come all the way out here. Too far a walk for them."

"Walking never did hurt me."

Moses motioned at another stump. "Sit a spell, won't you?"

"All right," I said and strolled over to the stump. My legs weren't tired, but I hadn't walked all the way out here just to turn around and go back.

Moses scratched at his arm. "Haven't seen you in a while. You been out of town?"

I shook my head. "No, actually, I've been in town. Staying with Jessie."

He grinned. "Bet you didn't mind that."

"No, that's good times. Only this morning I woke up and she was gone.'

"Maybe she went shopping, or for a walk. Women like to get out of a place from time to time, you know. Never did know of one what was content to stay at home."

"She didn't leave a note. I waited around all morning, but she never showed back up. Plus, it's happened before. Twice this week."

"Maybe she was visiting. Used to have an aunt who'd go visiting every chance she got. And once she got to talking, Lord God, I mean to tell you that it was nigh impossible to get her back home." Moses rolled his eyes. "That woman sure could talk."

"Jessie doesn't talk so much."

Moses studied me. "No, I'd say Miss Jessie was a right different sort of woman. Nothing wrong with that, of course. Matter of fact, I'd say lots of men like Jessie just the way she is."

There was truth in the old man's words. Not that I cared to hear it. I looked off into the trees. Beneath them the shadows looked blue.

I wasn't sure now why I had come. Maybe, way in the very back of my mind, I'd had the notion that Jessie might be out here. But that was crazy thinking. Maybe I was going crazy. I'd heard tell of men who went loco over a woman. There were times, especially when I was missing Jessie, that I felt like I'd slipped a cog myself. Perhaps I wasn't crazy, but I sure wasn't quite right either.

But all of that might not have been Jessie. I hadn't been the same man since I'd killed Brad Menifee. He was the only man I'd ever even hurt bad, least as far as I knew. Oh, like any man worth his salt, I'd had a few fist fights. But none had lasted long and a black eye or a bloody nose were about the worst results. Killing a man was way different. Knowing that you'd taken another man's life preyed on your mind. Especially if you were making love to a woman who'd made love to him. No wonder I wasn't sleeping good.

As if he was reading my mind, Moses said, "You think about that day much?"

I didn't have to ask which day. "Some," I said.

"Bother you?"

"A little." I turned my head and spat. "Be worse if I'd planned for it to end that way. All I really wanted was to talk. The other was his play all the way." That was the truth, too. All of it. Only to my ears it sounded like I was trying to convince someone of something I didn't quite believe. Maybe it was myself I was trying to convince.

Moses nodded. Off in the timber a woodpecker hammered away. "Any trouble?"

"Nope. Hear people asked some questions, but nobody acts like they suspect anything."

"What about Jessie?"

"What about her?"

"She suspect anything?"

"Not that I noticed," I said. But down deep I wondered.

"That's good then," he said.

"Reckon so," I said. "But she's out rambling this morning." I looked down the slope. Milkweed heads quivered in the wind. I could smell dust and leaves and stale sweat. All at once I wanted a cup of coffee.

Moses stretched out his legs and studied them. "Hard to say what Jessie's doing," he said. "Women, they always hard to figure. Leastways for me," he said and grinned.

I grinned back and nodded. I couldn't make sense out of much of anything that morning. Wasn't even sure why I'd come.

Moses leaned over and picked up a twig. He started drawing patterns in the dirt. "Course men can let their minds go wild, too. Get to thinking things they shouldn't. After a while, they get themselves so mixed up that can't even tell what is good for them and what ain't."

The back of my neck was suddenly warm. Seemed like the old man's words were aimed straight at me, even though his eyes were on the ground. "Meaning what?" I said.

He shrugged. "Don't mean nothing by it, only saying."

"You're saying Jessie's no good for me."

"Not exactly. It's pure impossible for one man to judge what's best for another. I've learned that the hardest way over the years. Only you can know what's right for you, brother. All I know is that Jessie is a hard woman for any man to hold." He stopped drawing in the dirt and held the stick up before him like a mirror. He studied it like there was message written on it. Then he shrugged and tossed the stick away. He glanced my way. Then he shrugged again and pushed off the stump.

"Think I'll go fix me some cornbread and milk. If you'd like some you're surely welcome." He turned and started walking to his

house. Today, he walked like an old man. Well, that was natural—
he was one, and right then I felt like one. So maybe we were in the
same boat after all. I thought about Jessie. Then I thought about the
man I'd shot. Then I thought about the boss. And then, for a second,
I thought about Marilee. Her smile rose up unbidden in my mind.
That image made me fell funny inside, so I stood and headed for the
old man's shack.

Fifty-two

"You look tired."

I'd seen her coming down the slope, but kept on chopping wood. After all, she was still paying me and I need money same as the next man. I straightened up and leaned against the axe handle. I was breathing hard and when I got that under control, I said, "I'm fine."

She'd been standing up the slope and she walked down and stood closer to me than I was comfortable with. Her standing so close made me suddenly conscious that I hadn't shaved that morning. There was a smile on her round white face.

"Are you sleeping all right?"

"What?"

"You have dark circles under your eyes," she said.

I shrugged.

"Is there something you'd like to talk about? After all, I'm a bit of an expert on not sleeping well."

What was I supposed to say to that? Anyway you cut it, times were rough. Knew she was talking about the boss dying, or the boy getting killed, or both. I could tell her I was sleeping fine, but that would be a lie, and we both would know it. In a way I wanted to talk to her, but in another I was afraid of sharing. Easy for a man to say too much. I straightened up and glanced down at the axe. "Reckon I ought to get back to chopping, Mrs. Ayers."

She turned and looked around. I let my eyes follow hers. On and off for the past couple of weeks I'd been chopping wood. I'd been a busy boy. Enough wood had been chopped and stacked to last two winters, maybe three.

She smiled up at me. For a heavy set woman she had a nice smile. Most of her teeth were good, although one in the front was crooked. "I wish you'd call me Marilee. And do you really think we need more wood, Judas?"

"Might be a hard winter," I said. "We're due for one."

She laughed at that. "Well, when you're finished, come on up to the house. I've made us some cocoa and was thinking of scrambling a couple of eggs. I know it's dinner time, but sometimes I get in the mood for breakfast this time of day. How about you?"

"I've eaten eggs for supper," I said. What I didn't say that the eggs were stolen and they'd been cooked and eaten in a hobo jungle outside of Leavenworth, Kansas.

"Good," she said. "Eggs it will be. Come on up when you're ready." She lifted her face and studied the sky. I knew what she was thinking. It was going to be dark soon and my wood chopping excuse was going to disappear. She smiled at me and started up the hill. I hefted the axe and drove it downward. The birch limb split with a satisfying crack.

Fifty-three

I pushed my chair back from the table and wiped my mouth with a real cloth napkin. We were eating in the kitchen and the room was full of light and good smells. It was warm, too, and I felt a drowsiness coming over me. I rubbed at my eyes.

"More coffee?"

"Maybe a splash. If you've got it made, that is."

"Have some right here in the pot."

I started to say I'd get it myself, but she was already on her feet. For a hefty woman, she moved right quick. Seconds later the coffee was streaming from the cup. Having her wait on me made me feel funny. I wasn't used to such.

"How about a piece of apple pie?" she said. Her hand rested lightly on my shoulder. I could feel the warmth of her hand through my shirt. That warmth traveled down to the center of my body. That, I couldn't explain.

"Maybe a small one," I said. Apple pie was okay, but it wasn't my favorite and besides, my belly was full of scrambled eggs. Still, she'd been mighty nice to me and I didn't want to hurt her feelings. Knowing how much she'd lost in the last year made hurting her seem downright sinful.

I looked out the window, out into the darkness. Night had fallen while we'd been eating. A light burned in the house next door. I wondered about the family. Being here in the kitchen with

Mrs. Ayers made it seem like I had a family. But I knew that was only another illusion. Seemed to me that life was full of those, and they did nothing but cause you heartache. Lately everybody seemed to be using everybody else. Way I figured it, Marilee was only lonely. Lonely I knew about. Reckon now she did, too.

She put the pie down before me and smiled. I smiled back. She turned and walked back toward the sink. Her dress brushed against the side of my face. Her perfume trailed after her. I forked pie into my mouth and tried to clear my mind.

But those illusions were still hovering. Maybe all of life was an illusion. Maybe shooting Brad Menifee had been an illusion. Even Jessie might be an illusion. At least it might be an illusion that she cared for me. Or maybe it was cared for me the way I wanted, needed, to be cared for.

A man could ignore the facts for only so long. Unless he was crazy, that is, and maybe everybody was crazy, at least a little. For sure I was for sitting here in the kitchen with the widow of the man who'd been damn good to me.

Sitting here made me feel funny, sort of sad and sort of nervous. Like the boss was still alive and I was cheating on him. Religion wasn't my strong suit, at least not the formal kind, and I wasn't sure exactly what I believed. Could be there was a heaven and maybe hell burned somewhere. Maybe the boss was like some kind of ghost, hiding in the corner or floating out in the dark or waiting for me down the street, seeing everything I did.

Just thinking about him being dead gave me the creeps, especially when his widow was being so nice to me. What made it worse was that I liked the way she was treating me. And I liked her smile. In spite of being heavy, she had a pretty face. Her lips looked real soft. I remembered how sweet they had tasted that one morning. I forked more pie in my mouth and thought about those lips. No denying the truth, part of me wanted to kiss those lips again. I slugged coffee and thought about the boss and Jessie and what kind of man I was becoming.

All my life it seemed like I'd lived hard, not having much and without prospects of getting more. I'd gone cold and wet and hungry, but I'd always tried to live right. Live the way the Bible said to. I'd slopped hogs, cut timber, and broke up rock for a road, but, except for a little vagrancy, which I didn't see how I could help, I'd never done a bad thing. At least not what I'd considered a bad thing.

But lately I'd taken to lying with a woman of the night and I killed a man over her and now I was eating pie and drinking coffee in the kitchen of my old boss who'd been real good to me, actually more like a friend than a boss. Granted, he'd been dead several months, but I still felt like a bum for the thoughts I was having about his wife.

I shot a quick glance at Marilee, aiming to study her on the sly, only she caught me and smiled. And that smile looked real nice. I took a deep breath and let it out and turned and drained my coffee. It was still right warm and scorched the fur off my tongue, but that was all right. That pain was a sort of a penance and it felt good to feel it.

I sat the cup back on the saucer and stood up.

"Getting late. Reckon I'd better be going,"

"So soon? I thought we might sit in the living room and talk a little while. Maybe play some cards. You play cards, don't you?"

"Draw poker's my game. Don't expect you know that one."

She rubbed my left arm up above the elbow. "No, but you could teach me."

"Maybe another time. 'Spect I'd better go." I reached for my jacket.

Her face sorta squeezed in on itself as she blinked and licked her lips. I watched her work the lump out of her throat. Well, her being disappointed was just too bad. Being alone with her and starting to get those certain feelings gave me the willies.

She rubbed at her eyes and turned toward the counter. "Would you like to take a piece of pie? I could wrap it up in wax paper for you."

"No thanks. I like to travel light."

"I see," she said. Her back had gone all stiff. I slipped my jacket on and started for the door. As I passed her, something made me stop for a second. I almost put a hand on her shoulder. She had been so nice to me I felt like I ought to do or say something.

But I was afraid. Afraid of a lot of things. Afraid of certain feelings. Afraid of caring too much. So I just said, "Thanks for the good supper. It sure beat my cooking."

She half turned around. A slash of hair had fallen down and covered the one eye I could see. I couldn't read her at all. Her chin worked a little and she swallowed again.

"I'm glad you enjoyed it, Judas. Be safe going home."

I felt like there was something I needed to say. Something important. Only I couldn't think of the right words. I wanted to stroke that fallen hair out of her eyes. All of a sudden there were a lot of things I wanted to do. Only, I was scared, and ashamed. Sore ashamed.

"Night," I said.

"Good night," she said and there was something in her voice that pierced me.

I made myself go out the door without looking at her again. Seemed better, or safer anyway, that way. The night was black and the wind was sharp and cold. I bent to it.

Fifty-four

Jessie wasn't in her room. I was there at dawn and when the desk clerk looked the other way I went up the back stairs. The room was cool and dark and I crossed it on tiptoe like I expected her to be sleeping in the brass bed. Her fragrance still lingered on the sheets, but the bed was as empty as the tomb of Jesus.

I lay my body across the bed and breathed deeply. Why, I wondered, didn't she care about me? Care even half as much about me as I did her. For a long time I lay very still and thought very hard. Then I did something I hadn't done since I was a kid.

I cried.

I don't why I did that. Not exactly, anyway. Maybe I'd been beating my head against a brick wall for so long that the frustration had to come out some way. Or maybe my nerves were simply shot. What with the boss dying on me and then me having to shoot Brad Menifee to death and then the way Jessie kept toying with me, I was real bad confused. Throw in all my mixed up feelings about Marilee and it was a wonder I hadn't had to have been committed to the state asylum.

Maybe if I could have talked to somebody it would have helped. But there wasn't anybody except Moses, who wouldn't have understood enough, and perhaps Marilee, who would have understood too much.

Thinking about Marilee got my mind working in another direction. She surely was one woman I couldn't get a handle on. She wasn't what you'd call pretty. She was too big-boned and fleshy and sinking into a too comfortable middle age to be attractive to a lot of men. But she had a pretty enough face and a nice mouth and she took pains with her clothes and with her hair. Maybe more important, she had a way of paying attention to a man that most men would find real attractive.

Granted, there were times she got on my last nerve, but there were also times she made me feel good. Good and warm and comfortable. In some ways she was a pain, but in others she was real nice to be around. It was during those times that I found myself caring more about her than I should have.

Way that I saw things, I still had promises to keep, especially to the boss—and those promises didn't include making love to his widow. Plus, she was lonely and I was handy. Seemed to me that Marilee was one of those women who are never happy unless they are taking care of a man or a child. Another man would soon come along and I'd go back to being Judas Cain, yard man ordinary. That's what I told myself, anyway.

My eyes were tired from the crying and I rubbed them. Then I curled up and pulled the sheet over me. Radiator pipes clanged and I could smell furniture polish. I lay there and wondered where Jessie was. Then I wondered what Marilee was doing. Finally I wondered about when someone would find Brad Menifee's body and what I would do when they did. All that wondering made my head hurt and I closed my eyes and tried to ease my mind by thinking back to when I was a kid and the warm summer afternoons when I lay along the banks of Crane Creek and watched the fish, blue and quivering in the deep pools.

After that I slept. The blare of a car horn out in the street woke me. Sunlight filled the room, but it was weak and pale. My checks were damp and I dried them on the sheet and got up and walked across the room to the window.

The street and sidewalks below were busy. I could see three cars, two trucks, and a motorcycle with a sidecar rolling down the street. At least a dozen people, men, old men, women, old women, kids, were walking down the sidewalks. A dog lay sleeping in a patch of pale sunlight on the sidewalk below the window of the barber shop. I hadn't seen the old hound that had followed me home when I'd left this morning. Some nights, like me, he liked to ramble. Maybe it was time for me to ramble on down the line. A vein in my temple throbbed.

None of the people knew I was standing at the window looking down on them. None of them even glanced up. Not the men driving the cars and trucks, not the women strolling down the sidewalks in the haze of morning. Not even the dog. I reckoned they were too intent on getting about their own business to think about looking up. For all they knew I was no more there than God or the Devil or the Man-in-the-Moon. To make sure I wasn't guilty of the same sin, I craned my neck.

All I could see was the overhang of the room and a sparrow sitting on the edge and above the bird a smoky gray sky. I wondered if God was up there looking down on me like I had been looking down on the people below. I'd had way too much wondering for one lousy morning and I turned from the window, walked across the room without looking directly at anything, then went out the door and down the hallway to the stairs that I took two at a time. The desk clerk was reading the newspaper and never looked up.

That struck me as funny. There he sat, enthralled in all that news. All those car wrecks and bank robberies and hurricanes and tornados and earthquakes. And right there before his very eyes walked a stone cold killer. Yes, indeed, there walked the man who had shot bad Brad Menifee dead. If it hadn't of all been so sad, I think I would have laughed out loud.

Fifty-five

I walked every street I knew she frequented, but all I saw were squirrels and old men wearing sweat-stained Stetsons and shiny trousers. I walked to the edge of town, cut across the tracks and started the swing back to my place. Half a mile down the road, it occurred to me that maybe I ought to check out the juke joint where I'd first seen Jessie. Without any more consideration, I climbed over an old wooden fence and walked across a field of grasses that grew to my knees. At the far edge of the field was a thin line of cedars.

Those cedars grew so thick that it was almost dusk beneath them. Their sharp odor was strong and the fallen needles turned the ground into a carpet. Sound was muffled here and it was hard to keep going in even a semi-straight line. Took longer than I'd figured to make the road and when I did I was too far south. I had to curl back to the north and by then I was getting hungry.

There wasn't much I could do about that. I was low on cash and there wasn't any sort of café or burger joint on this road. My stomach growled at me and I told it to shut up and picked up the pace. Crows cawed from the shelter of the trees and clouds thickened all along the northern edge of the sky. Out of the cedars, the wind was sharper and the air smelled like rain. There was a chill in the air, though, and I wondered if it was going to snow instead.

Before I saw the first building, I heard the music. There were four buildings, each standing sentry at one of the four corners of a crossroads. The wind hurried me along and I mentally rolled the dice and headed for the first place on the right, a concrete block building that had been painted white within recent memory. Gravel crunched beneath my feet as I slogged across the parking lot. Half a dozen cars were parked close to the building, and the newest one had to be ten years old.

The door swung open and a man stumbled out. He was short and so skinny his pants were about to fall down. A battered felt hat sat slanted on his head and his chin and cheeks were covered with raggedy whiskers. He bumped against me and lifted his face. He looked very surprised. He shut both eyes. Then he opened the right one. It was pale blue and bloodshot. He cracked open his mouth and licked his lips. Then he said very slowly and distinctly, "Are you a preacher?"

"No," I said, "why?"

He cocked his head to one side and his face assumed a very solemn look. "My wife said if I didn't quit drinking I was going to hell and I figured you might be a preacher come to save me or the devil come to claim my soul, and I was afraid to ask if you were the devil." He squinted his eyes almost shut and leaned back as though I were contagious.

"You ain't the devil, er ye?"

"No," I said, serious like, "but some say I'm close kin to old Scratch."

Both his eyes came open then and they got real wide. Then he shut his face down and began to side step around me. Once he got in the clear, he started making good time, even though he stumbled a couple of times and kept looking back. For some reason I didn't want to think about, scaring the drunk tickled me. Maybe I was turning mean as I grew older. Sure enough felt mean and mad inside. Mean and mad enough to bust up hell and half of Georgia.

I swallowed hard and counted to ten slowly. Then I pushed the door open and walked inside.

For a moment, I stood just inside the door, letting my eyes adjust, wondering what it was that I really wanted to see. On the jukebox, some cowboy with a Texas hill country twang was singing about drinking. Smoke was so thick it burned your throat. Three men and two women were sitting along the bar. Neither of the women was Jessie. I looked around the joint. That didn't take long. It wasn't a big place and there were maybe a dozen tables, and only two of those were occupied. A couple sat at one. Best I could tell, they were about the same age as Jessie and me. An old man sat at the other table with his head in his hands. Him, I could relate to.

I walked over to the bar and gave the bartender the sign. He was polishing glasses and he finished the one he was working on and wandered over. He looked down his nose at me. He had a nose like a badger.

"What can I do for you?"

"I'm looking for a woman."

He snorted and gave me a snide look. "Ain't we all, brother?" He laughed a little, then rearranged his face. "What's your woman look like, mister?"

"Tall for a woman, real pretty face, sorta heart-shaped, big dark eyes that don't have any bottoms."

"Slim or heavy?"

"Slim."

"Does she drink bourbon or beer?"

"A little of both, I reckon." I thought for a moment, then added, "Her name's Jessie."

The barkeep shook his head. "Names don't mean a thing to me." He glanced around the room. "Not that you'd know it by the crowd today, but way too many people pass through here for me to keep up with any, lest they make trouble or try to stiff me. Those I remember. I'm a good rememberer."

I nodded. He looked like a man who'd remember a wrong quicker than a right. Down the bar, one of the men laughed and one of the women, the peroxided blonde, giggled in return. I rubbed at my face.

"Well," I said, "you won't have any reason to remember me. Don't aim to cause trouble and, since I'm not buying, I can't stiff you. All I want to know is if you've seen the woman I described."

The bartender ran his fingers through his thin hair and looked up at the ceiling and then down the bar. "Hard to say," he said. "Least for sure." He shifted his gaze back to my face. "Besides, I ain't here to give out nothing for free, except maybe for some advice. If you're looking for something free head on down to Cohen's filling station. He gives away free air for your tires."

The bartender laughed at his own joke and showed me his teeth. Guess you could call it a smile, if you felt generous. He had crooked teeth. A couple of the ones on top were twisted around each other. I dug in my pocket and fingered out a quarter. I spun it on the counter. It came up heads. I gave him a look. His fingers closed over the two-bits.

"Woman who looked something like that was in here earlier. Seen her before, too. Heard she worked for Brad Menifee at one time. That her?"

"Might be."

"Funny about Menifee. Man simply up and disappeared one day. Never did hear what happened to him. Have you?"

"Never heard the first clue."

"Well, I hope he's all right. Heard he was mixed up in some rough stuff and maybe crossed the line on a couple of laws, but he was a customer. Good customer, too. Why I've seen him spend fifteen, twenty dollars a night in here. Now that's something, brother. Most of my customers come in and try to nurse a beer all night. Won't put up with that. Not that I rush any man on his drink, but business is business, you know."

"Sure," I said. "About the girl?"

"Oh, right. Well, like I was aiming to say, she was in here earlier. Left maybe two hours ago. Can't be sure cause that jukebox gets loud, but I think the fellow she was with said something about going to Scrappy's." The bartender leaned over. His breath smelled of onions, and odors I couldn't place.

"If you're interested, that's the place across the highway. Got a big old wooden Indian with one arm standing by the door. What a damn ugly thing. Don't know where he got it or why he'd want it."

I took my elbows off the bar. "Thanks," I said and headed for the door.

The bartender called after me, "Come back anytime, mister. Little conversation passes the time. Let me know if you ever hear what happened to Menifee."

I waved without looking back and pushed the door open. It had started to rain.

Not that it was much more than a mist, but my face was damp by the time I made Scrappy's. I hustled under the overhang and ran my fingers through my hair. As I did, I noticed they were trembling.

Fifty-six

Inside Scrappy's the music wasn't so loud, but the smoke was thick enough to cut. A quick look around showed me Jessie wasn't there. Four or five couples were slow dancing to a song that had been old when I was still young. Two of the girls looked familiar, and, after a bit, I figured out that I'd had seen them talking with Jessie.

The guy behind the bar I knew from somewhere. I leaned against a roof support pole and studied his face. At first he was in shadow, then a customer called and he came down the bar and into the light and I recognized him. He was Menifee's driver. At least he had been. Well, times were hard for everybody. I pushed off the pole and up to the bar. After a couple of minutes, he noticed me and came on down.

Two steps before he got to me, I saw the recognition in his eyes. It erased the half smile starting on his face. He had one of those long thin faces you see regularly in the piney woods down South. Put me in mind of a horse's head. He snarled up his nose at me, like I smelled bad.

"What the hell you want?"

"Just looking."

"If you're looking for trouble I can sure enough make it happen." His eyes drifted over to a fat man in a tight shirt standing on the far side of the room.

"No trouble," I said. "Only looking for Jessie."

He jerked his head at the door. "Get out. Last time I seen him, Menifee warned me about you. Said you was trouble walking. That was right before he disappeared." He gave me a long look down the side of his nose.

"So what? Menifee doesn't like me. You don't like me. Probably lots of people don't like me. So what?"

"So get the hell out of here. You're bad news from way back and I don't like you. Never did. Now get afore I call Bobby over." He nodded at the fat man who was waddling our way. He was fat all right, but he was also tall. Had to have been six or seven inches taller than I was and he must have outweighed me a hundred and fifty pounds. Right now, I didn't need a beating. And Menifee's old gang was only too ready to give it. If it wasn't for the other customers, they would have already started.

I told myself to turn around and walk out. After a moment, I did. All the way to the door I half expected burning holes in my back. Course that was pure imagination. I stepped out and shut the door behind me. It was raining harder. I stood under the eaves, trying to decide what to do. After a couple of minutes a man came out—the man I'd seen coming out of the first joint. He wasn't trouble, except maybe to himself. He was thin like he hadn't been eating right and his pants were stained and patched. His breath would have put kerosene to shame. He wiggled his lips into the sort of smile you see on an egg-sucking dog. I wondered what he wanted. Probably the price of the next drink. He didn't even recognize me.

"Heard you talking in there," he said in a voice that wasn't much more than a whisper.

"And..."

"And I think I seen the woman you want."

"Yeah."

"Sure, I seen her. Name's Jessie. She comes here right regular. Lots of girls that used to work for Menifee come in here lately. Think they're working for Dutch Stengel now."

"Never heard of him."

The little man's nose was running and he swiped at the end of it with his shirtsleeve. You could hear the rain striking the fallen leaves. It was coming down harder than before. The wind had a real bite to it now and was working down the neck of my shirt. I dreaded winter. That season was always a cold and lonely passage.

"Stengel was in Memphis before things got too hot for him. Least ways, that's the story. Guess he came to these backwoods till the heat dies down." The man coughed and spit. He tilted his head and looked directly at me. "Knew his daddy over to Vicksburg back before the war. Ran a freight operation. Honest man, far as I know. Probably seen Dutch around when he was kid, but never paid him no mind. Goes to show, don't it?"

I nodded, although I wasn't following the man's ramblings real closely. "What about Jessie?"

"Oh yes, that's what I was fixin' to tell you." He sniffled and rubbed at his eyes, shivering in his ragged britches. "Getting right raw out here, ain't it?"

"Too cold to stand around and shoot the breeze. You got something to say, say it."

"Sure, sure. Well, like I was saying, she comes in here right often and most times I see her leave with some fellow."

"Same fellow each time?"

He twisted his mouth around to one side of his face. I could almost see him trying to think what to say. If I hadn't been wanting to find out about Jessie I might have busted him a good one across the chops, aggravated as I was. If he didn't start getting to it I was going to bust him anyway.

"Not necessarily, no. Sometimes she'll walk out with a man she's walked out with before, but not always."

"Okay," I said, "so she walks out with a guy, so what?"

He nodded like I was a pupil who had asked the right question. "Getting to that. Yes sir, I'm a comin' to that." He quit talking then, rubbed his mouth.

The wind shifted then and drove the rain in under the eaves. "Get on with it," I said. "It's damn nasty to diddle-ass around."

"I'll be mighty thirsty after all this talking," he said.

I jingled the change in my pocket. "Let's hear it."

"Well, I saw her leave a little while ago. Maybe thirty minutes before you got here. She left with a guy." He shrugged. "Don't know his name, but he favors the Perkins boys from over around Alton Ridge."

I turned away and looked out through the rain, down to a line of pines looming dark. I couldn't make myself look at the little man.

"Where'd they go?"

"Can't say for sure, 'cause I didn't watch for long, but it looked like they were headed for the cabins."

"Which one?" I asked, still looking at the trees.

"Can't rightly say," the little man said. "But there's only six of 'em."

I turned then and looked at him and he had a hand out, cupped. I dropped all my coins in it. He nodded and mumbled something. Might have been "Thanks." I didn't bother to respond. The little man was already heading for the door. I took a deep breath, bent my neck and stepped out into the rain.

~ * ~

Like the little man had said, there were six cabins. They were scattered about a clearing in the woods. Appeared to be no rhyme or reason to where they stood. Looked like whoever had built them had flung a handful of shucked corn in the air and then built a cabin wherever one of the kernels had landed.

The roof had caved in on one and the door stood wide open on the one next to it. I started with the next one in the crooked line. Each cabin had one little window in front. Raggedy curtains only partially obscured the view of the inside of the cabin. I turned the collar on my jacket up and peered inside. Empty as the tomb on the third day. I moved on down the line.

As I got closer to the next cabin, I could hear noises. Not words, only sounds. Sounds somewhere between moans and groans. Then what sounded like two voices. The rain was coming down so hard I wasn't worried about them hearing me. I eased up tight against the cabin.

The curtains on this cabin were less raggedy than the others I'd seen, but there was still a gap in the middle and I curled my neck and leaned forward and placed my face against the fly-specked glass.

For a few seconds all I could see was a blurry darkness. Then my eyes adjusted.

The only furniture in the room was a bed and a straight-backed chair. Clothes, a man's and a woman's, were draped over the chair and scattered about on the plank floor. A man and a woman lay on the bed. Both were as naked as the day they were born.

The man on top of the woman had a strip of hair down his back that looked like it had been painted on by a semi-sober house painter. His ass was scrawny and wrinkled. His head hung over the woman's like a dirty moon and I couldn't make out her face. Then he swung his head to the right and I could see the woman real clear.

Guess a man always keeps hoping. Hoping until the hammer smashes his dream like it was cheap carnival glass. Even after I knew better, for a moment I kept on hoping. Letting go of something that has been deep in your mind for a long time hurts like hell. Don't let anybody kid you about being tough. Ain't nobody that tough.

Oh, I'd known what Jessie was. At least, what she was part of the time. But knowing it and seeing it are two different things entirely. Especially after seeing that scrawny-ass man humping on her. Especially after I asked her to go away with me. Especially after I'd shot Brad Menifee over her. Especially after I'd told her fifty times how much I truly cared.

Only caring doesn't signify. Fact is, caring's nothing but a heartache waiting to happen. One loving and the other not, or at least not near enough, was no damn good. No damn good. There was lump in my throat like I'd tried to swallow a fistful of gravel.

Jessie's eyes had a glazed over look. Then they swung over to the window and I watched her body stiffen. Her eyes widened and her mouth came open. She didn't say anything, though.

We just stared at each other. Her hands were on the man's back and her legs were locked around his. I saw all that in a flash and then I wouldn't look there anymore. I only looked at her face. I only looked right into her eyes. Right into those lying eyes.

No, that wasn't being fair. She'd never promised me anything. I'd been a fool. And a damn big one. Could see that now so clear it made my head hurt something awful. I wanted to hurt somebody, hurt them real bad. But the only person who really deserved it was me. Self-delusion is damn powerful voodoo.

She was trying to tell me something with her eyes, but I couldn't work it out. Maybe that was all for the best. I took one final look, whirled on my heel and stepped out into the rain, pushing hard for a dark stand of pines that lined the road. The wind was blowing stronger, pushing the pine scent across the clearing, driving the rain, chilling me to the bone. In the dying afternoon my face was wet. Not all that wetness was rain.

Fifty-seven

In the morning I went there.

As I came up the drive, I could see her standing by the living room window, fooling with her African violets. I was halfway to the house when she looked up and saw me. At first she looked frightened, sorta like she'd seen a ghost walking. Then she smiled and waved at me like a little girl. I waved back and kept walking.

I curled around to the back door. It was closed against the chill. For maybe twenty seconds, I stood on the back step, catching my breath, wondering, remembering, working up my nerve. Then I took a long look around and twisted the knob and walked in without knocking.

Marilee was standing by the stove, wearing a blue print dress and white apron that emphasized her stomach. She smiled. Her hair was brushed and her round face had been scrubbed. I felt grimy and wished I'd heated water for a good wash before I'd left the house.

"Good morning, Judas. Have you had breakfast?"

"No," I said. There were other words I wanted to say. But all I said was "No."

She motioned at a chair. "Well, have a seat and I'll fix you some eggs. Do you like them fried or scrambled for breakfast?"

"Fried," I said, "over easy." I didn't look at her. Not directly anyway. Only glanced at her out of the corners of my eyes. I kept remembering the boss and I felt funny. But somewhere in the

Bible—Luke, if memory served—Jesus had said, "Let the dead bury their dead." Maybe I was misapplying scripture, but that phrase kept running through my mind.

I sat down and she came over with a china cup on a white saucer and set them down in front of me. Her hair brushed against my face and I wanted to stroke it.

I could smell the coffee before she poured it. I could smell the coffee and heating grease and her perfume.

She put one hand on my shoulder. This time I let it stay. It was soft and warm and she smelled like early spring. The feeling that I'd finally come home welled up in me until I wanted to cry. I didn't though. Only stretched out a hand and covered hers.

Meet Chris Helvey

Chris Helvey's short stories have appeared in numerous reviews and journals, and he is the author of *Claw Hammer, A Gathering of Stories,* and two novels: *Whose Name I Did Not Know* and *Snapshot.* Chris lives and writes in Kentucky and currently serves as a writing coach and the editor in chief of *Trajectory Journal.*

Made in the USA
Monee, IL
01 January 2020

19725240R10173